D1058825

227 Main Street
Lovell, ME 04051

THE
HEXED

Heather Graham

CENTER POINT LARGE PRINT
THORNDIKE, MAINE

This Center Point Large Print edition is published
in the year 2014 by arrangement with Harlequin Books S.A.

The text of this Large Print edition is unabridged.
In other aspects, this book may vary from the original edition.
Printed in the United States of America on permanent paper.
Set in 16-point Times New Roman type.

ISBN: 978-1-62899-235-9

Library of Congress Cataloging-in-Publication Data

Graham, Heather.
The hexed / Heather Graham. — Center Point Large Print edition.
pages ; cm
Summary: "Devin Lyle moves into an eighteenth century cabin in the
woods of Salem, haunted by dead bodies and ghostly apparitions"—
Provided by publisher.
ISBN 978-1-62899-235-9 (library binding : alk. paper)
1. Witches—Fiction. 2. Apparitions—Fiction.
3. Murder—Investigation—Fiction. 4. Salem (Mass.)—Fiction.
5. Large type books. I. Title.
PS3557.R198H49 2014
813'.54—dc23
2014026321

To Pearl Riley and Kelly Riley
with lots of love and thanks.

THE
HEXED

PROLOGUE

"Help me, Rocky! Help me!"

Craig Rockwell—Rocky to family and friends —was seventeen, a high school senior. It wasn't that he didn't like Melissa Wilson; he just wasn't interested the way *she* was interested.

He rolled over restlessly on the bed, her voice— frantic as always—pushed to the background as his half-sleeping mind returned to the thoughts that had occupied him earlier as he'd drifted off over homework.

He'd been waiting to leave here as long as he could remember. He wanted to head to Boston or New York. Not that there was anything wrong with Peabody, Massachusetts. It was fine. It was filled with old houses, history and die-hard Yankees, though sometimes the people around him seemed uptight. He'd been drilled in the history of Pilgrims and Massachusetts all his life, so maybe—since many of the people in the area were descendants of the Puritans who had first settled in the state—it was natural that people here took a *wicked* long time to progress.

He played football, and he was good. Six-one, strong and sleek and quick, he had set his mind on being the best quarterback possible, and it looked as if he was going to have his choice of scholarships. But that meant hanging in and hanging tough with football and his grades. He was lucky, too. Well, lucky in a way. He had leading-man looks, and when the school drama club was doing *The Crucible*, he was cast as John Proctor. He would give all of it up, though, to have his dad back.

On Friday nights when training was over, he met up with friends and they went to a movie or sat around a coffeehouse, or occasionally went into Boston for a concert. It was the same group of friends he'd hung out with forever. Haley Marshall, who he'd more or less gone out with until they'd recently called it quits; Jack Grail, lineman; Vince Steward, guard; Renee Radcliff, captain of the cheerleading squad—and Melissa.

They'd known one another since they were kids.

Peabody was fairly small. Population just about fifty thousand, give or take a thousand or two. The town had once been part of Salem, but it had become a separate entity as time went by and the world grew. But there was more out there, and he intended to see it.

He was good, and he wanted to make the pros. If he didn't make the pros, he wanted to join the FBI. While his mother could trace her family back to the damned *Mayflower*, his father had hailed from Texas, where he'd been a sheriff. Late in life he'd fallen in love with Rocky's mom, so

10

he'd been almost seventy a year ago when he'd died of a heart attack. The pain still assailed Rocky often, but he was grateful for his father. It had been better to have him for sixteen years than anyone else for a lifetime.

And he was definitely going to be a lawman, with or without a football career first. FBI. An agent had come to town when he'd been ten and spoken to an assembly, and he'd known since then that was what he wanted to be.

The sound of Melissa's voice rose, interrupting his restless thoughts.

"Rocky!"

There was a sudden banging at his bedroom window. He started and sat up, staring. Melissa was there, her face white. He couldn't hear her anymore, but when her lips formed a word he knew what she was saying.

Rocky.

His name, nothing more.

He heard more banging and realized it was coming from the front door. He leaped out of bed and checked the clock. It was still early, just after 8:00 p.m.

He looked back to his bedroom window, but no one was there.

Too many teen slasher movies, he decided. They were fun, though. The girls crawled all over you after a slasher movie, and Haley, completely at home with her sexuality, had been no exception, for which his raging hormones would be eternally grateful. But she had realized he was really planning on leaving, while she just wanted to get married and have babies, so now when the movie ended she was all over Vince or Jack as she tried to figure out who was the best candidate for marriage and settling down.

He didn't care—he knew he wasn't what Haley wanted. He just didn't like it that now Melissa Wilson, apparently with Haley's blessing, was yearning after him all the time.

It was odd, he thought. If it was slasher movies that unnerved him, it should have been some kind of a homicidal monster at his window. A killer in a human skin mask or something. Instead, he saw the face of Melissa Wilson. She was five-three and a hundred pounds, tops. Not too scary.

Whatever. She was gone. And the banging at the front door continued. He got up and went to see what was going on.

It was Vince. "Hey, man," his friend demanded, "your mom's working late?"

His mother was a "vice president" at a small ad agency. In reality she was a glorified assistant with a title instead of a decent salary.

"Yeah," he told Vince. "They're shooting that Welcome to Salem ad tonight—in Peabody."

"Close enough, I guess. I got a couple of beers. Come on out—we'll hang in the truck, and that way we can toss 'em quick if she shows up," Vince said.

Rocky shook his head. "My mom can smell beer a mile away."

"Chicken!"

"Yeah, well, that and our English test is tomorrow, and I have to ace it," Rocky said.

"Wow. Some wild and crazy hotshot you are," Vince said.

Rocky shrugged. "You said you're going to community college until you figure out what you want to do. Well, I *know* what I want."

"NYU or Harvard," Vince said, grinning. "Maybe Yale."

"Notre Dame. But, hey, I'll sit in the back of the truck and watch you down a few."

Vince shrugged. "Suit yourself." Vince was huge. Six-four, close to three hundred pounds. He was great to have on the football field. He might have taken it somewhere—he just didn't have the ambition.

"I don't get you, buddy," Vince said, opening the back of his Ford pickup and crawling into the bed.

As he did so, another car drove up. It was an ancient Toyota. Best Jack could buy, and then only with his dad's help.

"Hey!" Jack called. He wasn't as big as Vince; he was lean, with wiry muscles.

"Come and join us—back of the pickup," Vince

said as Jack got out and greeted them with a grin. "Haley hasn't got you cornered?"

"Don't know what's up. I think the girls were going shopping. Now hand me a beer."

"See, Rocky? That's what boys do when the girls aren't around—they drink beer and watch football," Vince said.

"There aren't any games on," Rocky reminded him.

"Okay, so we settle for drinking beer," Vince said.

"School night," Rocky said. "And I have plans to get out of this town."

Vince looked at Jack and Rocky, grinning. "Rocky, you got it all wrong. Peabody is a great place. Close to the action in Boston when you want action. Away from people when you don't want a crowd."

Jack laughed. "I think you're talking about the wheat fields of Kansas or something. We have neighbors almost on top of us."

Vince popped a beer and lay back on one of the plastic cushions he kept in the truck for "entertaining," as he called it, looking up at the sky. "Yeah, in some places you got old Victorian on top of old Victorian. But there's still some wooded land available. And reasonably priced, too. I get some trust money when I graduate, and I'm buying land."

"To do what?" Rocky asked.

"I don't know yet—I just know I'm buying it."

"Yeah, well, I don't have any trust money coming," Rocky told him. He crawled up into the bed of the truck, but he didn't lie back.

"Witch's moon," Jack said.

It *was* huge and full, Rocky noticed. The local Wiccans were probably all out forming circles or whatever it was they did.

"Werewolves a-howling," Vince said, laughing.

Rocky frowned, listening intently. Just as Vince had spoken, he could have sworn that he *did* hear something. Not a howl, exactly. More like a sob.

"What was that?" he murmured.

"You hear a werewolf?" Vince laughed.

"No," Rocky said, glancing at Vince and rolling his eyes. "But something. Shut up and listen."

Melissa. Melissa Wilson. She was calling his name again. She was trying to tell him something. Help me, Rocky. Help me!

"Don't you hear her?" he demanded, looking around. His next-door neighbor's house was close —not fifty feet away. The sound, however, seemed to be coming from farther than that. He gazed toward the playground across the street and beyond . . . where a small forest of pines led down to the pond.

"Hear what?" Vince demanded.

"Melissa," Rocky said. "I could swear I hear Melissa—and she's calling for help."

Vince laughed. "Melissa? What the hell are you

talking about? I'm the one doing the drinking and *you're* hearing things? You hear anything, Jack?"

Jack shook his head. He looked worriedly at Rocky. "You okay?"

"Yeah," Rocky said. "I'm fine. I'm not hearing things. It's Melissa, and she's asking for help."

"You're crazy, man. The pressure is getting to you. Hell, you'd help yourself out if you'd have a beer," Vince offered.

"He may be right," Jack noted.

Rocky jumped off the bed of the truck and listened. He couldn't really tell, but the voice seemed to be coming from across the street and . . .

From inside his mind.

He walked across the street, so intent he forgot to even look for traffic. Thankfully, it was a quiet neighborhood.

"Rocky, what the hell?"

Vince hurried after him, with Jack following behind.

Rocky sprinted across the grass and into the pines.

"Rocky, wait!" Vince gasped. He was bigger, but it was hard for him to run as fast. Jack was quickly catching up.

But Rocky kept going until he finally stopped in the maze of pines, holding his breath, listening.

Rocky!

Melissa's voice again.

He walked through the trees, grateful for the

full moon, whose light filtered through the branches. Branches reaching toward him like skeletal arms.

Yup. Too many slasher movies.

Fallen pine needles were brittle beneath his footsteps as he moved through the trees. Something brushed his face, and he almost gasped aloud before he realized it was just a spiderweb.

"Rockwell, where the hell are you going?" Vince yelled from somewhere behind him.

"Come on, man. What are you doing?" Jack demanded as the other two caught up to him. "You're scaring me."

Rocky didn't know. He kept walking through the woods until he came to a barren circle surrounded by pines. A little area of dust and rock and bracken, and . . .

Melissa. Melissa Wilson.

She was lying on her back, arms and legs stretched straight out. She was staring up at the night sky, at the full moon. Her eyes, he realized, were frozen open.

A red line extended around her throat and dripped to the forest floor.

Melissa Wilson was dead.

"Mr. Rockwell?"

Rocky started. He'd been sitting in the front office of the Virginia office of the FBI special division called the Krewe of Hunters, waiting for his appointment with Jackson Crow. He was the assistant director of this branch of "special" investigations. The titular head of all the Krewe units was a man named Adam Harrison, but he was seldom seen. He seemed to "direct" from some kind of lofty haven.

The events that had filled his mind—as fresh as if they'd just happened, although they had been almost thirteen years in the past—faded with the sound of the receptionist's voice. Until recently, he'd buried the memories of Melissa Wilson deep in the darkest recesses of his mind.

He'd forgotten about football after finding her. He'd concentrated on law enforcement in college and gone to work first with the Boston police, and then he'd made it into the FBI Academy and taken a position in L.A. after graduation. Since his mother had remarried—a great guy, a retired fireman—he didn't suffer from the only-child guilt that would have made him feel he needed to be near her.

Over the past ten years, he'd learned that Hollywood really was a world of illusion, and that only made the area a hotbed for mayhem and murder.

And now . . .

And now here he was, seeking a new position with a vengeance. He'd followed the Krewe of Hunters for the past few years. His curiosity had been piqued from the first time he'd read about their cases—and heard the rumors in the field offices. No matter how the members of the special unit were mocked, they were also respected, because they had a batting average that was off the charts.

And that was what he needed now.

Because it had happened again. A murder so much like Melissa's that it gave him chills—and practically in his hometown.

"Special Agent Crow will see you now."

As Rocky walked into Crow's office, the man rose to greet him. He'd known Crow was Native American, and he wasn't surprised the man was tall and fit. He hadn't expected him to be quite so striking, though. He studied the man he hoped would be his boss, and he knew that Crow was studying him in return.

"Sit down. I've been reading your file and the clippings that you sent about the case," Crow said.

Rocky sat. "And?"

"I see that another woman has been discovered in circumstances exactly like the girl you found."

"Swampscott this time," Rocky said. "Practically next door."

Crow looked gravely at Rocky. "You were personally involved with the original case as a teenager."

"Yes."

"Do you think that will affect your work?"

Rocky hesitated.

One wasn't supposed to be emotionally involved

in the field; it could jeopardize the ability to make the best decision possible in a tough situation.

He let out his breath. "Yes," he admitted.

Crow looked back down at the file before him.

"This woman was left just as your friend Melissa was. Arranged in a very specific position —almost as if her body was meant to create a pentagram."

"Five points," Rocky agreed. "And there was a silver medallion lying on her chest—the same as in Melissa Wilson's case."

Crow leaned back, stared at him for a long moment, then nodded slowly.

"I'm assuming you've studied up on the Krewe of Hunters and that's why you wrote to me."

"Yes."

"And of course, we've studied up on you, too."

"I'm damned glad. I'm sure I wouldn't have a chance here if you hadn't."

Crow actually smiled. He leaned forward and said, "My boss—our director, Adam Harrison—is like a magician. It will still take me about twenty-four hours to get you transferred over. But," he said, looking up, "feel free to head on up to Massachusetts right away. I'll inform you when the transfer goes through."

He stood. Rocky did the same, and Crow held out his hand.

"Welcome to the Krewe of Hunters, Agent Rockwell."

1

Every once in a while Devin Lyle couldn't help herself. People did such outrageous things sometimes that she just had to step in.

She stepped forward, positioning herself a little closer to the group standing by the memorial so she could hear what they were saying.

"Burn, witch! Burn!" a young man said. Despite his words, he was actually reverently placing a flower on the bench dedicated to one of the victims of the witch trials.

"How horrible. I can't even imagine burning to death," an older woman said.

"Excuse me," Devin said. "None of the condemned in Salem were burned. Nineteen were hanged, and one man, Giles Corey, was pressed to death."

"Really?" The older woman sounded relieved. "Not that hanging must have been less than horrible, but to burn . . ." She shuddered.

"Almost any tour you take in Salem is going to tell you about the victims—and tell you that no one was burned," Devin said. They were all staring at her, and she suddenly felt self-conscious. She wasn't a tour guide, after all. She wrote sweet, fun children's books about a slightly crazy "witch."

But Salem was her home. And she hated the misinformation about it that spread far too frequently.

"I saw it in a movie," a kid said, nodding sagely. "They burned them in the movie."

"That movie took license with history, I promise you," Devin assured him.

"And men were called witches, too? Not warlocks?" the older woman asked.

"Yes, they were all accused of being witches. And at the time, witchcraft was punishable by death," Devin said. "So, if you 'hexed' a neighbor—just cursed him, or say you had a voodoo doll, whether there was any real magic there or not—you were considered a practicing witch and subject to execution."

"So they were all guilty?" someone else asked.

"No, not all of them—you have to remember, even just saying that you had cursed someone was considered to be witchcraft. Kids would read their futures in broken eggs, and that was witchcraft, by the standards of the time. Those who were condemned and hanged refused to plead guilty, because they were innocent and feared for their souls if they did. During the hysteria, all kinds of crazy things happened. You really need to take a tour—or just start at the Witch Dungeon and get a good overview of the entire situation.

"People were at odds politically, creating an

atmosphere ripe for petty arguments. It was winter, it was bitter cold and it was, frankly, miserable. Most scholars believe that the tales Tituba—a slave from the Caribbean—told to a group of girls started them making up their own stories. And since people not only believed fiercely in the devil but that he also lived in the woods, they . . ." Devin's voice trailed off, and she smiled as she saw an old friend, Brent Corbin, standing nearby. He owned an occult and souvenir store on Essex Street, and led one of the best night tours of the city.

She could see that he was grinning at her, with a teasing light in his eyes. Brent was a little stout, but he had a cute thatch of blond hair, beautiful bright blue eyes and a great smile. He was clearly as bemused as she was by the conversation.

Ten years ago Brent had graduated with her from Salem High. They'd fought like crazy when they'd been kids, teased and tormented each other over dating as they'd gotten older, and now—especially with her living back in Salem—they laughed over their old squabbles. It had been great to spend time with him now that she was back to town, and no way was she letting him get away without an introduction.

"Hey," she said, smiling. "We've got one of the city's best tour guides right here. This is Brent Corbin. He owns Which Witch Is Which just over on the mall and no one—seriously, no one—

knows Salem's history better than Brent. I'll leave you in his capable hands."

She waved to him, laughing when the smile disappeared from his face. But then it was back, and he shook his head in amusement as he watched her go.

A few minutes later he sent her a text message. I'd throw you in the stocks for that—except half of them signed on for the tour tonight. Thx. See ya later.

Devin laughed and continued on to Essex Street, where one of her best friends carried Devin's books in her shop, the Haunted Dragon. She not only carried books, but toys and Salem T-shirts, as well as finely made cloaks, clothing and jewelry. Beth Fullway was a practicing Wiccan. She had graduated a few years before Devin, then stayed in the area and, like Brent, opened a shop. She was open from 11:00 a.m. to 7:00 p.m. daily, with two employees to help her cover all the days of the week. When seven at night rolled around, she was done. Unless, of course, it was October and they were in the middle of Haunted Happenings. In Salem, Haunted Happenings was one of the year's biggest events—a money event. People came in droves, and all the rules changed. Stores stayed open later, and there were more special tours, historical events, haunted houses and whatever other manner of "spooky" entertainment an up-and-coming entrepreneur could imagine.

A little bell tinkled when Devin went in; the store was about a thousand square feet, with curtained rooms in the rear where Beth and her employees sometimes did readings.

"Hey!" Beth said, rising to greet Devin with a hug. Beth was about five-eight but so slim she appeared small. Even with Devin being an inch taller at five-nine, they had to stretch over the counter to greet each other.

"Glad to see you," Beth said. "I mean . . . now. I'm always glad to see you." Her verbal confusion was a frequent result of her effervescent sincerity. "I have to tell you—I sold out of the last batch of your books in two days. Of course, it's summer and this town is teeming with kids. But still. . . ."

"That's great," Devin said. "I'm impressed— and flattered."

"Anyway, if you happen to have any extras, can you bring them by?" Beth asked her. "I've ordered more, but I could use a few to tide me over."

"I'll bring my author's copies."

"Great, thanks."

Devin looked in the display case by the counter as they talked. She wasn't really much for costly jewelry—diamonds, platinum, elegant pieces— but she loved artistic costume jewelry. Silver. And, okay, sometimes silver with stones.

"Wow!" she said, and looked up at Beth.

"You're looking at the Sheena Marston series, right?" Beth asked.

25

"They're gorgeous pieces, aren't they?" came another voice.

Devin looked up. Theo Hastings, one of Beth's employees and mediums, had come from the back. He waved at the young women to whom he'd been giving a reading and smiled at Devin. He was about forty, devilishly handsome and great at his work. He was a practicing Wiccan—though Devin suspected that he was "practicing" more because it was good for his image and his work than because he believed the way Beth did. He had the right look, with dark hair that fell to his shoulders and was highlighted with just a touch of gray, dark eyes and perfectly sculpted features. And of course, he always wore black suits that hinted at the 1800s without being costume pieces. He was always nice, but she hadn't known him all that long, and he wasn't an open book like Beth, so Devin always kept a little distance.

"Take that one," he said, pointing to a gorgeous silver medallion hanging from a delicate chain, a pentagram entwined with enamel glass-green leaves and tiny stones. "Beautiful—truly beautiful. So many people come in here thinking that the pentagram is evil, but it isn't. It even symbolizes the Freemasons, who do a lot of good things and fall under suspicion, too. Pentagrams were important religious symbols for the Babylonians, and they were also used in ancient Greece.

Christians have even used the pentagram to represent the five wounds of Christ. It's no different than the cross or the Star of David or any religious symbol. How do people get these things in their minds . . . ?"

His voice trailed off as he shook his head.

"Hey, you're asking that question in a place where 'spectral' evidence was considered proof of guilt," Devin reminded him.

"Amazing, right?" Beth asked. "A kid said she was being pinched by the astral projection of some poor old woman, and people believed her."

"Different times," Devin murmured. "And sometimes I'm not so sure we've evolved very far. Look at the prejudices we still practice."

"Hey, not me," Beth protested. "I love everyone."

Devin laughed. "And everyone loves you. I mean, as a species, we can still be pretty wretched. You can make prosecuting witches illegal, and we can enact laws against discrimination, but that doesn't mean we can change the human mind."

"Well said," Theo told her. "But to get back to what's important, you should buy that piece. Your hair is so dark, a perfect contrast to the silver, and your eyes are such a deep blue—like the sapphires. It practically screams your name, Devin."

"It *is* gorgeous," she agreed. "I may."

"It really does scream your name," Beth agreed.

"You have the perfect creamy skin for it, too. I'll wrap it up."

"Hey, thanks for the compliments, but I don't even know what it costs," Devin said, laughing.

"Not that much, really. Just bring me your books—if you have a box, we'll wind up about even."

Devin laughed again. "Okay, done deal."

Beth took out the medallion and put it in a small box.

"Well, I've got to get back to writing. I just came out to buy birdseed—which I still have to do—and wound up walking around," Devin said. "Seems like every time I look, something's closed and something new has opened."

"And we grow more commercial every year," Theo said sadly.

"It's a commercial world," Devin said lightly. "They want you to pay your power bill no matter what."

Beth put the box in a decorative bag and handed it to Devin. "So how are you doing with that wretched old bird?"

"Poe?" Devin asked.

"Other people are left cats and dogs—and your great-aunt left you a raven!" Beth said, shaking her head. "You know, I watched him until you came home after your aunt Mina died."

"I do, and I'm grateful," Devin assured her. "He's doing just fine."

"How the hell long do those birds live?" Beth asked.

"I think they can get to be about twenty in captivity. Aunt Mina rescued him when he was a baby, so I'd say he's about twelve now," Devin said. "He's a very cool bird. I like having company. I mean, it's not that the cottage is so far out of town, but it *seems* like there are a lot of woods out there."

"You need a cat," Beth said.

"Or a dog," Theo suggested.

"For the moment, I have Poe," Devin said.

Theo set a hand on hers. "It's been nice to see you. We'll all have to go to dinner one night."

"Sure," Devin said, smiling and quickly extracting her hand. "See you all later."

Her car was in the public garage off Essex, and she hurried to it. It wasn't a long drive down Broad and out to her cottage, but it did involve avoiding crowds of jaywalking tourists.

Parking, she studied her "cottage in the woods." Technically, it was an old house, but it did have the white-walled, thatched-roof look of a cottage, and she was surrounded by a small forest of trees. When she had the fire going and smoke was drifting out of the chimney, it did look as if she lived in a home that belonged in a fairy tale.

As she opened the door and stepped in, Devin found herself smiling. Poe immediately let out a loud squawk. Unlike Poe's raven, this bird didn't say "nevermore." He only squawked. But he liked to sit on his perch and watch her. Sometimes—though he was nowhere near as attached to her as he had been to Aunt Mina—he would even sit on her shoulder. She didn't mind; Aunt Mina had trained him. He kept his droppings discreetly deposited in his cage onto newspaper that was easy to replace.

"Hey, buddy," she said, putting down her packages and walking over to the bird. She stroked his head through the bars the way he liked. "Got your birdseed. All is well."

His cage was near the mantel, so she set the bag of birdseed on top while she fed him. When she was finished, she stepped back and smiled, thinking that it was time to make some changes. But it was hard. She'd spent so much of her childhood here in the cottage. Her parents had traveled frequently for work, and since Devin had loved Aunt Mina and her aunt had loved her, it had made sense for her to stay here.

She'd loved how different Aunt Mina was from her own parents and everybody else's—that she collected unusual and beautiful things. Once, in school, Brent Corbin had told her that if she'd just add a few more wacky family members she could join the cast of *The Addams Family*.

That was okay. She'd grown up with love, both here in Auntie Mina's cottage and in the house her parents had owned—and still owned, actually—

an old Victorian near the wharf and the House of the Seven Gables. It had been rented out for years now, and it was completely different from the way she remembered it. While the cottage . . .

Despite the years, little had changed here.

Devin opened the box holding her beautiful new silver medallion and hung it around the neck of a marble bust of Madame Tussaud that sat on a pedestal near the fireplace. The bust had been made from a life mask of the tiny woman who had created so many wax images, including death masks of some of the victims of the guillotine. Aunt Mina had loved the woman because she had been so talented—and such a survivor. The pentagram suited her marble neck.

"Guess I should get to work, huh?" Devin asked the bird.

He was too busy eating to reply.

She booted up the computer. The world seemed silent. Too silent. She turned on iTunes and set the music to play randomly.

For long minutes she actually concentrated.

Then she heard the crying.

It was soft and heart-wrenching—so soft, she wasn't sure at first that she was really hearing anything at all. Next she thought it might have been part of the song that was playing.

But then a Bon Jovi hit came on, and she knew there was no soft sobbing in that hard-hitting rock song.

She muted the volume and listened. She was certain she heard it again. Very strange, since her nearest neighbor was a quarter of a mile away.

She walked to the door and opened it—and thought she saw a woman in white disappearing into the trees.

"Hello?" she called out. "Can I help you?"

There was no answer. The leaves rustled as the breeze picked up, nothing more.

"Please, do you need help?" She stepped out onto the stone path that led from her house to the road.

No answer.

Because no one was out there, she told herself.

She turned and looked back at the bird. Poe was still playing with his seed, unconcerned.

And of course, the idea that there was anyone out there had almost certainly come from the fact that she'd spent half her childhood, her most impressionable years, growing up with Aunt Mina. Not that her aunt had been crazy—unless being delightfully full of fun and life could be called crazy. But Aunt Mina had been forever telling stories—stories about leprechauns and banshees and forest folk, and the arguments that went on between the tooth fairy and Santa's elves.

Devin walked back in the house, trying to forget the sound of sobbing and give her attention back to *Auntie Pim and the Belligerent Gnome.*

It was wonderful that her books had sold out, she thought.

Thanks to her aunt, she not only had a wonderful place to live but she'd found her true vocation. She'd done her duty as a junior reporter, but when Aunt Mina had suggested she try children's stories, she had sat down and written one. She'd set her sights on reaching ten-year-olds—the age she'd been when Aunt Mina had first enchanted her.

Auntie Mina had been a practicing Wiccan. Her garden—while now in need of a woeful amount of care—was filled with a wide selection of herbs. Long before it had been popular to be Wiccan in Salem, Auntie Mina had been a healer and devotee of the old religion. While some in town mocked her, others came to her for advice, and with their aches and pains.

Devin's parents were good Anglicans, but they were also a pair of hippies and were all for everyone believing as they felt they should, so they'd respected Aunt Mina's religion. According to Devin's father, "There are real Wiccans, and they're just as decent as everyone else—or not. And then there are commercial Wiccans. You know—those people who come to Salem and open shops and claim to be Wiccans for a living. Hey, who's to judge? Your aunt helps everyone, whatever their beliefs. In my opinion, like she says, it doesn't much matter what we call the path or the light at the end of that path as long as we're good people while we walk it, doing our best to help our fellow travelers."

Devin loved her parents. When she'd left for school, they'd rented out their old home off Front Street and moved west to enjoy the mountains and sunshine of Boulder, Colorado.

Her own cottage was small but charming. It dated back to the early 1700s. There were just six rooms, all on the ground floor, with the parlor having a grand stone fireplace and old, unfinished woodwork all around. The room was decorated with Aunt Mina's various treasures: crystal balls, elf-shaped incense holders, gargoyles, raven bookends, a pair of medieval mirrors—the bust of Madame Tussaud, of course—and all sorts of other items suited to a slightly crazy but very sweet Wiccan.

Devin's first book, *Auntie Pim and the Gregarious Ghost*, sat nicely in the shelf alongside her second book, *Auntie Pim and Marvelous Martian*, contained between the raven bookends.

Looking at the books, she was glad that Aunt Mina had lived to see the first one published. She'd been so proud. Thinking of her aunt made Devin smile. She couldn't be too sad—Aunt Mina had died at the grand old age of one hundred and one. She'd enjoyed great health until the night she'd said she was tired, sat in the old maple rocker before the fire and simply died. Devin had still been working for the paper at the time, but her mom had come for a visit because Aunt Mina had called her. Aunt Mina hadn't been alone. Devin was glad about that, too.

Sometimes Devin thought she saw her aunt peeking out at her from around a corner with a mischievous smile.

But then, thanks to Aunt Mina, she'd thought she'd seen the dead before. That was because she really did owe everything to Auntie Mina, who'd been the best storyteller ever. When she had taken Devin to the Howard Street Cemetery where old Giles Corey had been pressed to death and told his story, Devin could have sworn that she saw the old man standing among the tombs, leaning on a cane, his expression thoughtful as the breeze rushed through his thin gray hair.

Auntie Mina had often told her with a wink that it was possible to speak with the dead—but only when the dead wished to speak. And of course, she'd added, with another wink, only special people received the talent to see through time and space, and hear the dead when they spoke.

"The books are doing so well, Auntie Mina," she said aloud. "They're really your books, you know."

It helped, of course, that she worked with a wonderful artist, Drew Wicker, who lived in nearby Marblehead.

She sat back down at her computer, but just as

she got comfortable, the sound came again. It was a woman crying. Definitely.

"Poe, is that you?" she demanded aloud, even though she knew the crying was coming from somewhere farther away.

The bird, as if indignant, looked up, cocked his head and squawked in protest.

"Okay, that's it—no way I can concentrate now," she murmured to herself.

She started out of the house again and then remembered that while she considered her neighborhood safe, bad things did happen. They'd found a murdered woman just two weeks ago in Swampscott.

Most of the details had been kept out of the paper, but she knew the woman had been young. Maybe in her early twenties.

Something itched at her memory. And then she recalled the incident that had been nagging at her.

It had taken place a little more than a decade ago. And it hadn't been in Salem; it had been in Peabody or Marblehead or somewhere. A high school girl had been found murdered in the woods.

The details had been kept out of the paper then just as they had been now—the newest victim's name hadn't been revealed yet—but she knew one factor both women had in common.

Both women's throats had been slit.

Surely, it was impossible that the two incidents could be related, not with so many years in between.

"Okay, Poe, freaking myself out here, huh?" she said aloud.

It was only about nine at night, and since they were on daylight savings time, there was still a little glow of light in the sky.

"It's still light out, for heaven's sake," she said.

Poe squawked.

"Maybe I *do* need a dog. A large one," she murmured.

Poe protested again.

"Okay . . ."

She looked around and then headed into the bedroom and grabbed one of her old hockey sticks out of the closet and started out. "No sense in being stupid. I can wield a wicked hockey stick."

She heard the sobbing again. It was coming from the trees to the west of her house, from the little stand of trees that separated her from her neighbor.

"Please, I'm trying to help you," she said softly. "Hello? Are you lost? Are you hurt? If you'll just let me help you . . ."

She walked into the trees, then began to question her own wisdom.

The sky was darkening. Beneath the trees the light was all but gone.

She tightened her grip on her hockey stick.

And then she saw her.

She was young, a slight blond woman, wearing a black dress and a shawl that looked to be of the Puritan period. She was peeking out from between two trees.

There was nothing unusual about her outfit. This was, after all, Salem.

"Hey, there you are. I don't know what's wrong, but you can come in and we can call someone—someone to come get you. Someone who can help," Devin said.

The young woman looked at her with enormous brown eyes. She shook her head and began to sob again.

And then she disappeared into the trees.

The woman might have been twenty or twenty-one—or she might have been a teenager—but she certainly didn't look dangerous. Determined to help her, Devin headed back to her cottage and swept the electric lantern off the mantel. She hurried back out, turning the light on as she went.

"I'm not leaving you out here!" she called. "Come on, speak to me, please."

She headed toward the spot where she had first seen the woman. She didn't hear sobbing anymore, but the woman couldn't have gone far.

Maybe she was a foreign tourist who didn't speak any English and had gotten lost.

Maybe she'd been on a date or gone out with friends who had decided it would be fun to explore the old cemetery down the road from Devin's cottage, and she had gotten lost and ended up terrified.

Maybe some jerk had just driven her out here and dumped her.

Or maybe . . .

Devin let out a shocked, ear-piercing scream.

The woman lay in a tiny open area between several large trees with gnarled branches. She was faceup, arms and legs outstretched, so her body resembled the design of a pentagram.

Her sightless eyes stared up into the darkness of the night. On her chest was a silver chain with a medallion.

Much like the silver pentagram she herself had just purchased.

But that seemed like nothing.

Because . . .

Around her throat . . .

There was a ribbon of blood.

2

The road was dark. The day had been long, but when it had finally ended the night had gone almost stygian. There was a moon, but it was hidden behind billowing clouds that promised summer rain for the northeast.

Rocky nearly hit the woman who ran out into the middle of the road.

His lights caught her, and for a moment he thought he'd entered some kind of nightmare region in his mind. She stood like an ancient icon in the glare, but was she goddess or demon? No matter what, she was beautiful, like an elemental force emerging from the darkness. She wielded something in her hands as she forced him to stop. A scepter?

No. A hockey stick.

Rocky quickly turned the car off, leaving the lights on, and stepped out. He was never unarmed, but he didn't pull his Glock from the holster at his side. He lifted his hands to show her he meant no harm.

She was tall, and the dress swirling around her in the rain-scented breeze made her appear especially regal and elegant. She had long black hair that whipped around her face. It was almost like seeing the perfectly fashioned heroine of a video game come to life. There was no way any healthy male could ignore her presence. She aroused every fantasy his mind had ever come up with, and she drew on every ounce of lust that coursed through his body.

He quashed the wanderings of his mind, reminding himself that she was clearly in trouble. This was no fantasy. They were standing in the middle of the road in the dark, with a storm on the way.

"Are you all right?" he demanded.

"I'm fine, but . . . phone. Do you have a phone? Call 9-1-1, please!"

"What's your emergency? I can help you if you'll just tell—"

"Dammit, are you stupid? *I* don't need help! Dial 9-1-1—there's a dead woman in the woods!"

He dialed. Then, slowly and precisely, he identified himself and their location—and the situation.

"Did you discover the body, sir?" the operator asked.

"No—I was stopped on the road by the woman who did." He looked at Devin. "Who are you?" he asked.

"What?"

"Your name. They need to know who discovered the body."

"Devin. Devin Lyle."

"Devin Lyle found her," he said into the phone. "Please send someone." He knew the operator would keep him talking while the police were dispatched and he needed to find out what was going on, so he hung up.

"Where?" he asked Devin Lyle.

She pointed toward the woods. "But . . . but don't go in there. The cops . . . they'll want the crime scene intact, right?"

"Ma'am, I'm an FBI agent. Are you sure she's dead?"

41

"Yes."

"Did you try CPR or just take her pulse?"

"Sir, she's dead."

"Agent," Rocky said by rote. "Agent Rockwell. Do you have any kind of medical training? Are you certain that she's dead?"

"No," she said. "And yes, I'm sure."

"Where is she?"

Devin Lyle's finger rose, and she pointed.

Rocky hurried through the trees.

And found the victim.

She wasn't far from the road; there was a break in the trees, and there she was.

For a moment he forgot his years of training and fieldwork. He simply froze. Body . . . and soul.

It was déjà vu.

She was lying just like Melissa had lain, limbs and head creating the five points of a star.

And on her breast lay . . .

A silver medallion. A pentagram.

Around her throat . . .

A red ribbon of blood.

He didn't move to her side, only stood rigidly and stared.

Devin Lyle came up behind him. He suspected she thought he was being respectful of the dead woman.

That wasn't it, though. He was simply frozen by his memories.

"Are you going to try to revive her?" she asked

quietly, only a small note of irony in her tone.

He could hear sirens; the police were on the way.

He turned to face the dark-haired woman who had stopped him. "When did you find her?"

"Seconds before I stopped you."

"How did you find her?"

She pointed. "My home is just there—on the other side of the trees."

"How did you know to look for her here in the dark? Did you hear something? Did she cry out?"

"Yes, I—I don't know what exactly. I heard something. Sobbing—a cry. Something."

He broke his paralysis and moved forward carefully, hunkering down to set two fingers on the flesh of the woman's wrist. She was cold. She'd been here awhile.

No attempt at resuscitation would have helped.

Her eyes had been green, her hair a soft brunette. She was clad in a simple halter dress and light sweater. At least the dress was pulled down decently, almost tucked between her outstretched legs.

He heard car doors slamming. The cops had arrived.

"Hey!" he said loudly, so he could be heard. "In here!"

A moment later two uniformed officers came through the trees and into the little clearing. They were competent and compassionate at the same

43

time, the first checking the victim and securing the scene, the second speaking with Rocky and Devin Lyle. It was while they were in the midst of the conversation that more sirens sounded, and Rocky was surprised to look up and see that a third officer, this one in plain clothes, was coming his way.

He was even more surprised to realize that he knew the man.

"Hell, Rocky—you're back in town?" the newcomer demanded.

"Jack Grail," Rocky said, shaking Jack's hand. "And you're still here." He grinned; it had been a good ten years since he'd seen Jack.

"Come on, I moved a bit. This is Salem, not Peabody."

"Right. You working these murders?" Rocky asked.

"This one, anyway," Jack said. They looked at each other for a long moment, both of them remembering a long ago day.

When they'd stared at the same scene that was before them now.

Rocky arched a brow. "Just like Swampscott, right?"

"Don't go talking that way, Rocky. People will think we have a serial killer on our hands, and the last thing we need is mass panic. Kind of suspicious, though, isn't it? You leave town not long after Melissa Wilson dies, and now you're back and we've got two more dead women."

Rocky stared at him and realized Jack wasn't serious—not about *that,* anyway. He *was* serious that he didn't want anyone yelling "serial killer" right now.

No, he didn't seriously suspect Rocky.

But they knew. They *both* knew. They had been there. They had seen Melissa's body, and they couldn't deny the eerie similarity of the newest murders.

"So you grew up to be a detective with the county?" Rocky asked Jack. "Good going."

Forget the past. They both had to shake off this feeling of déjà vu. They'd been boys back then. Now they were men—and the men assigned to work these newest killings.

Jack nodded. "And you just happened to discover this body, too?"

Rocky shook his head. "I just got back into town. Jack Grail, this is Devin Lyle." He nodded toward her. "She found the body. She flagged me down in the road."

"My house is over there," Devin said, pointing through the trees. "I heard a noise and ran out without my phone, and when I . . . when I saw her, I ran for the road to get help. I guess I should have gone back in and called, but . . . I just ran for the road," she finished lamely.

Jack turned his attention to Devin. As he spoke to her, the crime scene techs got to work and the

45

night seemed to come alive with flashes as pictures were taken.

Rocky waited while Jack talked to Devin and let his mind wander.

Jack looked good. Funny, Rocky had always thought that he'd wind up flipping burgers by day and smoking pot by night.

Finally Devin's interview was finished and an officer escorted her back through the woods to her house.

"So I heard you're a fed, like you planned," Jack said.

"Yeah. And it's good to see you, Jack. Bad circumstances, but it really is good to see you."

Jack grinned. "You, too, Rocky. Last I heard, though, you were working the mean streets of L.A."

"I just transferred to a new unit."

"We have a unit here?" Jack said, frowning.

Rocky smiled. There were field offices all over the country, with the one in New York City being the largest. "I was assigned to a behavioral unit out of Boston, but we go all over."

"And you were sent *here?*" Jack asked him. "To work *this* case?"

Rocky wasn't sure the assignment was official yet—whether Adam Harrison had cleared the way for FBI involvement—but he decided to be honest.

"I read about the woman in Swampscott," he said.

Jack looked grave as he lowered his head and nodded. "Yeah. Freaked me out," he admitted quietly. He looked at Rocky again. "None of us ever got closure, did we?" he asked.

"Not me, that's for sure," Rocky said. He studied Jack. "That why you became a cop?"

Jack nodded. "Yeah—worked my way up from the streets to make detective." He hesitated. "I study the old case sometimes. Okay, a lot of the time."

He looked at Rocky with an odd mixture of emotions, shrugged and started toward the crime scene. He turned back. "You coming?"

Rocky followed him. They hunkered down by the body and the medical examiner.

"Dead about four hours—give or take thirty minutes. Not too cold tonight, but not hot, either, so I think we're looking at just about five o'clock," the M.E. said.

"Broad daylight," Jack muttered. "Sexual assault?"

"No. Probably pretty quick—merciful, under the circumstances. Looks as if she was standing here when her killer came from behind and slashed right across her throat. See the pattern of the blood spray—almost a straightforward gush. Then he just laid her down and arranged the body."

Jack looked at Rocky. Neither of them spoke. Everyone knew how Melissa had died. She'd had her throat slashed. That much had leaked out; though, as far as he knew, only he, Jack and Vince, along with the cops and medical personnel who had worked the case, ever knew the details of the killing. With law enforcement and the powers that be afraid of both repercussions on the Wiccan community and that the investigation could be compromised, all the specifics had been kept quiet by the police, rather than let out for any would-be copycats to act on.

At the time, they'd all been so stunned and devastated, they'd never even spoken of it among themselves. They'd prayed and they'd waited for the murderer to be found. . . .

And waited.

The killer eluded all efforts by the police to discover his—or her—identity.

Back then, the cops had talked about cults. Maybe they'd do the same now.

Within the hour, the body was on the way to the morgue. The crime scene unit continued to comb the woods, and Rocky stood with Jack by the side of the road.

"Shit," Jack muttered, looking at Rocky. "I don't study this kind of stuff—you know, the psychology of a killer. I guess you do. But my wife watches those shows all the time." He paused and looked at Rocky a little sheepishly. "My wife—Haley."

Rocky smiled. "Congratulations. I'm sorry I

missed it. I guess I should have come home more."

"We sent you an invitation to the wedding."

"I never saw it. I was probably working out west and it never reached me."

"Yeah, well, anyway, Haley is hooked on all the crime shows. She's relentless—trying to tell me how to be a better cop all the time. I guess it doesn't hurt. But how could this be the same guy? Melissa was killed, what? Almost thirteen years ago? I thought serial killers escalated, getting more violent and killing more frequently."

"Usually. But there have been cases where a killer starts, stops, then picks up years later. Sometimes it turns out he was in prison for something else, but sometimes he just loses the urge until something happens to trigger it again. No one has ever really cracked the puzzle of the human mind. We can look for patterns, we can base our investigations on what we've learned, but we're surprised all the time. This looks like the same killer, but we don't know yet that it *is*."

"Copycat?"

"Possibly. Are you lead on the case in Swampscott?" Rocky asked him.

Jack nodded. "They've taken everything else off my plate. They want this one solved." He shook his head. "Nothing to do with Melissa. It's just my job."

"So," Rocky said, "tell me about her."

"Carly Henderson," Jack said. "She was a red-head. We found her in the same kind of situation, small patch of woods in a semiurban area. She was a local. I don't know who this woman was, but I'm willing to bet she'll prove to be local, too."

"Like Melissa," Rocky said.

"Like Melissa," Jack agreed.

"I definitely need a dog," Devin said, leaning back against the door. It was locked and bolted. She'd checked the back door and the windows, too. She still felt on edge. "A giant dog. Or maybe an attack cat—like a tiger."

I just found a woman with her throat slashed!

She suddenly wondered at her own courage—or stupidity—in running into the road. She might have flagged down the killer instead of an FBI agent. A normal person would have run back to the cottage, locked the door and called the police.

But what if the killer had hidden in her house?

At least she knew the killer wasn't inside with her now. The young officer who had walked her back had made a thorough search. He'd gone into her closets and looked under the beds. And the cops would be nearby, searching the scene, for a while, she knew.

Poe squawked.

Her hands, she realized, were still shaking.

She could still see the woman all too clearly in her mind's eyes. Lying there. Dead.

Poe let out another cry.

"I'm sorry. You're a great bird. You just don't have fangs and claws," she told him.

It was all right. She was locked in, and she wasn't opening her door to anyone.

Devin walked to the entertainment center—artfully hidden behind lattice doors—and turned on the television, wanting company.

She sat down at her computer, thinking that if she went back to work she would concentrate on the wonderful magic of her aunt—both her real aunt and her fictional Auntie Pim—and get lost in the joy of writing.

Except she didn't.

Work? Was she kidding herself? She wasn't going to get any work done now.

She looked up the murder in Swampscott.

The first site she opened, the local paper, gave her as much information as was available to the public.

The police have identified the victim found dead in the Swampscott woods on Saturday as Carly Jane Henderson. Ms. Henderson ran a local beauty salon and was a longtime resident of Essex County, though she was born and raised in Danvers. She was last seen leaving the O Club in Salem at eleven o'clock on

Friday night, after enjoying dinner and cocktails with friends. Her car was parked at the local garage, where it remained until found by police. Police are seeking help to solve her murder. Anyone with any information regarding her whereabouts after she left the O Club is asked to please call the county sheriff's department.

While police are closely guarding information regarding the murder itself due to the ongoing investigation, some local residents remember the murder of Melissa Wilson thirteen years ago. Melissa had left a friend's house at around five o'clock, after a study date. She was later found the same evening in Peabody Woods. However, while Miss Wilson was seventeen, Carly Henderson was thirty-two.

The clock on the mantel struck twelve. Devin jumped, then stared at the softly chiming clock.

The two men had talked about ... both murders. Or two murders. Or ...

They'd known each other, she thought. The cop and the man she'd flagged down. Agent Rockwell ... and Detective Grail. The two knew each other and ...

She turned back to the computer screen.

Melissa Wilson.

She remembered the murder herself. She'd been

about thirteen. Her parents had gone crazy with worry, of course. She'd barely been allowed out for weeks. But then events in the rest of the world had overshadowed one murder in little Peabody, and Melissa's death had faded from the collective memory.

She'd jumped when the clock chimed; when her phone rang, she nearly flew off her chair.

Who could be calling at midnight?

She stared at the caller ID. She didn't know the number. She didn't even know the area code.

For some reason, though, she answered it.

"Hello?"

Images from books and movies swept through her mind. It was the killer. He was going to tell her that he was watching her. . . .

"Miss Lyle?"

For a moment she didn't reply. She couldn't.

"This is Agent Rockwell."

Sometimes the handsome cop was the killer, she reminded herself.

"I asked Detective Grail to make sure that an officer was posted outside your house tonight."

She found her voice. It was a squeak. "You think—you think he's still out there?"

"Frankly, no. Whoever this is, he carefully stalks and kills his victims. It's very possible he gets to know them, one reason why Carly Henderson might have left willingly with him, and why the victim you discovered may have stood unsuspectingly with her back to him."

She didn't know what to say, so she didn't say anything, just waited for him to go on.

"I think you're fine—I promise. But I thought you might be nervous, and that it wouldn't be a bad idea to have a patrol car in front of your house."

"Thank you."

She walked to the window, pulled the drapes and looked out. There was a patrol car, bearing Salem's famous witch logo on the door.

"Thank you," she repeated.

"Have the best night you can," he told her, and hung up.

There was something she liked about his words, she realized. He hadn't said anything inane like *Have a good night.*

No. He'd said, *Have the best night you can.*

She'd barely noticed anything about him earlier, but now memory kicked in.

The man was tall and well built, though it was hard to really tell what lay beneath the suit. He'd looked strong. A good man to have around when a murderer might still be lurking in the woods nearby.

Unless *he was the murderer.*

Oh, God, her imagination was making her crazy.

She hovered by the computer a while longer and then rose at last. She was too nervous to undress for bed. She turned out her bedroom light but left the other lights in the cottage on.

Sensible, she thought. She could see out, no one could see into her room.

She was finally beginning to drift off to sleep when her half-closed eyes turned toward the bedroom door.

Maybe she was asleep already. Dreaming. She could swear she saw Aunt Mina there with her delightfully rosy cheeks and her long white hair rolled into a bun.

"Sleep, my little darling, I'm here," her aunt said.

And Devin managed to fall into a real sleep at last.

"Are you two ever calling it quits and going to sleep?"

Rocky looked up. He and Jack had spent the past several hours poring over everything they knew about Melissa's murder, and the murders of Carly Henderson and the as-yet-unidentified woman whose body had been found that night.

The question had come from Haley—Haley Grail, Jack's wife.

Haley, too, had aged well. She'd gone from being a cheerleader to a dance instructor. She and Jack had married five years ago. They had one child, a toddler son named Jack, after his father, and called Jackie.

Haley had been pleased to see him, genuinely pleased. Not surprising. They'd parted as friends. Tonight she had her pretty blond hair pulled back in a ponytail and was wearing sweats.

"Wow, I didn't realize how late it was. Sorry," Rocky said, rising. "My fault. I drove back into town and into a murder. And with the similarities to Melissa's death, well . . ."

"It's not all your fault," Haley said. "Jack has been obsessed, as well." She looked at her husband affectionately. "And I understand. You have to remember, Melissa was my good friend back then." She straightened and went into parental mode. "But you two, if you're going to be worth anything to anyone tomorrow, should get some sleep." She smiled at them even as she nodded firmly. But then her smile faded. "He's back, isn't he?"

"Haley, we really don't know—" Jack said.

"He's back. The Pentagram Killer is back," she said.

Rocky looked at Jack. He hadn't known they'd given a nickname to the man who'd killed Melissa.

Jack shrugged. "You never heard that?"

"I never knew the news about the pentagram was out there," Rocky said.

"It's not. That's just between us. Those of us who were there." He stopped, flushing. "Of course, Haley and Vince and Renee and I have talked over the years. I guess we didn't start using the nickname until after you went to college. It's just between us. You never heard the term because . . . you were gone, and once your mom moved . . . you never came back. The kids growing up around here just call him the Backwoods Slasher. I think I heard it first at Salem College, where I wound up going. You know how urban legends start. In the dorm hallways people would see the ghost of Melissa, her throat red and bleeding, and she'd say, 'Help me.' When kids went parking out by the woods, they were warned to beware of the Backwoods Slasher."

Rocky knew all about urban legends and ghost stories.

It was just different when you'd been there. When you'd really seen a woman lying dead in the dirt, a necklace of red around her throat.

When you'd really heard the words from somewhere in your mind.

Help me!

And when you'd completely failed to do so.

"Haley, that was thirteen years ago," Rocky said. "We don't know what's going on here yet. We *will* find out this time, though."

She smiled at him. "I know you will," she said. "Meanwhile, you know you're welcome to stay here. We have a little room behind Jackie's. It's yours, so long as you don't mind tripping over Legos now and then."

"That's nice of you, Haley," he said. "Thank you. But I'm at the new hotel on Derby Street. I'm okay. And now it's time for me to go."

"I'll walk you out," Jack told him.

As they headed to the car, Jack said, "Hell, you even look like a fed. Black suit, perfect tie."

Rocky laughed. "And you look like a detective."

"Oh, yeah, how's that?"

"Nondescript," Rocky teased. "I'm joking, of course. You look good. I'm sure you can still 'go long.' "

"It's softball for me these days," Jack told him. "I'm a damned good first baseman." He hesitated. "Vince is on the team, too. You can imagine what that's like. When he hits the ball . . . well, if he gets a piece of it, we're all rounding the bases."

"I have no problem believing that. How's the rest of our old gang?" he asked, then added softly, "You and Haley are married. What about Renee?"

"Renee is the eternal cheerleader—she's coaching now. Obviously Vince is still in town, too. Believe it or not, he's running for city council. He became an attorney," Jack told him.

Rocky laughed. "Well, hell—Vince is going to show us both up. Good for him."

Jack was thoughtful for a moment. "It changed us, you know? Melissa changed us. We were all cutups—except for you. But . . . maybe we realized how short life could be. I don't know.

But after the night she was found . . . after the grief counselors came to school . . . and after watching . . . waiting . . . for something horrible to happen again. I don't know. We changed. Actually, I thought about you a lot. You could have done anything. With your grades, you had it all made. But all you wanted was to be a cop. Like your dad."

"Did it have anything to do with wanting to solve Melissa's case?" Rocky asked. "You deciding to become a cop?"

Jack shrugged. "Maybe. That's why you're here, isn't it?"

"Yeah," Rocky admitted.

"And you walked right into another murder."

"Technically, I was driving. Miss Lyle walked into the murder—or sort of, anyway."

"How do you figure that?" Jack asked him.

"That she sort of walked into a murder?"

"Yeah."

"She said she heard something. But according to the medical examiner, the woman was killed around five, and Miss Lyle didn't even get home until it was at least six. By then . . . who knows what she heard. I'm going to talk to her again tomorrow—with your permission, of course."

Jack grinned. "You have my permission, though I have a feeling you're not going to need it. Someone on high is going to tell the sheriff to invite the FBI—and you're going to be it."

"I doubt I'll be alone," Rocky said. After his meeting with Jackson Crow, he'd met the other members of the local Krewe. Crow's wife was also one of his agents; her name was Angela Hawkins, and her main job was to assess reports and determine which agents should work each situation, according to their talents as well as their availability. She would undoubtedly be sending someone else to work the case with him.

Jack nodded. "Autopsy tomorrow, if you want to observe. Carly Henderson was released to her family a few days ago for burial. You've seen all the records and reports, though."

"Thanks. And good night, Jack. Good to see you. I just wish . . ."

"I know. You should have shown up for the reunion," Jack said. "Except even then . . ."

"Melissa was on everyone's mind."

"Yeah," Jack agreed.

Rocky slid into the driver's seat.

Jack called out to him one last time. "I'm glad you're here, Rocky. I'm, uh, ready to go long."

Rocky waved to him. "Takes a team," he replied.

A little while later, in his room at the hotel, Rocky laid his Glock in its small holster on the bedside table, stripped down to his shorts and lay back on the bed, staring at the ceiling.

Three. Now there were three.

That they knew of.

Why one all those years ago—and two more now, so many years later?

He could ask himself the question all night and it wouldn't matter. He didn't have the answer.

Yet.

Finally he slept.

And he dreamed. He was a kid again, following a voice. A voice that said, "Help me."

He ran—ran hard and fast. This time, he had to save the victim. He came to a graveyard and hopped over and around stones, trying to reach the summit of a little hill right in the middle of the graves. Because he could see her there.

It was Devin Lyle.

She was facing him. The wind had caught her raven-black hair and swept it around her face. She was tall and sleek, and her dress was caught by the whipping breeze, as well. The night sky was a deep blue, with black shadows. He could hear her calling to him, asking for help, and he couldn't reach her.

There was a presence behind her, but she didn't know. She didn't see.

It was the killer.

For a moment something glittered in the starlight.

A knife.

Rocky jerked awake drenched with sweat. He looked at the bedside clock. It wasn't quite 6:00 a.m.

Screw it. He got up and showered. He thought of the different investigative paths he might take.

By the time he was dressed, he knew exactly where he was going.

The old saying was right. Daylight *did* make everything better.

Devin rose, showered and dressed, then brewed coffee. Looking out, she saw that there was still a patrol car in front of her house, just as she had been told there would be.

She poured a cup and went outside. Unbidden, an image came to her mind. *She was going to get there and find out that the officer was dead. There would be a bullet hole through his forehead or a knife stuck through his throat.*

Her imagination playing tricks again, of course.

He wasn't dead. And he was young, maybe twenty-three or twenty-four, tops.

"Thought you might like some coffee," she told him.

"That's wicked cool of you, thanks," he said, smiling.

She nodded and dropped her estimation. Maybe twenty-one and fresh out of the academy.

She handed him the cup. "It's black, but I have sugar and creamer inside."

"Black is great."

"Are you hungry?"

He didn't get to answer the question, because a black SUV drove up behind him and parked.

Agent Rockwell got out, and she noticed details she'd missed the night before. His eyes were direct and green, and he kept his dark auburn hair short and well groomed. And he was impeccably dressed in a dark suit that fit him perfectly.

He walked over to them, displaying his badge for the officer in the car.

"I'm Officer Fitzpatrick," the young man in the car said. "Glad to see you, sir. I've been told I could head home at nine, but I don't know if I'm getting a replacement or not."

"I don't believe so," Rockwell said, and looked at Devin. "Not enough manpower, and we don't believe that Miss Lyle is in any danger—especially now that the night is over." He smiled reassuringly at Devin. "We don't actually believe you were ever in any danger, but I thought that after the trauma you went through, the reassurance of an officer out front might be welcome." He stared at her assessingly. "It looks like you made it through the night quite well."

Fitzpatrick handed back her mug with a thank-you, then turned his key in the ignition and drove off.

"Thank you for sending him."

"Sure. May I ask you some questions?"

"I guess," she said.

He was staring at her house curiously. Suddenly

he looked at her and smiled. "I just realized . . . this is the Witch of the Woods House."

Devin felt her muscles tightening at the reminder of the way some locals had mocked her aunt and the cottage.

"I don't know what you're talking about," she said coldly.

"Sorry, just growing up so close—in Peabody— there were rumors about this place, that's all. It was owned by an older lady, by all accounts a lovely woman, who was a Wiccan and grew herbs and . . . every girl I went to high school with wanted a love potion from her. I guess she passed away—she was quite elderly even then. Did you know her?"

"Yes. She was my great-aunt, Mina Lyle," Devin said. She couldn't help the chill in her tone.

"I'm sorry. I didn't mean to offend you. About those questions . . . ?"

She shrugged. "Come in. The house doesn't bite."

"I didn't think it did."

She led the way in and offered him coffee, then went to get it, leaving him in the parlor, studying all her treasures.

When she returned, Poe was sitting on his shoulder.

She looked at the bird. *Wretched traitor!* she told him silently.

And yet . . .

She didn't know what it was. She'd been so terrified after her discovery in the woods that she'd thought he was an idiot when he hadn't immediately dialed 9-1-1.

Now . . .

Now she couldn't help but note that he was extremely good-looking in a masculine but rather . . . *federal* way. He could have walked onto the set of a new *Men in Black* movie and fit right in.

"He's great," Rockwell said of the bird. "What's his name?"

"Poe."

"Of course. Well, let's set you on your perch, Poe," he said, and easily urged the bird back onto the white pine perch in his large cage. He looked over at Devin. "And thank you. For seeing me, speaking with me—and for the coffee."

As he sipped, his eyes wandered, then lit on the marble bust of Madame Tussaud.

He walked over to it, and she realized that he was staring at the pentagram medallion.

He turned to her. He was tense. Hard. Everything about him had changed.

"Where did you get this?" he demanded.

And she realized that the icy stare that he was aiming her way was filled with . . .

Suspicion.

3

None of the pentagrams were the same. No one of the three was like either of the other two. Rocky had seen all three medallions, and they were firmly etched in his memory.

The first, the one he'd seen on Melissa Wilson's body, had been a very clean design, with only a thin line of silver vines winding around the angles at each point of the star.

On the second—found on Carly Henderson—the points of the star were themselves formed by green-tinted vines.

The third—found on Jane Doe last night—had intricate little flowers at each point.

And now this . . .

It was probably one of the nicest pieces of jewelry he had ever seen. Enamel delicately decorated the silver to create slender elegant leaves around the points of the star, and there was a tiny stone at each point—a sapphire. There was something so fragile and beautiful about the piece that it was instantly arresting. In a city where there were probably thousands of similar pieces for sale, this one was exquisite.

And enough like the others that they all just might have been created by the same artist.

He stared at Devin Lyle, and she stared back at him. Maybe she thought he'd lost it. She hadn't trusted him much from the get-go, he thought, even though *she* had flagged *him* down.

"Who are you—really?" she asked him.

"Agent Rockford. Really." By rote, he produced his badge.

She looked at it, then at him, and said, "You do realize that badge doesn't mean much these days. We—the innocent public—are conditioned to accept any kind of forgery because we're accustomed to seeing official badges everywhere."

"It's real," he told her, smiling.

"So I really flagged down an FBI agent—by accident—after stumbling across a body?"

He nodded, but he wasn't about to get distracted from what really interested him. "Where did you get this piece?" he asked her again.

"My friend's shop. She has a number of them. I'm not much for diamonds, but I do love colored stones."

"Like rubies, emeralds and sapphires?" he queried. It wasn't an attack, though he could tell from the way she looked at him that she had taken it as one. She seemed to believe that he suspected her—or her friends—to be guilty of something.

"Citrine, aquamarine, opals—fire opals are my favorite," she said. She set his coffee on the

67

natural-wood coffee table that stood between what Rocky was pretty sure was a grouping of eighteenth-century carved chairs and a love seat.

"Your questions can't be about my likes and dislikes when it comes to jewelry," she said, sitting down. "I don't know what else I can tell you. I heard a noise outside. I grabbed my hockey stick and went out into the woods, and there she was. My first instinct was to get help—to get the police. I was closer to the road than I was to my house. Okay, I was panicked and afraid the killer might be around and follow me home, so maybe that's why I ran to the road. I saw her, but I didn't know her," she added quietly.

He took a seat across from her.

"What did you hear?" he asked her. "The M.E. reckoned that the time of death was around five o'clock. You found her hours later. That's why I'm asking."

She shook her head. She was evading him, he thought. "I don't know exactly. I just thought that someone might be hurt or something, so I went out."

He could press it, but he could tell she wasn't going to say more. So far he'd called her beloved deceased great-aunt a crazy witch and jumped down her throat over a medallion. Not good. He wanted her help.

She turned the tables. "So you're from here?"

she asked him. "You said something about Peabody."

"Born there. My mother could trace her family back to the *Mayflower.* She's proud of it. I have more of a tendency to think the ship was filled with hypocrites. They wanted freedom, so they came here and persecuted others, and, as we both know, their descendants tangled themselves up with the witchcraft trials. My father was from Texas, but he loved my mom, so I was born here. What about you?"

"I grew up in an old Victorian right here in Salem. I could see the House of the Seven Gables whenever I went outside."

"And you never left?" he asked.

"No, I left. I was a reporter in Boston for a while, then I came back. But I'm sure you didn't come here to chitchat about growing up in New England."

She had blue eyes—deep, direct blue eyes. The color of the sapphires on her pentagram. He lowered his head for a minute, hiding a dry smile. She was the perfect image of a witch, or of the Hollywood version, at least. Her hair was as dark as the wings of her pet raven. She was tall and slender, with elegant curves and perfect posture. She was in jeans today, and a soft sweater that hugged her form nicely, but—given a cloak and a scepter—she could have stood on a hill in the wind and, with an evil chant, lifted her face to the heavens and demanded that the lightning strike and the thunder roar.

And there was something she wasn't telling him.

"I wish there was more I could tell you. I so wish I could have done something to help that poor woman. If I knew anything that might help assist you, I would be writing it down to make sure you had it right," she told him.

"Thank you. I do need the name of your friend —the one you bought that medallion from—and her store."

She nodded. "You know, there was another woman killed in Swampscott two weeks ago," she said.

"Yes."

"The police aren't giving out much information. And they aren't saying much about the woman I found, either," she said. "It was the same killer, wasn't it?"

"They aren't giving out information because they're trying to weed out all the crackpots who want to confess to murders they didn't commit. They're also trying to avoid—" He stopped abruptly.

"To avoid?"

"Copycats."

"The officer last night asked me not to give out any information about the body," she said.

"And that's important. Luckily, we managed to have the scene sealed off and most of the work done before the press showed up last night. They don't know that you're involved, so hopefully there won't be anyone trying to get information out of you."

"I can keep quiet," she assured him. She hesitated. "But . . . this is also like that other murder . . . the one that happened thirteen years ago." She looked at him with that direct blue stare of hers. "In Peabody," she said.

"Yes," he said quietly.

"You . . . were there?"

"I was a senior in high school at the time."

She rose and walked over to the mantel. "Were the other women found with medallions like mine lying on their breasts, as well?"

He hesitated, then realized that having seen one victim, she was smart enough to draw conclusions.

"Yes. But that's something else I hope you'll keep to yourself."

She turned and looked at him. "Are you thinking they're some kind of Wiccan sacrifice? I ask because I know that might be a lot of people's first impression. But you'd be really wrong. Half my friends are Wiccans. They're . . . like flower children. They believe in good things. People have a tendency to think that Wiccans follow Aleister Crowley's tenets, but you grew up around here, so you must know that's not true. Crowley was a hedonist who used whatever suited him to create his own brand of religion. He even homed in on Masonic principles, and the Masons I know are great people. My dad is a Mason, and he and his friends bowled a lot and raised money for children's charities. Trust me, no real Wiccan committed these murders."

She was passionate and clearly convinced of the truth of what she was saying. And of course, he hadn't grown up in the area for nothing.

"Do no harm to others lest it be returned to you threefold," he said.

She seemed a little startled. "Yes."

"No true Wiccan did anything like this, no," he said. "But there are still other people out there who could have, and could have made it look like Wiccans were involved. Satanists, or plain old nutcases. We don't know yet. But hunting down the source of the medallions will be important, and with three of them, we finally have a shot."

"Well, I can assure you that my friend Beth Fullway, who owns the shop where I bought *my* medallion, isn't involved. She and I were thirteen when the first murder occurred. We went to school together."

"But did she create the piece?" he asked.

"No," Devin admitted.

"What's the name of her shop?"

"The Haunted Dragon. It's right on Essex."

He picked up his cup and finished his coffee. It

was excellent. Black and strong, with no bite or aftertaste. He set the cup down regretfully.

"Thank you."

"Of course, Agent Rockwell."

"Rocky," he said.

"Pardon?"

"Please, just call me Rocky."

"Your name is Rocky Rockwell?"

"Craig Rockwell. But I've always gone by Rocky." He turned toward the door, then stopped and extracted a card from his wallet. "Please, call me if you think of anything."

She accepted the card and slid it into the pocket of her jeans. "I will."

"And keep your doors locked."

"Of course," she said again, stepping forward and opening the door for him.

He had started toward his car when she called him back.

"Agent Rockwell. Um, Rocky?"

"Yes?"

"Maybe I could come with you. I've known Beth all my life. I'm afraid if you just go in and start questioning her . . ."

"You think I come on too tough?" he asked her.

"Well, when you first asked me about the necklace—the medallion—I thought you were going to arrest me."

He was thoughtful for a moment, not sure how much he wanted to involve this woman.

"I really can help," she said. "You'll find out more if you let me introduce you and play it cool."

Maybe she *could* help him. Like Jack Grail, she was a lot more closely tied to the area than he was.

He let out a breath.

"Sure. Let's go."

"Wait, give me a second," she told him.

She ran into another room and came out with a large box. He reached to take it from her.

"It's okay," she said. "I have it."

"Please."

She let him carry it. "Crown jewels?" he asked her.

"Books."

He looked at her questioningly.

"I'm a writer."

"Oh."

She didn't elaborate.

"Of what?"

"You mean you don't just assume that because I live in Salem, I must write about ghosts or monsters?"

"You could write anything. Fiction? Nonfiction?"

She blushed. "Witches—for children."

He grinned knowingly, and her blush deepened.

"They're based on my great-aunt."

"The good witch."

"The Wiccan. As you know."

Once they were in his car, she turned to him curiously. "Don't you think it's awfully coincidental that you came back to town just in time to be on the road when I ran out?"

"Not really. I'm here because of the murder in Swampscott."

"Ah," she said, looking at him. She was waiting for more.

"And because of the murder thirteen years ago. Because of the similarities."

"You must be pretty high up—to be able to pick your assignments, I mean."

"I got lucky," he said simply. He should have added that he wasn't sure he was even official yet, he just happened to be friends with the lead detective on the case.

They headed to the pedestrian mall on Essex and he parked in the public garage. As they walked out to the street Rocky looked at the old Civil War building that was now the National Park Visitors' Center. When he'd been growing up, it had been under reconstruction. As they reached Essex Street he reflected that while specifics changed, the town didn't. Shops had different owners and offered different delights, but the overall effect was still the same. He paused, allowing himself a small moment of pride. Yes, the town was commercialized. But even so, most places—even the shoddy museums with less than stellar mannequins—made a point of getting the history right. They offered theories on what had caused the mass hysteria that led to the witch trials, but they didn't profess to have the definitive answer. They reported history.

He listened to the chatter on the street. Some of the tourists were talking about the news—about the fact that a second woman had been murdered in just two weeks.

"Young women," one man said. "Out alone." He looked at the teenage daughter walking next to him. "*You* won't be going anywhere alone."

"Dad!" she protested.

"How dreadful," a woman passing by said to her friends.

"Yes, but we'll all stay together and be safe," offered one of them.

Devin undoubtedly heard them, too, but she just watched him instead.

"Beth's shop is this way," she finally told him, taking the box from his arms and starting to walk away.

He followed her. When they entered the shop, a little bell rang and a pretty petite woman behind the counter looked up.

"Devin! You have my books. Thank you," she said. "I had a mom in here a while ago asking about the new *Auntie Pim*. I have her number. Now I'll be able to call her back and—Oh, hello." She was clearly surprised to notice that Devin wasn't alone.

"Devin! Who is this?" she asked.

"Rocky. Um, Rocky Rockwell," Devin said.

She'd probably already forgotten the "Craig" part, he thought.

Rocky took Beth's hand in a firm grip and said it was a pleasure to meet her.

"A friend from Boston?" Beth asked.

Before Devin could answer, Rocky seized on the opportunity.

"Yes. And Devin has told me that you have the best shop in town."

Beth flushed, while Devin stood silent.

"Thank you, and welcome to Salem," Beth said. "I hope you enjoy our city."

"Thank you. Your store looks to be as wonderful as Devin said."

"Thank you again. And where are you from, Rocky?" Beth asked him.

He grinned—charmingly, he hoped. "Peabody."

Beth laughed. "Of course you are. No one who isn't ever says it right."

While the rest of the world pronounced all the syllables, locals said it more like Peab'dy.

"Small world," Beth went on, delighted. "I wonder if we ever met at a concert or something, somewhere along the line."

"He's older than we are," Devin said. "And he's been gone a long time. He and I never knew each other locally, either. Until now." She blushed. "I mean, he's here now."

"Oh," Beth said. "Ohh."

Clearly she had heard an implication of intimacy that Devin had never intended. Rocky was amused. Devin wasn't. But Beth quickly went on to other matters.

"Devin, you have to be careful. Have you seen the news? Another young woman has been killed. They haven't identified her yet, but . . . it sounded as if she was found not far from your house."

"Yes, I know," Devin said.

"Want to come and stay with me?" Beth asked her. "I mean, I live right here in the middle of the city. A lot safer, don't you think?"

"I'm okay right now. But thank you for the invitation."

"I guess you need to be home in the cottage to write. I mean, Auntie Pim *is* Mina. Did you ever meet her, Rocky?"

"No, I'm sorry to say that I didn't," Rocky said.

"That's too bad. She was a remarkable woman." She turned back to her friend. "Devin, please be careful," Beth urged.

"I will be. I promise."

"Buy some pepper spray or something."

"I'll think about it."

They were interrupted as two women, one noticeably tall and the other much shorter, walked toward them from the back of the store. The tall woman appeared to be about fifty. She had shoulder-length snow-white hair that curved around an attractive face and wore a black dress that fell to the ground. The other woman was clutching a number of shopping bags. She thanked her companion, waved cheerfully to them at the counter and left the shop.

"Hello," the white-haired woman said as she walked over to Devin and gave her a quick kiss on the cheek. "Delighted to see you. Did you bring books?"

"Yes, I brought the box," Devin said.

She didn't get a chance to introduce Rocky, because Beth stepped in.

"Gayle Alden, this is Rocky Rockwell, a friend of Devin's. Rocky, Gayle is one of the two best mediums in the city. The other, of course, is my other employee, Theo Hastings, but Theo is off today."

"How do you do?" Gayle said politely, then turned to Beth with a twinkle in her eye. "I don't suppose he's here for a reading, is he?"

"Actually, I'm here about a piece of jewelry Devin bought from you," Rocky said.

"The silver pentagram. Or pentacle—whatever you choose to call it," Beth said. "Technically, it's a pentagram when it's just the symbol and a pentacle when the star has the circle around it, but people mostly just say pentagram these days."

Rocky smiled. "Whatever you call it, it's a beautiful piece."

"I'm sold out for the moment. They go as

quickly as Devin's *Auntie Pim* books," Beth said. "But they're done by a local artist. Sheena Marston. I can order one for you. In fact, if I special order it, you can have input on the design, if you want. She only works with silver, but she can add enamel, and precious or semiprecious stones. I had one with black onyx that was spectacular."

"Is it possible to meet with Ms. Marston?" he asked. "It would be easier for me to explain my ideas in person."

There was a slight pause. Gayle and Beth exchanged a long look filled with something he couldn't decipher.

"She doesn't actually see people," Beth said.

"She's something of a hermit," Gayle added.

Gayle Alden was *Sheena Marston,* Rocky thought.

"Are the pieces exclusive through you?" he asked Beth.

"They are now. In previous years, a number of shops carried her work, but I convinced her that being exclusive would be to her advantage," Beth said.

"I'm sure Beth and the Haunted Dragon will have more soon," Gayle said.

"Are you a Wiccan, Rocky?" Beth asked.

"No, but I think the pieces are beautiful," he said.

"I'm so glad you like them," Gayle said. "I'm guessing you're thinking of getting one as a gift for someone. So many people think that only Wiccans should wear them. And a lot of others think they're associated with devil worship, or that they're just plain evil. In fact, there's nothing evil about them." She pointed to a pentagram-shaped paperweight on the counter. "From the top and moving clockwise, the points represent spirit, water, fire, earth and air."

She met his eyes and continued. "There's nothing evil about the pentagram or the modern practice of Wicca, which was established by a man named Gerald Gardner in 1954, with practices based on ancient pagan traditions. Laurie Cabot, arguably the most famous Wiccan high priestess, came to Salem in the 1970s and popularized Wicca here. And just as Christianity has many sects, so does Wicca. Some are traditional, others revere figures a lot like Christian saints. But none of them are evil."

"Are you a Wiccan?" Rocky asked her.

She flushed. "No. Congregational church. But people here in Salem respect everyone's beliefs. Or those of us you'd want to know do, anyway."

He smiled. "Gotcha."

The little bell rang as a group of tourists came into the shop. Gayle excused herself, and then Beth went to help a couple who were interested in the jewelry under the counter.

"Did that help you any?" Devin asked Rocky as they left.

He didn't get a chance to answer her, because she'd been looking at him as she spoke, and now she plowed straight into another man.

"Devin! Hey, sorry."

"No, I'm sorry," she said quickly, backing away.

The man was almost Rocky's height; he had slightly silvered hair, which somehow added to an impression of being debonair—or a lecher, one or the other.

"Completely my fault," the man said. He looked at Rocky with raised brows.

Was that jealousy? Rocky wondered.

"Theo, meet Rocky Rockwell. Rocky, Theo Hastings. Theo works for Beth, too."

They shook hands.

"Old friends?" Theo asked lightly.

"From Boston," Rocky said, avoiding a direct answer.

"Oh, well, pleased to meet you," Theo said. "Devin, always wonderful to see you."

He smiled and moved on.

"Interesting character," Rocky said.

"I think pretty much everything about him—including his claim to be Wiccan—might be an act," Devin said. "His way of making it here. Anyway, I should get back."

"Of course."

"If you're looking for a restaurant later, I can suggest a new one for you. It's at the old jail. The place is apartments now, with the restaurant on the ground floor."

"Thanks."

They headed to the car, and he drove the short distance to her house. He got out and went around to open her door, but she'd already opened it by the time he got there.

"You've got my card, right?" he asked her.

"Yes, of course. And I'll call you if I think of anything that might help," she promised.

Still, he hesitated. "How well do you know Gayle Alden?" he asked her.

She arched her brows. "I've known her forever. She was one of my teachers in high school. She retired last year and went to work for Beth."

"What did she teach?"

"History." Devin was silent, a smile playing across her lips. "You don't think that *Gayle* could possibly—"

"I think that Gayle Alden is Sheena Marston."

That genuinely surprised Devin, who shrugged after a minute. "I have to say, that's possible. We did a lot of reenactments in class, and she made a lot of the jewelry and things for the costumes."

He nodded. "What about the old guy?"

"The old guy?" she asked.

"The one you crashed into."

Devin laughed. "Oh, Theo. He would be devastated that you called him an old guy."

"How long have you known him?"

"A year or so. I think he's from Ohio." Her smile faded and she frowned thoughtfully. "Do you really think . . . I mean . . . is it possible that the person who killed thirteen years ago is back?"

"I don't know, and that makes me nervous. I'm sure you don't have anything to worry about, but even so, be careful. If something seems suspicious, call the cops. Or call me. Do you have anything you can use for protection?"

"I really do wield a wicked hockey stick."

He smiled. "I'm going to get you some pepper spray. I'll call you before I bring it over so you'll know it's me."

"Sure. Thanks," she told him. "Well . . ." She smiled again and headed toward her door. He followed her up the little stone path.

"I just want to make sure—" He began.

"That I lock the door."

"Yes."

"I will," she promised.

They both hesitated.

"Want me to walk through the house—just check it out?" he asked her.

"Um, sure. That's not a bad idea. Ever. I guess."

She moved to one side so he could enter first, then followed him as he went from room to room, and looked in closets and under the beds. He checked all her windows and the back door. At last he was satisfied.

"You're alone—well, except for Poe, of course," he told her.

"Thank you."

He could tell that she was waiting for him to leave, so he did, but he waited outside the door until he heard the bolt slide into place.

As he walked back to his car, his cell phone rang.

It was Jackson Crow. He was official. And several other agents would be joining him shortly.

Devin finished cutting up bits of fruit for Poe and walked back into the parlor. "Hey, boy, you know what? I'm not so fond of Mr. FBI. I was living this nice happy life, just getting back into something approaching a social life with old friends, and now he has me doubting all of them."

Poe had no answer. He was interested only in the fruit she was offering him.

"Meanwhile, I need to get back to the computer. My publisher wants a new *Auntie Pim* adventure out there every six months."

There were a number of places in the house where she might have chosen to work. Auntie Mina might have been an herbalist and a Wiccan and slightly crazy, but she had also loved technology. There was cable television, and a wireless network. Auntie Mina had loved her little tablet that had let her watch her shows in any room.

After giving it some thought, Devin had chosen the parlor as her office. She loved the old mantel and the way the fire burned when the nights turned chill. She liked to look out at the stone path that led to the house and the gardens—now in need of work—that grew on either side of it.

Last night, though . . . She hoped never to go through anything like that again. She had discovered a murder victim.

A sight she would never get out of her mind.

But she wasn't a cop. She wasn't even a reporter anymore.

She made her living writing children's books, and she needed to get back to *Auntie Pim and the Belligerent Gnome.*

She started to work. The gnome was angry with one of the dwarfs who lived in the woods and wanted a potion from Auntie Pim to make the dwarf grow a giant nose. He begged at first and pleaded—but Auntie Pim told him that magic must never be used to hurt people. The gnome threatened her next, telling Auntie Pim that he would send a plague of locusts to eat all the herbs in her garden and then she wouldn't be able to do anything. So Auntie Pim told the gnome that she would make a potion that could cause a nose to grow. But she warned the gnome that any harm he caused would come back at him threefold.

Devin had read her initial draft to children at

the library, and they had actually been on pins and needles—horrified that Auntie Pim would use her magic for evil. But Devin had assured them that they shouldn't be afraid, because Auntie Pim always had a plan. What would happen, of course, was that the dwarf's nose would grow by a fraction of a fraction of an inch, while the angry gnome's nose would blossom out like a double-size volleyball. At the end, of course, the gnome, having learned his lesson, would beg for for-giveness. And after Auntie Pim returned his nose to a normal size, he would help her in her garden.

Devin looked out at the garden, wishing that she had a belligerent gnome to help her now. She'd intended to get outside today, but that didn't seem like such a good idea anymore.

Her phone rang, and she jumped.

It was Beth, who skipped right past hello and said, "You've been holding out on me!"

"What?"

"Rocky Rockwell. Wow. You sure can keep a secret. I can't believe you've had that man in your pocket all this time and haven't said a word. Now I know why you don't want me fixing you up with anyone. He looks like he walked off the cover of *GQ*. I have to admit, I couldn't have found you someone like him anywhere around here."

Why the hell hadn't she introduced him as an FBI agent, here to investigate the recent murders?

She massaged her temples with her thumb and forefingers.

The last "*GQ*" man she'd dated had worked with her at the paper. He'd been stunned—shocked—but not emotionally devastated when she'd broken it off with him. He'd scooped her story, and people who cared about other people didn't do that. In his mind, it had been his right. She was just a woman, while he was a serious reporter.

But this man . . .

Yes. He was a sharp dresser, tall and well built and . . . okay, gorgeous. Neatly clipped auburn hair, searing green eyes. Of course, it was easy for Beth to think . . .

"We're friends," Devin said.

"With benefits?" Beth teased.

"Friends," Devin repeated firmly.

"Well, if you're not interested in the benefits part, bring that boy back around!"

"Oh, Beth . . ."

"Sorry. Sorry. I didn't call to tease you. Okay, yes, I partly did. But I really called because I wish you'd come stay with me. I just had lunch over at Rockafella's—I love their food—but they had the televisions on, and there was a police spokesman telling young women to be careful, not to go out alone. You really should think about staying with me. Please?"

"I will, Beth. I promise I'll think about it."

"Okay. Hey, the new Brad Pitt is playing at the mall. A few of us are going tomorrow night. Why don't you join us? Bring tall, auburn and handsome if you want. I promise—no more teasing. And I won't drool on him or anything."

"Let me call you?"

"Sure."

Devin hung up and went into the kitchen. She hadn't eaten anything all day, and Beth's mention of lunch made her hungry.

She had just pulled out the bread and sandwich meat and was standing by the refrigerator, a bottle of mayonnaise in her hand, when she had the uneasy feeling that she was being watched.

She looked toward the kitchen doorway.

Her heart seemed to stand still.

There was Auntie Mina. She was wearing one of her pretty black dresses that came just below her knees; her white hair was swept into a bun, and her spectacles were in place. Her cheeks were rosy; her lips were pursed into a smile.

Devin blinked. Aunt Mina didn't go away.

Instead, she spoke.

"Yes, I'm here, child. Now please put that mayonnaise down before you drop it."

4

The drive to Boston wasn't a long one, but Rocky, sitting in the passenger seat beside Jack Grail, found that he resented the time the trip would take. Still, when Jack had called him over lunch, he knew it only made sense to go.

He didn't like being away from the active investigation, because this case was a confounding one. The murderer had struck once and stopped, and then again almost thirteen years later, when he had struck twice in two weeks.

Either that, or they had a copycat on their hands.

But how could a copycat mimic Melissa's murder so precisely, when many of the details had never been made public?

Now he and Jack stood in a sterile room that smelled of antiseptic and death, and listened to the report being given by Dr. Samuels. Dr. Samuels hadn't performed the autopsy on Carly Henderson; that had been Dr. Smith, who was currently on vacation. His report was in Carly's file, and she had been buried in Salem just three days ago.

Their Jane Doe lay on the table. If she weren't such a strange color and didn't feel like ice—and didn't have the Y incision that was the most obvious sign of autopsy—she might have been any young woman catching a few rays. Dr. Samuels droned through the necessary information. Female, between the ages of seventeen and twenty-three, five feet six inches, one hundred and fifteen pounds. There were no signs of rape or sexual molestation; she hadn't even been sexually active in the days before her death. She had no tattoos or identifying scars, and she had nearly perfect teeth.

In fact, other than the slice across the throat—performed, according to Dr. Samuels, by a double-edged blade of about six or seven inches and made from left to right—she had been unharmed. No one had beat her, strangled her, dragged her or done anything else to her. Her stomach contents were being tested. However, Dr. Samuels had read the report on Carly Henderson and believed that the two women had consumed identical meals—clam chowder and fish and chips—before they had met their demise. If that turned out to be true, Rocky thought, it could be a clue as valuable as the pentagram medallions.

"So," Rocky said, moving to use Jack as his mock victim, "the killer came up directly behind her, placed the weapon so—and slashed?"

"Yes, that appears to be what happened," Samuels agreed.

"The same as Carly Henderson?" Jack asked.

"From what I've read, yes."

"And what about Melissa Wilson?" Rocky asked.

Samuels frowned. "I don't think I know that name."

"She was killed thirteen years ago—she was found the same way."

"I'll have to look up that report. I was working in San Francisco thirteen years ago," Samuels told them.

They thanked him for his time and headed back to their car.

"None of them was molested," Jack said. "I guess there's a small comfort in that."

Small comfort? Rocky thought. *Maybe. They were all still dead.*

"Yeah," Rocky muttered. "I guess. I don't think they had any idea they were going to die. It must have been quick."

"I don't understand how he pulls it off. This guy has to be covered with blood once he's done," Jack said.

"Not that much. He's behind the victim, and the spray would go forward."

"But then he's lowering his victim to the ground —laying her out. And placing the medallion on her," Jack said.

"Yes, some blood, but not so much that he couldn't cover it if he'd stashed a jacket nearby. Soon as he's done he goes home and cleans up. And since we don't know where home is . . ."

"Gotta be Wiccans," Jack said.

"I don't think we can automatically suspect an entire community. It might just as well be someone who wants to cast blame on the local Wicca community. Maybe some nut job who believes that they're Satanists and it's up to him to get rid of them."

He might have been away from the area for a long time, but he knew enough to know that Wiccans didn't practice human or animal sacrifice, and did not in any way, shape or form condone murder.

"Yeah, I guess. Everything about this case is one thing or the opposite, isn't it?" Jack asked. "Either it's the same killer or a copycat. Either it's a misguided follower of a nontraditional religion or it's someone trying to pin it on them. Thank God the witch trials are over, that's all I can say. All we need is another witch scare."

"That alone makes it imperative that we keep a lid on the details," Rocky said.

"Some of them have gotten out, you know," Jack told him.

Rocky looked at Jack and waited.

"The boy who found Carly Henderson. Luckily the kid was terrified—he saw her and ran. But people know she was splayed out and covered in blood."

"I have it on my list to talk to the kid, anyway," Rocky said.

"No problem. Whenever you want to go."

"How about now?"

Their timing was good. School was out, and Manny Driscoll, the fourteen-year-old boy who had discovered Carly Henderson when he was out on his after-school job delivering Chinese food, was home.

"I'm not letting him work right now," Manny's mother, Martha, told them. "Chow Chang, his boss, understands. When this is all over, maybe Manny can just mow the yard for allowance," she said firmly. She sat with Rocky and Jack while they questioned her son.

"Did you see anyone leaving the woods or hanging around anywhere nearby?" Rocky asked him.

Manny was a sober boy. He looked at Rocky seriously. "No. I fell off my bike onto the road and . . . and that's when I saw her through the trees. Man, I fell down when I got a look at her. I . . ." He paused and looked around, as if he wanted to make really certain none of his friends were there. "I screamed like a girl—like a little girl," he said, sounding disgusted with himself.

"That's all right, Manny. I've screamed like a girl, too," Rocky said.

"Really?" Manny asked him.

"Really," Rocky echoed.

"You fell, though, because a car almost side-swiped you, right?" Rocky asked.

"Yeah."

"What kind of car?"

Manny stared at him blankly. "Um, I don't remember."

"Was it dark, light? Old, new?"

"Not too old, I don't think," Manny said. He perked up. "It was dark—maybe a truck, but maybe not that big."

"A big SUV?" Jack asked him.

"Yeah, maybe," Manny said.

"Did you see who was driving?" Rocky asked.

"No. I just saw how close it was coming."

"My boy is lucky to be alive," Martha said, setting a protective arm around his shoulders.

"Of course, and we're very grateful," Rocky told her. "What then, Manny?"

"Well, I fell. And the orders fell, too. Mr. Chang is really nice, and I didn't want all that food to end up on the ground, so I was picking it all up— and then I saw her. I just threw it all away and grabbed my bike and got out of there. Fast."

"As soon as he got home, we called the police," his mother said. "We didn't believe him at first," she admitted. "I thought he'd maybe been playing too many video games. But . . . she was real."

"Thank you, Manny, you really helped us," Rocky said. He left the boy with a card—which, of course, his mother took. But Rocky thought it was important to make kids know they were respected and believed. "Call me if you think of anything else."

"I can't believe you got something," Jack muttered as soon as they were outside.

"The car?" Rocky asked.

Jack nodded. "When my men questioned him, they never asked about it. It's not a lot, but it's something. Or could be. It might just have been some idiot speeding home. Asshole might not even have realized he almost ran down a kid."

"True. Can you take me by the scene?"

"At your command," Jack told him.

The crime scene tape was down, the fact that Carly Henderson had died here only a memory for many. Two weeks ago she had been planning her future.

Now . . .

Now she was underground and the soggy tape that had fallen from the trees was all that was left to mark the place where she had passed, a sign of nature regaining control.

Jack led him the ten feet off the road to the spot where Carly had been found. He stooped down over the faint depression that told him where the body had once been. He could see the point of the star that had been marked by her head, the indentations made by her arms and legs, and was grateful the ground had been soft and muddy from a recent rain the day of her murder.

What the hell did the position and the penta-gram mean, though? A killer who was pretending to a belief he didn't share? A killer who was sending a message, or one who was pointing a finger?

He closed his eyes in thought.

Help me.

He thought he heard the words in his head.

The victims knew, he realized with a sudden certainty, despite the absence of proof. They knew that something was wrong, there in the woods. But the killer was there with them—hiding. Either he brought them there or lured them there. Then left them. And he would wait—and watch. He wanted them to realize something was wrong, and only then did he slip up behind them.

"What is it?" Jack asked. "You've figured something out, haven't you?"

Careful not to sound too certain and raise suspicion, Rocky said, "Here's how I think it plays out. Most likely the killer gets there first, then he hides and watches his victim arrive."

"We found Carly's car in town," Jack said. "It was right where she'd left it, in a garage."

"Then she got a ride here somehow. Maybe even with the killer, and then he left her here on some pretext. Or maybe he has an accomplice." He looked at Jack. "He picks his victims carefully. He convinces them that he has something unique to show them or give them. Or maybe he romances them or comes up with some other reason for them to come to the place he's chosen. But he's already there, and he watches. Maybe he takes them when they're still calm and just waiting—or perhaps he waits until they get impatient, maybe even angry, and finally afraid. Then he attacks."

Rocky looked around and noticed one of the trees where the bark had peeled away.

"He waited there," he told Jack quietly, pointing.

"What makes you think so?"

"The way the bark is worn in places and plucked at. I believe that's where he was."

"I can get a crime scene unit back out."

Rocky shook his head. "No, you won't get any physical evidence. Not now. I've got to get into his head, Jack."

"Or *her* head," Jack said.

"Or *her* head," Rocky agreed.

He was pensive when they returned to the car.

"Want to come home with me for dinner?" Jack asked after a while. "Haley would be delighted."

"Not tonight. Thanks," Rocky said. "I'm going to go over everything one more time. I'm expecting some more members of my team soon, too. So . . ."

"You going to want a room at the station?" Jack asked him.

"Thank you. That would be perfect."

Jack drove to Rocky's hotel. There was a group of men in business suits standing out front, finishing up a discussion.

"Hey, an old friend!" Jack said.

Rocky studied the group and recognized Vince Steward easily. He had to be six-four, at least, and he was still built like a brick wall.

He stood out in any crowd.

"I'll park," Jack said. "Vince is going to want to say hello to you."

Vince saw Jack before he saw Rocky. He grinned and waved. He'd come a long way from the kid who drank beer in the back of a pickup truck.

His suit was custom cut; his hair was neatly clipped. His eyes flashed with good humor when he saw Rocky.

Vince strode over to throw his arms around Rocky. "The prodigal son returns. No, wait, can't use that. You were never a prodigal anything. Good to see you, buddy. What brings you back to town?"

"He's working the murder," Jack said.

"Oh," Vince said, and his grin faded. "Yeah, sad thing, huh? So, you still a fed, huh? That's the last I heard, anyway. You know, old friends can keep up. They have this new thing called Facebook. Oh, yeah, there's also a great invention called email."

"I guess I spend too much time working," Rocky said. "But hell, if I'd known you were going to go to law school, I'd have come back just to see it," Rocky said with a laugh.

"Well, I'm glad you're here, anyway. Let's get

together before you leave town again." He called out to his group. "Hey! Got an old friend in town. Craig Rockwell. Rocky, come meet the boys."

"The boys" were a group of maritime attorneys, as it turned out, and they met once a week at Rocky's hotel.

There was conversation all around for a few minutes. The men asked Jack about the murders, but he was an experienced cop and said very little.

"It's good to see you," Vince told Rocky when the conversation wound down. "We should all get together soon. No one can work around the clock."

Actually, Rocky thought, *he often did.*

"Has Haley seen our old shining star?" Vince asked Jack.

"She has," Jack told him.

"Renee will want to see him, too. We have to get together."

"We'll make a plan," Rocky promised.

"Yes, but for now, I'd better be going," Vince said. "Court bright and early tomorrow—I'm defending Harwell Marine. Meanwhile, if you need me, buddy, for anything, don't hesitate," Vince said sincerely.

Rocky thanked him, and the three of them said their goodbyes.

As Rocky headed into the hotel, he was glad that they'd run into Vince.

The rest of his old crowd was doing great.

Even Vince had developed ambition and made a real success of his life.

Melissa.

She had changed them all.

He went to his room and set his briefcase on his desk. He liked the hotel. It was near the waterfront and offered inexpensive mini-suites with all the necessary conveniences. He had a coffeemaker, a wet bar and a large dining room table that allowed him to spread out the reports for all three cases.

It had been good to see Jack, but he was obsessed and he knew it.

Back to work.

The women and the circumstances were all similar.

The women were all young. They were all of similar height and weight, but with different coloring. All Caucasian, though. They had all been fully clothed, no sign of molestation.

They had all been found with a silver pentagram on a silver chain lying on their breasts. Cause of death appeared to be the same: throat slit by a double-edged blade that was six or seven inches long. The crime scenes had yielded no clues. No footprints, not even near Carly's body. The killer must have taken the time to obscure them. No gum wrappers, beer cans, condoms or wrappers, not even any cigarette butts. No evidence that anyone had used any of the crime scenes for anything at all.

Frustrated, he picked up the photographs of the medallions. They were similar—and very much like the one Devin had—but from the photos, he couldn't even prove that they'd been made by the same designer.

He stood. He wanted to see the medallions again. It was time for a trip to the evidence lockup.

Somehow Devin managed not to drop the mayonnaise. She groped toward the counter and set it down, never taking her eyes off the apparition still standing just inside the kitchen doorway.

"Come on now, Devin, dear," Aunt Mina's ghost said. "You didn't think that a loving aunt would leave you so easily, did you, child?"

Aunt Mina sounded both sincere and worried.

A thousand responses ran through her mind. They ranged from, "You almost made me waste good mayonnaise" to a scream of pure astonishment. Or terror.

No, not terror. How could she ever be afraid of Auntie Mina?

Maybe she was just hallucinating, she told herself. After all, she'd recently discovered a dead woman. She was still not herself.

"Auntie Mina."

The words came out like a croak.

"Make some tea, dear. That always helps everything." Aunt Mina smiled broadly. "I'd be delighted to help you, but frankly, I'm just learning this ghost stuff. Manifestation isn't easy. And I did die when I was over one hundred. But the good thing is that nothing hurts. Nothing at all." Her smile faded. "I think I'm here for a reason, Devin. I think I'm here to help you."

Devin was shaking. She walked forward and reached out to touch her aunt. She felt a slight chill in the air but nothing more.

"You can't touch me, child," Aunt Mina said sadly. "Don't you think I wished I could stroke your hair last night? Try to soothe you?"

"You know what happened?" Devin asked.

"I saw the face at the window," Aunt Mina said.

"A face at the window?"

"You weren't looking or you might have seen her, too. You heard her, though—and then you found her. I haven't managed to leave the house yet, but I did try to stop you from going out, but . . . well, you are the child I helped raise. Kind and compassionate. So you went in search of her. And when you came back with that officer, I figured out what had happened." She shrugged. "And you did turn on the television and your computer."

She might have died at a hundred and one, but Aunt Mina had known her electronics.

Devin's knees felt wobbly. She wasn't sure she could make tea without breaking something. She swept past the great-aunt she couldn't touch and made her way to the parlor, sinking down on the sofa.

She was imagining things.

No, Aunt Mina had followed her.

Poe squawked. He flew over and tried to light on Mina's shoulder, then ended up fluttering to the ground in confusion.

"Poe, my poor Poe," Aunt Mina said.

"I'll get him," Devin muttered. She rose and scooped up the bird, who flapped agitatedly for a second and then settled into her hold.

The damned bird was seeing the same apparition!

"I can't stay long, my dear. I haven't mastered the skill yet, though I'm getting better and stronger every day. I practiced speaking when you were out, but . . . I had to pray that you would hear me when I finally showed myself. Not that I doubted you for a minute. Not really. After all, last night you heard the dead. And once you hear them . . . well, dear, I'm afraid you can't just turn them off."

Devin stood stroking the bird and staring at her aunt. Suddenly tears welled in her eyes.

"I loved you so much," she said. "Still love you, of course."

"Love lasts forever," Aunt Mina told her. "And I love you, too. So very much. Since I never had children of my own, you are, in spirit, my child. Not to take anything away from your lovely mother, you're just my child in a different way. And your books! They're getting better and better. I'm so proud of you. What are you working on now?"

Devin told her, and Aunt Mina clapped her astral hands. Then she looked down and sighed. "The house is locked up tight?"

"It is."

"Good. Oh dear, I'm fading already. Well, at least now you know I'm here."

"Auntie Mina . . . ?"

Too late. Aunt Mina was gone. And, Devin realized, darkness was falling quickly and she was still standing by the love seat, stroking the raven.

The night shift was on; the evidence room was quiet.

An Officer Buckley was manning the desk while Rocky sat at another desk in the back, studying the three medallions.

It had taken some doing to find the first. While Jack had been looking into the old case, he hadn't gone so far as to request the medallion, which had been misfiled and hard to locate. After half an hour of studying the three pentagrams on their silver chains, Rocky shook his head.

Having them right there in front of him didn't tell him anything that the photographs hadn't. None of them carried an artist's mark, which was what he'd been hoping to find.

Had they been designed by the same person or not?

He couldn't tell. But he did know that he was going to have to get to know Gayle Alden and find out if she really was Sheena Marston, not to mention whether she'd created these pentagrams as well as Devin's.

At nine o'clock he locked up the medallions in their boxes and got ready to head back to his hotel.

Since he knew he would be plagued all night if he didn't, he called Devin Lyle.

"I'm just checking on you," he admitted immediately. "I hope you don't mind."

"Not a bit, thank you. And I'm fine," she told him.

He hesitated. He should just hang up. He'd checked; she was fine. But he took a chance.

"I'd like to get to know your friends at the shop better," he said.

"Oh?"

"I need to learn more."

"About pentagrams?"

"Yes, and Wiccan traditions and—"

"Wiccans didn't do this!" she snapped.

"And Christians aren't bad people, either—until they take religion and turn it into the excuse for an inquisition," he told her. "I'm sorry—I'm not trying to fight. And I'll defend this nation's Wiccans just as I would her Christians, Jews,

Buddhists and Muslims. It's possible that someone is trying to make these deaths *appear* to be
part of a Wiccan ritual of some kind. The more
I understand today's Wiccans in this city, the
better I can figure out what's happening."

She was silent for a moment and then told him,
"We're going to a movie tomorrow night. You
can pick me up around six-thirty."

He was stunned. And appreciative.

"Thank you," he managed.

"I'd ditch the suit, though," she muttered.

And she hung up.

Rocky headed back to the hotel. Luckily, the bar
there served food until eleven. He ate and went
up to bed.

That night when he slept, it was Melissa Wilson
who entered his dreams.

*He was standing by her graveside in Peabody
when she came up behind him, setting a hand on
his shoulder.*

*"You couldn't hear me," she told him. "I kept
crying out for you, but you didn't hear me."*

*"I did hear you," he told her. "I just didn't
understand."*

"You have to listen," she told him.

"I'm listening. Who did this?"

*"He comes in the dark, he comes from behind,"
she said.*

He turned to her.

But she was gone.

He awoke sweating. He found a bottle of water and drained it, and looked at the clock. It was only four in the morning. He lay back and prayed for dreamless sleep.

5

Agent Craig Rockwell had taken her advice— he'd shed the suit.

When he picked her up he was wearing jeans and a light sweater. He wore them well.

She hadn't ventured so much as a foot outside her door that day. Aunt Mina had appeared a few times, but now she was accustomed to her great-aunt appearing and disappearing. They'd had an enlightening conversation about ghosts. Aunt Mina had explained that spirits stayed because they had a cause, something or someone they had to take care of.

Aunt Mina's cause, of course, was Devin.

"Some of those I saw when I was living . . . they stayed because they wanted to watch over the world they once knew, doing what they could to make folks remember the past and its values. Others stay because they have to finish some-thing, in many cases finding justice for their own deaths. That poor woman the other night—she came for you."

"Maybe she came for you. Maybe she knew you were a ghost and—"

"Oh, Devin. No, no. She came for help from the living. She needed you to find her. To make sure that the police started looking for her killer right away."

"I never saw her," Devin said.

"But you heard her. If you'd looked, you would have seen her. She was leading you where you needed to go."

After that Aunt Mina had faded out again, as she was wont to do, but Devin knew she would be back again, most likely asking Devin to change the channel to one of her favorite programs. She was especially fond of *Monk*, and thanks to cable and the internet, Devin was always able to find it for her.

Aunt Mina wasn't there when Agent Rockwell came to take Devin to the movie, as she had suggested, but just as he was closing the door behind them, she saw Aunt Mina hovering just inside.

"I approve," Aunt Mina told her with a wink.

Devin rolled her eyes, but she doubted Aunt Mina saw, because by then the door was shut.

It seemed that either by instinct or training, Rocky moved with natural authority and had the manners of a gentleman. He set his hand lightly at the small of her back to guide her, then opened the car door for her. She wondered if he even realized what he was doing; he seemed to be distracted.

"Long day?" she asked him.

He set the car in gear and flashed her a quick smile. "Tedious day. Fact finding, reading missing-persons reports. Frustrating." After a moment he admitted, "Long."

"Do you usually solve cases in a day?" she asked.

He opened his mouth, closed it and then said, "No."

She wasn't sure why, but she wanted to set a hand on his arm and tell him that she knew he was going to get to the truth. She barely knew the man. There was just something about him that she liked. He had integrity. He was able to work with clear-cut determination and yet feel the emotional impact of the situation, as well.

Or, she wondered, looking at the road, was Beth right? Had she simply not realized just how attractive the man was when they'd first met? In the dark, sitting next to him, she wished that they were on a date. Going to the movies . . . dinner. That exciting time early in a relationship when you met someone and made sometimes inane conversation, even exchanged bad jokes as you got to know each other, all the while wondering if you were going to end up together or out again at all—much less go home together.

She was appalled by the thought. She never went home with anyone on a first date. In fact, for her grand old age of nearly twenty-seven, she was woefully behind. But she'd always wanted something real and serious; she'd just never been the type to go out and party, and hook up just to hook up—whether for fun, companionship or even to satisfy the biological instinct for sex. Sadly, her two "great affairs" hadn't ended well. She didn't even want to think about her last— there were many ways to betray someone, and her last lover had betrayed her both emotionally and professionally. Before that? Well, there had been her three-year college fling that had sizzled . . . and then just fizzled.

She didn't regret the way she felt about relationships, about them needing to mean something.

Except for tonight.

"You okay?" he asked.

"Yes, of course." She turned back to him. "So, you want to find out about the local Wiccans? As you probably know, there are a number of covens in Salem. Some—most—are very traditional. Wiccans are just like everyone else. They eat and drink the same things you do, they wear what they choose and they don't tithe their income to some mystical spirit. You could have one as your neighbor and never know."

He looked at her, smiling. "I swear, I am not against anyone believing whatever they see fit to believe. I just want to solve these crimes," he finished softly.

"But you really think that Gayle makes those pentagrams using a . . . a pseudonym?"

"I do."

"Why?"

"Body language."

"You saw that much body language in a ten-second conversation?"

"When I asked, Gayle and Beth exchanged a glance. Beth was asking Gayle if she wanted to own up to being the artist. Gayle didn't, so Beth kept quiet about it."

"All that from one glance?"

"Yes. Aren't writers observant?"

"Apparently not all," she said.

They parked in the same garage as last time and made their way to the shop. Gayle and Theo were outside waiting for them.

"Beth is just closing up," Gayle said. "She'll be right here. Rocky, so glad you're joining us."

"I'm delighted to be invited," he said.

"How long are you staying in town?" Theo asked him. "Long enough to look around and get to know the area?"

"I'm not really sure yet—and I already know the area. I grew up in Peabody. I might take a tour, though," Rocky said. "Just to catch myself up."

"If you do, I know just the one. Mine."

Devin was surprised to see Brent Corbin coming toward them, grinning, his hand outstretched toward Rocky.

"Hey. Brent Corbin. I heard about you from Beth. You're a friend of Devin's. Great to meet you."

"Pleasure. You do a tour?" Rocky asked him.

"The best in town. Right, Devin?" Brent asked.

"Wow, put me on the spot," she teased. She turned to Rocky. "Brent and Beth and I went to school together."

"They were incorrigible," Gayle said. "They drove me crazy."

"Yeah, but we were still her best students, sadly," Devin said.

"Hey, we were good students," Brent protested. "Gayle taught politics and history—and she was a fantastic teacher. She made it fun. And she was pretty dramatic, which made us pay attention."

"Thank you," Gayle said.

Theo lifted his hands. "I can't comment. I wasn't living here at the time."

"Brent's tour company is excellent," Devin said to Rocky, bringing the conversation back to the present.

Rocky laughed. "Then I'll be happy to take it."

"Speaking of which, why aren't you giving it? I thought Friday night was your favorite," Devin said.

Brent grinned at her, then looked assessingly at Rocky. "I came to meet your mystery man. Why have employees if not to cover for me when I want time off?"

113

"Hey! We're going to miss the movie," Gayle protested. "Chitchat after."

"Right, right, just . . . Devin, you're okay, right?" Brent asked her soberly.

"Yes, thank you, why wouldn't I be?" she asked.

"Maybe because they found that poor woman right by your house?"

"Thanks for reminding me," Devin murmured.

"Don't make her nervous. She's okay, and she has Rocky to see her home," Beth said cheerfully.

"You all need to be careful," Brent said.

"I'm not worried," Gayle said. "I'm sure one of you fine gentlemen will escort me home. And the same for Beth," she added sternly.

"Of course," Brent said.

"You know it," Theo agreed.

It was an easy walk to the theater from Beth's store. Rocky bought the tickets quickly, before anyone could protest. "Newcomer's treat," he said. "I've heard in some places it's the law."

"That leaves me with the refreshments—way more expensive," Theo said.

"We'll split the cost," Brent told him.

They were there in plenty of time for the movie, but the theater was already crowded, thanks to its central location and the movie being a big action picture featuring an equally big star.

Rocky sat next to her as if it was a matter of course.

She was surprised by the way the night had

gone so far. He seemed at ease. Her friends were having fun.

Only *she* was tense.

The movie barely distracted her.

When it was over, the others were excited; it had apparently been a good movie.

They chose a late-night restaurant/bar at the end of the pedestrian mall for dinner and drinks.

Devin wasn't sure how he did it, but Rocky managed not only to end up next to her but across from Gayle, the perfect place for conversation.

Devin placed her order, and when she turned back to the table she realized that the conversation had turned to human sacrifice.

"Well, for years," Brent, sitting beside Gayle, said, "everyone assumed that the belief that druids engaged in human sacrifice was all a lie spread by their oh-so-civilized and advanced Roman conquerors. But scientific discoveries proved them wrong. 'Lindow Man' was discovered in England in the 1980s—so well preserved that they know he had manicured nails, and that he ate well and might have been one of the druid elite himself. And the evidence made it very clear that he was a victim of ritual sacrifice. There was a rope around his neck, his head was bashed in and his throat was slit. Scholars believe that when the ligature was tightest, that was when they cut his throat. That would mean a lot, lot, lot of blood, right, Gayle?"

Gayle rolled her eyes. "I'm sure I wasn't that grisly back when I was teaching. I can't speak to the amount of blood, since I'm not a doctor, but I *can* tell you that current thinking is that he was sacrificed to halt the Roman troops, probably about 60 AD. Obviously the sacrifice didn't work very well, since the Romans wiped them out pretty thoroughly, but there's plenty of evidence that the druids kept trying. About one hundred and fifty victims were found in a mass grave cave in Alveston, England. They'd had their heads bashed in, as well. There are also signs on the bones that suggest cannibalism. But, due to the deterioration of soft tissue, there was little else they could tell."

"Hey! We've just ordered dinner," Theo said.

"Now you all understand why I'm a vegetarian," Beth said.

"The problem is," Theo said, lowering his voice, "some people think of it as a direct line. You know. Druids are pagans are witches. Druids practiced human sacrifice, so witches—*Wiccans* —must practice human sacrifice, too."

"Oh, please!" Beth said.

"Hey, don't jump down my throat. I'm a Wiccan," Theo said. "I'm just telling you how some people see it."

"There are always people who will see what they want to see all the time, on any subject," Rocky said.

"That's true," Beth agreed. "I've seen it myself.

A group of us were setting out for our Midsummer Sabbat one night and right here—right on Essex Street—I heard a mother telling her little girl that I carried a knife so I could kill goats."

Theo laughed. "You? You won't even kill spiders that come into your store."

"Perception—especially when it's wrong—can be frightening," Rocky said. "Do all Wiccans carry knives?"

"We call it an athame, and like a sword, it's a symbol of fire," Beth explained. "The five points of the pentagram stand for the soul or spirit, then the elements—fire, earth, wind and water. And each one has a symbol. In whole, it stands for the soul, with each point being one of the elements of the world we live in. We don't walk around with swords, not in my tradition, because our circles can be small and we don't want to accidentally stab one another. The cup, or chalice, is like the cauldron of folklore, and it symbolizes water. The wand symbolizes air, and the pentagram, the earth. Our religion comes from ancient traditions. It's about the earth and drawing strength from the earth, and finding magic—good, positive magic— in our faith. It's about our care of the earth."

"So all practicing Wiccans would have those tools?" Rocky asked.

Devin couldn't stop herself from jumping in. "Wiccans might have them—but so would anyone else who wanted one and had a few dollars to

117

spend in a store or on the internet," she said, realizing too late that her tone sounded more aggressive than she'd intended.

Beth looked at her strangely and then smiled. "I don't think Rocky was attacking me or Wiccans in general." She looked at him. "Devin isn't one of us. I think she's just an out-of-time-and-place hippie, like her parents. I love them, but they're not entirely part of the twenty-first century."

Rocky smiled at Devin, then turned to Beth. "I'm still so enchanted by those necklaces—like the one Devin got from you. Silver stands for purity, doesn't it? And you said the artist only works in silver?"

Beth nodded.

"Is there symbolism in the silver?"

"Well, silver is associated with the moon, femininity and with clarity, single-mindedness, purpose. . . . I particularly like the idea of purity," Beth said.

"It's a beautiful metal, and easy to work with," Gayle said. "And I think the association with purity explains its popularity in the Wiccan religion. It's associated with the color white, snow . . . things that are themselves considered pure."

"And this association between silver and purity has been around a long time, right?" Rocky asked.

"Oh, yes, back to the Greeks, the Celts . . . the Romans," Gayle said.

"Please do tell me as soon as you have more of Ms. Marston's jewelry in stock," Rocky said to Beth.

"I will," she promised.

The conversation turned to other topics at that point, and eventually they all parted for the night. Theo was going to make sure that Beth got home safely, and Brent would walk Gayle home. She actually lived in the old jail. Though it had once been slated for demolition, the haunted structure that had witnessed many an execution had been saved and turned into very nice apartments.

Devin and Rocky headed to his car. As they drove, she was pensively silent. When they reached her house, he came around to open the car door for her, but she was already out. He walked her to the house. When she opened the door, he said, "I'll check the place out for you, if that's all right."

"Um, yes, sure. Thank you."

He went through the same ritual as he had the other day. Devin decided to wait for him in the parlor. As she stood there, she saw the ghost of Aunt Mina peeking out from the kitchen.

"Everything all right, dear?" Aunt Mina whispered.

"Yes, fine," Devin said, waving at her aunt to please disappear for the moment.

Rocky joined her in the parlor just as Aunt Mina disappeared.

Still a little unnerved by her aunt's strange comings and goings, Devin said, "So now you're convinced that the women were murdered by a Wiccan with an athame?" she asked.

"The weapon could have been an athame, yes," he said. "That doesn't mean that a Wiccan used it—anyone can buy one. As you so charmingly pointed out," he said, smiling to take the sting out of the words.

"And you really believe that?" she asked him.

"Yes, I really believe that's a distinct possibility," he said.

"Are you any closer to finding the killer?"

"I wish I could say yes," he told her.

There was a strange moment of silence as they stood there looking at each other. Devin had the wild thought that she should pretend that it had been a real date. That she should walk to him, smile . . . and lean up and give him a kiss.

She suppressed the insane desire. And yet it seemed that even from a distance she could smell his scent. Nice, not like a sweet perfume, just something clean and woodsy and a little bit musky.

Then she reminded herself that the ghost of her great-aunt was haunting the house even as she was picturing him undressed.

"Well, thank you," she murmured.

"My pleasure," he told her, and headed to the door.

She followed and as she was about to close it behind him, he caught hold of it and smiled, then indicated something behind her.

"Great-Aunt Mina, huh?" he said over Devin's head before turning his attention back to her. "Next time I'm here, you'll have to introduce me."

Before she had a chance to do more than stare at him wide-eyed, he closed the door behind him. She spun around, and of course, there was Aunt Mina.

Devin could have fallen down, she was so stunned.

Aunt Mina was not. "How delightful!" she said. "He sees me. Now, quit standing there like a dime-store dummy, child. Lock that door."

As he drove, Rocky smiled.

It was intriguing to discover that Devin also saw ghosts. Of course, he hadn't given her a chance to respond to the fact that he'd seen Mina. He'd just let that sit with her awhile.

He was glad that Devin was like him. Damned glad. Surprised, yes, but pleased that they could be free to speak about things they'd learned from the dead—a boon in this situation.

Rocky wondered again as he returned to his room if he had done the right thing; he might have gone on his way living a normal life. Well, something that resembled a normal life, anyway.

He was a good agent; he was focused and methodical—and passionate in his search for justice for the victims of violent crime.

He'd seen things over the years, things most people didn't even believe existed. He'd probably never had a chance of avoiding it, having been born and raised in an area of the country where people seemed to carry the past in them like a genetic trait. Sometimes he'd been able to use the . . . people he saw.

Because he hadn't been involved. Because he could say, Hey, it's all in my mind, but it's working, so just go with it.

Except for Melissa. Except for her face in his window, her voice in his head.

But tonight . . .

The things he saw were real. Dead, but real. And at least in his experience, they weren't out to do harm, as they supposedly had been in the days of the witchcraft trials. Hell, if the accused really had been witches, they could have pulled out their wands, whipped them through the air and shut up the likes of Cotton Mather.

Then he told himself to pull back. The "witches" he had known growing up were no more bizarre to a kid growing up in a Congregational church in New England than a Hindu or a Buddhist. They couldn't magically will themselves down from a hanging tree. But that didn't mean the so-called "other world" wasn't real.

He'd seen Mina Lyle tonight. As clearly as he had seen Devin. And he knew that he'd approached Jackson Crow in hopes of joining the Krewe of Hunters for reasons other than Melissa—though the fact that the memory of her had haunted him for more than a decade was the main factor.

He looked out his window for a long time before he went to bed. And in his heart he willed her, *Come back to me now. Now I can help you.*

He turned and headed to bed. He needed sleep.

He prayed that he wouldn't dream.

But he did.

The three dead women were there. And in the deepest regions of his mind, where REM sleep ruled, and the subconscious mingled with the conscious, they were caught in the breeze beneath the moon.

They wore white shrouds that whipped around their bodies and they had come to him where he kneeled over a grave. He looked at the headstone and realized that it was Melissa's grave. She reached out to touch him.

"Old friend," she said softly. "Now we are three."

When he woke up, he recalled the dream and thought he should be feeling off in some way, as if the dead had given him a hangover of remorse.

But instead, he found himself feeling more determined than ever. He headed straight for the police station and started setting up for the Krewe members who would be arriving later that day. He set up whiteboards where he wrote out time lines and set down the facts regarding each victim. When he stood back and studied his handiwork, he was more convinced than ever that the current killer was not a copycat. There were too many little things that a copycat simply couldn't know. The way the fingers of each victim had been stretched out, as if she were reaching for some-thing. The way the silver chain that held the medallion had been carefully curled. The way the feet had been pointed out, as if replicating the points of a star.

And he wondered once again why each victim had gone to the woods completely unsuspectingly.

Not a single defensive wound had been found on them.

Either they had been with a friend, someone they trusted, or they had gone there to meet a friend.

He was mulling that point when his cell phone rang. It was Devin.

He was surprised by the way his heart leaped.

"Everything all right?" he asked her.

"Yes, yes, I'm fine. But I'd like to see you."

She hesitated, and he realized that she was whispering even though she was in her own house and the only person who might hear her was . . .

"I know you saw . . . what you saw. And Auntie

Mina saw a woman in the window. That night, I mean. You asked me how I knew to go into the woods. I heard someone crying. But Auntie Mina *saw* her. And it wasn't the woman I found. She didn't tell me before because she didn't realize they were different people, but now that she's seen so many images . . . anyway. It was someone else. And I think she was murdered, too."

Devin was on edge. Maybe it was something she should have accepted all her life.

That sometimes she could see the dead.

But she hadn't accepted it. She'd gone into journalism, for God's sake. Facts and figures.

But now an FBI agent as cool and stoic as the *GQ* man she'd initially compared him to was sitting in her parlor—along with her dead aunt. And they were all talking as if this were a perfectly normal conversation. Rocky was interviewing Auntie Mina with sober consideration, listening to her words as if she were a living witness.

"The victim's picture is in the paper, you see—and of course, on the television," Auntie Mina said. "I do love television," she told him. "Why, when I was a girl, it didn't even exist."

Rocky grinned. "I love TV myself. Especially *The Big Bang Theory* and reruns of *Frasier.*"

Auntie Mina was delighted. "Excellent shows."

"So you saw pictures of the victim and realized

she wasn't the woman you'd seen in the window. Do you know who she is? Or recognize the woman you *did* see?"

Aunt Mina shook her head sadly. "No. I'd never seen her before. Except that I feel certain that she was a reenactor of some kind. I'm sure you've seen some of our local Wiccans. I'll admit, most of my clothing was black, and if you were to go into my closet now, you'd see that I had several gorgeous cloaks for our circles and Sabbats. But she was dressed differently. Like a Puritan. Perhaps she really *was* a Puritan, a woman from . . . some other time."

"Thank you, Mina," Rocky said. "I'm not sure what it means, but it's definitely a new avenue to explore."

"You mean, we have another dead woman somewhere?" Devin asked him.

He looked over at her. There was something gentle in his eyes. "Maybe not. Maybe she died a long time ago and stayed to try to save others."

"Oh," Aunt Mina said.

"I have to get back," he told them. "The members of my team are coming in later."

"You have a team?"

"I do."

She nodded. "Good," she told him. "A whole team to help out will be very good."

He rose and thanked Aunt Mina. Devin walked with him to the door.

"Lock it," she said. "That's what you're going to say to me, right? I would do it, anyway, you know, without you telling me."

He nodded and hesitated. "I think I'd like to take a tour with that friend of yours I met last night—Brent Corbin."

"Okay. I can set it up, if you like."

"Sure. Want to come with me?"

It was her turn to hesitate.

Sure, let's see a friend of mine. Let's pretend we've known each other before now, that you're here because I live here, that you're here to be with me. . . .

You could *just ask me to dinner.*

Great. Three women were dead, two of them in the past couple of weeks, and she . . .

She couldn't stop thinking about Rocky.

Each time she saw him, she was more fascinated by him.

"Of course. Except . . ." she said.

"Except?" he asked.

"I'm not sure why you're so focused on my friends."

"I'm not. You're friends are just up to speed on what's going on locally, and I need to catch up."

"*I'm* up to speed on what's happening locally. And don't you have your own friends?"

He laughed. "I do. And maybe I'll drag you to meet them."

She moved to close the door and their fingers

brushed. She felt as if sparks sizzled through her, warming her flesh, and she knew that a blush rose to her cheeks. She met his eyes, trying not to jerk her fingers away, trying to appear casual.

There was something in his solemn green gaze, and she wondered if he had felt it, too. If he . . .

He smiled. "I'm serious," he said softly. "My old gang wants to get together. It would be great if you'd come with me. We might learn something from them."

"Learn what?"

"Information we may not have—gossip that could lead to something," he said.

"Are any of them Wiccans? Or historians?"

He shook his head. "Jack is a cop, Vince is a lawyer, Haley is a dance instructor and Renee is a cheerleading coach."

"Ah. The in crowd. I bet you played football."

"Guilty," he said. "Until . . ."

"Until?"

"Melissa."

"She still haunts you, doesn't she?"

"We're all haunted, aren't we?" he asked.

He left, and she locked the door.

"What a delightful man," Aunt Mina said, coming up behind her and making her jump.

"Auntie Mina, he's an FBI agent trying to solve a series of murders."

"Yes, and we're just trying to help, aren't we?"

6

Rocky's phone rang on the way back to the station, alerting him to the fact that his fellow agents were waiting at his hotel. They wanted to meet in private before going to the station.

He discovered that he was being joined by Crow's wife, Angela, and agents Jenna Duffy, Sam Hall and Jane Everett.

He had a feeling Jackson had sent Angela, his right-hand "man," to assess the abilities that had gotten him into the Krewe—the unofficial name for the special units, and so called because their first case, a few years back, had been in New Orleans. Rocky wasn't offended; the Krewe of Hunters was unlike any other division in the FBI.

Once he got to the hotel they all headed for the restaurant to get to know one another.

Jenna and Sam were from the area. Just a few years earlier they'd solved the case of a massacre at Lexington House and exonerated a boy— supposedly haunted by demons—who'd allegedly murdered his family and several other people. Rocky had met Jenna and Sam already. The day of his interview with Jackson he'd met the other agents who made up what were loosely called the Krewe of Hunters and the Texas Krewe, names derived from the fact that Adam Harrison—the overall director of the Krewes—had first put a team together in New Orleans and then expanded their numbers into Texas.

Sam was an attorney as well as an agent. He had the size and bearing to be a good backup man in a pinch and also had the careful, ever-vigilant mind of a well-trained attorney. He still owned a home in Salem, one that had been in his family and was now rented out.

Jenna, a bright pretty redhead with large hazel eyes and tremendous energy, as well as abilities that had proven themselves time and again, had been one of the first Krewe members. It was obvious, though they were careful *not* to be obvious, that she and Sam were a couple.

Jane, a tall and attractive brunette, had been sent specifically because she was a forensic artist; she didn't have a law enforcement background, but she had been a consultant on many cases in San Antonio before heading to the academy and then joining the unit.

"We're going to have a 'Yankee' Krewe before long, the way our numbers are rising," Angela told him. She was a beautiful woman. After his interview, she'd been the one to show him around and he had learned that she felt she had found her true calling when she'd first joined the New Orleans Krewe. And of course, she'd added with a rueful smile, she'd also found Jackson Crow.

The five of them sat around the table, and at first Angela and Jane just listened as the others discussed growing up in New England.

"We both knew about Melissa Wilson's death," Jenna told Rocky. "You couldn't live in this county without hearing about it. But I was a teenager and Sam was just off to college. When you're that young . . . you hear about terrible things, but you don't feel like there's much you can do about them."

"I hadn't thought about it again until Jackson Crow brought you in to meet us," Sam said.

"So who's the lead detective?" Angela asked him.

"An old friend of mine," Rocky said. "A guy named Jack Grail."

"So does that mean he's being helpful?" Jenna asked.

"Completely. I was in before we got the okay," Rocky said. He turned to Jane. He'd heard about the Krewe. Hell, he'd *investigated* the Krewe before seeking out Jackson Crow. But it still seemed odd as hell to say certain things out loud.

"Devin Lyle, the young woman who found the Jane Doe, has a . . . dead aunt who lives with her. It used to be the aunt's house. The aunt saw someone at the window, and it wasn't our dead woman. She could be another victim." He waited. No one laughed; no one questioned him.

"Is the aunt an outgoing spirit?" Jane asked him. "Is she easy to talk to?"

"Yes, very."

Jane looked at Angela. "How about you and I head over to meet the ghost and her niece after we all go to the station?"

It was agreed. Angela and Jane took their rental; Sam and Jenna went with Rocky. At the station they met up with Jack Grail and were introduced to the other officers working on the case. Jack accompanied them when they gathered in the "feds' room," and Rocky went over his charts and explained why he was so certain they were looking at one killer, not a copycat.

"Do you think it could be someone who comes and goes from the area?" Jenna asked. "Because that would make this really, really hard."

"Yes, it would—except that I believe the killer's from the area, and that he doesn't necessarily come and go. Or, necessarily, that he's a 'he.' The victims don't distrust their attacker or even see him coming. Angela, if I may . . ."

Using her as his mock victim, he demonstrated the killing technique they'd discerned from the autopsies.

"So a woman *could* be the killer," Jack mused.

"A tall woman," Jenna noted. "Or the angle of the blade would be different."

"You're right," Rocky said. "Based on forensics, the killer stood between five-eight and six-one, possibly six-two." He shrugged. "I've played with a dummy at different heights, but I haven't been able to narrow it down any further. We need to go at this from all angles. With all of us on it, we can dig deeper, looking for connections and similarities between victims, or trying to come up with a psychological profile and pinpointing people who fit."

"So it's computer time," Sam said.

"I'm good at that kind of thing," Jenna offered. "I can search Essex County residents from thirteen years ago till now, just give me something to look for."

"Our killer might have come and gone," Jane said.

"I'll take that into consideration."

"Jenna," Rocky asked, "can you do a search for residents who purchased athames in that time frame?"

"Of course. But if they used cash . . ."

"I don't think they would have. Most people I know don't even use cash to buy a latte anymore. There are always outside possibilities, but let's go with this. And an athame is too common a purchase here for someone to be worried that they'd be targeted for buying one," Rocky said. "And truthfully, alone it means nothing. But when things start to add up, it will be another piece of the puzzle—assuming our killer even used an athame. Still, it's a good guess based on the ritualistic nature of the murders, so it's a place to start."

"The population of Essex County is over 760,000," Jenna said. "Any ideas for narrowing it down?"

"Our killer could live anywhere in the area, but start with the towns most directly associated with the witch trials," Rocky said. "Salem, Danvers, Andover, Peabody and the rest."

"You think this could have something to do with those executions?" Sam asked.

Rocky thought about how Mina Lyle had described the woman in the window. A Puritan.

"A hunch," he said. "Also," he added, "look for people on your athame list who own a dark SUV. The boy who found Carly Henderson wasn't sure what kind of car knocked him off the road, but he thinks it was a dark SUV. It might just have been a lousy driver, but it could have been our killer."

"All right—age ranges?" Jenna asked.

"I'd say anyone who was fifteen and up at the time of Melissa's murder," Rocky said.

"That young?" Sam asked, then shook his head ruefully. "Yeah, you're right—that young. Sad to say."

Jack left them to speak with his officers, Sam settled in to go back over the missing-persons reports, Jenna started finessing the computer and the other three each took one of the victims' files and started back over it, looking for any detail that might have been missed before now.

• • •

With Auntie Mina there in the house to keep it from feeling so empty, Devin found that her work seemed to fly, but Aunt Mina had more for her to do once she got a good look at her herb garden.

Aunt Mina shook her head. "You know, a lot of old wives' tales are just that, but not all. A lot of what our ancestors thought was good for us really was. The garden needs work."

"I've only been back a few months, Auntie Mina," Devin reminded her. "But I'll go out and pull some weeds right now."

"You will do no such thing! You've got to remain inside—and be vigilant," Aunt Mina said.

Devin *had* been careful. Very careful. But the two murdered women had been killed in different parts of town, only one of them near her house. And if they were counting the girl who had died thirteen years ago, she'd been killed in Peabody.

"I don't believe I'm in any danger, Auntie," Devin said. She couldn't help but wonder if she was talking to herself. Seriously, how easy was it to imagine her aunt, who had been such a huge part of her life, might be lingering at the cottage that had been her home?

But Rocky had seen her, too.

It was amazing; Rocky had . . . something special. A sense about such things. It made her feel closer to him, somehow.

She realized that she'd forgotten to call Brent

and make reservations for tonight's tour. She grabbed her phone and was relieved to find out there was still room for them.

He told her to be there by 7:45 p.m., then said casually, "I looked him up, by the way."

"What?"

"I ran a search on your friend. He *is* from Peabody, and he was a big shot on the high school football team. Then a girl he knew was murdered and he just quit playing. They say he was headed for the NFL."

"I guess he didn't care that much about a pro career." She had the feeling he had decided that going into law enforcement was more important —especially after losing a friend that way.

"He looks like he still plays. Bet the guy spends half his life in a gym."

"I don't know. We're friends, but—"

"I don't trust him, Devin," Brent warned her.

"What? Why would you say that?"

"His friend dies, he goes away. I can trace him through college and then . . . he disappears. I found some of his classes. You've got to hear the titles. Things like 'Women Who Kill,' 'Defining the Psychotic Mind' . . . the list goes on."

"He majored in criminology," Devin said.

"Yeah? Are you sure he didn't major in being a criminal?"

Devin kept her mouth shut. Rocky hadn't told the others what he did for a living, and though she didn't think he was trying to hide it—he wasn't here undercover or anything—it didn't seem like it was her place to say anything.

"He's a good guy, Brent," she said.

"Don't be fooled just because you think he's hot."

"Brent!"

"Okay, sorry. But friends have to look after friends. And I'm just saying, he leaves after a friend is killed—he comes back and two women are murdered."

"I don't believe he was back in the area yet when Carly Henderson was killed."

"You may not *believe*," Brent said, "but you don't *know*."

He hung up before she could reply. Exasperated, she almost called him back to tell him she wasn't coming.

But she didn't.

She was about to get back to work when her phone rang. Rocky. He wanted her to know that two of his fellow agents were on the way. One was a sketch artist who wanted to work with Aunt Mina.

"What?" Devin said.

"She wants to work with your aunt," he repeated.

She stared at the phone. "My aunt is dead."

"That's fine. They won't mind. They're both great, and I know you'll like them. So will your aunt." She felt his hesitation before he spoke again. "We're all with a special unit of the FBI, Devin. The Krewe was formed because there are people out there who can see and talk to the dead. By working together, we're able to do better work. We don't have to pretend to one another, or come up with some ridiculous explanation for why we know something. And of course, as we're seeing, it doesn't solve everything. Some souls do stay as ghosts, and some don't, but . . . well, I can't tell you how great it is that you're one of us."

"One of you?"

"That you can see," he added quietly.

"Yes, I suppose. I mean . . . it's not easy."

"No," he agreed. "See you soon."

That was all. He was gone.

And he hadn't given her much warning. She'd barely hung up when she heard the doorbell chime.

"Who is it, dear?" Aunt Mina called from the back room, where she was watching television.

"Two more FBI agents, Auntie."

Aunt Mina giggled. "I'll behave. I promise."

"No," Devin said dryly. "They're coming to see *you*."

"How lovely," Aunt Mina said.

Devin wasn't sure that any of it was lovely at all. She gave her aunt a weak smile and went to the door, looking carefully through the peephole before opening it. The two women on her doorstep were attractive and dressed in what people called business casual. The blonde introduced herself as Angela Hawkins, and the brunette was Jane Everett, the forensic artist.

To Devin's absolute astonishment, even though she knew from what Rocky had told her that they could see ghosts, they greeted Aunt Mina as if she were as corporeal as they were.

But she prepared coffee and tea, then—when she wasn't quick enough and Aunt Mina reminded her that they should offer their guests something to eat—went back to the kitchen and found some scones.

Jane was sitting on the sofa with Auntie Mina, working on a sketch as Aunt Mina described the woman she'd seen. Angela smiled at Devin and said softly, "It looks like you're in shock."

Devin admitted, "A little."

"Are you having trouble accepting your gift?"

"I'm not sure I see this as a gift," Devin said.

"Have you seen spirits before? Before your aunt's reappearance, I mean?" Angela asked her.

"She did, she just didn't admit that she did," Aunt Mina piped in. "Comes from me, of course. And my family line. It skips a generation in our family. But the ability is very strong in Devin."

"Now, Miss Lyle, I need you to focus," Jane said.

"Of course, dear, of course," Aunt Mina said.

Angela grinned at Devin. "So . . . you accepted

your talent late, I take it? Not to worry—many of us did. And it's not always easy to understand what's really going on, since there are spirits out there we never see, and others are shy or just haven't learned yet how to make themselves visible—not to mention audible—to the living. Even the most gifted among us." She shook her head and smiled. "Those of us in the Krewes have been at this awhile, and we still don't understand everything. We try, and then we hope for the best."

Devin glanced over at her aunt. "I don't know what to think. Aunt Mina saw a woman in Puritan dress. It might have been an actress, of course—there are reenactors all around the city. But . . . if she saw a ghost, what would that mean? Whoever the killer is, he or she might have been around thirteen years ago—but not three-hundred-plus years ago."

"No, that's very true. But if we can identify the woman you found or your aunt's Puritan, we might be able to find out how they're related, and that could help us solve our case."

"Okay," Jane announced, breaking into the conversation. "Here's what I have so far," she said, then turned her sketch pad around, showing them what she'd drawn.

The woman in the sketch was pretty and delicate. She had fine features, and large, light-colored eyes. She wore the cap typical of the

Puritans and a white pinafore over a dark dress.

"Close?" she asked Aunt Mina.

Aunt Mina sighed softly. "Close? She's nearly exact. But I've never seen her before—or since—that night."

"Have *you* ever seen her?" Jane asked, looking at Devin.

"No, I don't know her," Devin said.

"Well, then, I guess we're set here," Jane said. She rose and smiled at Devin. "You have a lovely home," she said.

Devin didn't respond. It was still Aunt Mina's home, really.

But Aunt Mina seemed to be disappearing.

"Thank you," Devin said distractedly, her eyes on her aunt's fading form.

Jane followed the direction of her gaze and said sympathetically, "It takes a lot to appear and speak, and your aunt had to really focus to give us so much information. She'll be back."

"Don't be startled when she arrives out of the blue," Angela warned.

"Oh, I've gotten used to her," Devin said.

Jane and Angela got set to leave, and Devin walked them to the door. When she opened it, she had to stifle a scream.

Because standing there was Rocky.

"Hey, how did it go?" he asked.

Jane produced her drawing. Rocky studied it for a long moment. Then he looked at Devin.

"Anyone you've ever seen before?" he asked.

She shook her head. "No, I don't know her."

"We'll find her," he said, his eyes holding hers. "Thank you," he told Jane. "Are you ready?" he asked Devin.

"For?"

"It's after seven," he said. "The tours all start around eight, right?"

"Oh!" she said, amazed that the afternoon had gone by so quickly. "Oh."

"So . . . ready to go?"

"Yes, yes, of course." She turned to the other two agents. "Would you like to join us? Brent is a friend of mine, he won't mind."

"We were going to go back to the hotel and assess what we have so far," Jane said. "I think a tour—a refresher course—of the city's history is actually a good idea, but we'll go another night. Witchcraft does seem to be the key to solving this case, doesn't it?"

Devin didn't let herself reply, reminding herself that Jane wasn't attacking the city's Wiccan community, only stating the obvious. Because one way or another, witchcraft *was* at the heart of these killings.

It was the pentagrams found on the victims.

Devin grabbed her purse, let the others out ahead of her and locked the door. The other women took their rental, and she went in Rocky's car. As they drove, he seemed preoccupied.

"Your friends—your coworkers—are very nice."

He flashed her a smile. "They are. I'm just getting to know them myself. But what I know already is that they're pretty amazing."

"Oh."

"New assignment," he told her. "I just joined the Krewe. I'd been working across the country."

"It must feel strange to come home to . . . this," she said.

"Not at all—I asked for this assignment."

Of course, he had. He had said it: he was haunted. Had been for years.

And now . . .

"Have you come up with anything?" she asked him, then smiled. "Or is that classified?"

"We've followed every lead, and we're running some computer searches. But as to answers . . . no, none yet."

"It makes sense that you wanted a sketch of the woman Aunt Mina saw."

He glanced her way. "Of course. I'm trying to figure out how the victims are chosen, because I do believe there's a reason they're being targeted. I just keep thinking . . . our killer's not a sexual sadist. The women aren't being molested. It's more like a ritual—a sacrifice."

"Which is more proof that the killer's not Wiccan. Today's Wiccans don't sacrifice—no matter what the Druids might have done. And if you're looking to history to clarify what's going on, the accused at the witch trials weren't even witches. They were the innocent victims of paranoia. So if you think tonight's tour is going to point a finger at the big bad witches, think again."

"I know that."

"Then . . . ?"

"I don't know. But I keep feeling . . . Well, I have been gone awhile. I just keep thinking that something in tonight's tour will dislodge a clue from my memory."

"Well, you'll like Brent's tour even if it doesn't solve the case for you. There's no hocus-pocus. No pun intended."

Brent's tour began at the Salem Witch Trials Memorial and ended at his shop—which, being a clever businessman, he opened for business as soon as they arrived.

It was a busy night. Over twenty people had gathered to take the tour. As they waited, Devin watched Rocky's face. He was listening intently to those around them.

"I don't think tourists really have to worry, do you?" one woman asked another.

"No, of course not. The victims were all locals," her friend replied.

"They haven't identified the second victim yet," a man standing nearby pointed out. "And if she were local, wouldn't someone know her? They posted her picture in the paper, and it's been all over TV."

"Hush, Henry, the children," said his wife.

"They need to know to stay with us at all times," Henry said gruffly.

"How do you feel about the memorial? Or do you remember when it wasn't here?" Rocky asked Devin.

"Yes, I remember," she told him, grinning. "You're not *that* much older than I am." She'd been very young when it had been erected for the tricentennial of the trials, but it had been a big deal in town, the kind of thing that stuck in your memory.

There was always controversy when the powers that be made a big change in town, but Devin personally liked the little area—adjacent to the cemetery—where twenty individual stone benches were each engraved with the name of one of those who was executed during the witch craze, nineteen of them hanged and Giles Corey pressed to death. Most tours began here, but she particularly liked the way Brent began his tours at this spot, with the real history of the time and an explanation of the situation.

The memorial was atmospheric at night; the moon and city lights cast a glow over the graveyard—closed at dusk, but easily visible over the low stone fence. None of the victims was buried there in the Old Burying Point Cemetery, but Nathaniel Hawthorne's ancestor—John Hathorne, the only witch trial judge never to repent of his actions—was interred near the memorial. Sometimes a low fog would roll in, which made the stories especially poignant and a bit eerie.

"Hey! You two made it. And on time," Brent said, smiling, as he found them in the crowd.

"I'm always on time, Brent," Devin said.

"That's right—Beth is the one who never seems to know what time it is," Brent said. "I'm glad you're here," he told Rocky. Suddenly he turned around and started coughing.

"Brent, are you sick?" Devin asked him.

"Allergy. And I don't even know to what," Brent said with disgust. "But if I yell for help, you take over, okay? And you might as well have a seat while I do my intro."

Devin sat with Rocky on the bench dedicated to Bridget Bishop. She'd always felt empathy for Bridget—she'd actually worn a color other than black at times and had some sass in her. It had proved to be her undoing.

Brent stepped forward, welcoming the crowd, checking his watch—and moving right into his first speech.

"If we're going to think about the deaths of people, first we have to think about the lives they were living. So think about Salem back then—a divided place, one town loosely divided into Salem and Salem Village. The first was near the coast—more urban. The second was made up mainly of farmland. The farmers closest to town didn't want to break away. They were economically tied to the seaport. Others wanted to separate and make Salem Village an official town of its own.

"The Putnam family—one of the most affluent in the area—wanted to separate. To that end they hired Reverend Samuel Parris to come and lead services near them. If that didn't make relations with those in town bad enough, they gave Parris a house and grounds to go with the stipend and firewood they provided. That seemed outrageous to people who felt a minister shouldn't be compensated to such an unheard-of degree. So even before the claims of witchcraft and pacts with the devil began, the community was at odds.

"On top of that, remember that it was winter. If you've been here for a Massachusetts winter, you know it can be brutal. Imagine winter with no electricity and only a fire for warmth. Such darkness and cold. Not so long ago they had been at war with the Indians, and many still found the woods a terrifying place. There was a devil out there, the strict Puritans believed, and he was ready to seize those who showed signs of moral weakness. And anything fun was a sure sign of sin. I've got to say, I'm awfully glad there aren't any Puritans still living in the area today."

Laughter followed Brent's last statement. He grinned and looked at Devin. "Pipe in here for a minute, will you?"

She was surprised. Brent loved to tell his stories. She started to demur, but then, as he pointed to his throat and reached for a bottle of water, she remembered what he'd said earlier about helping out. By then, the crowd had turned to her, and Brent, coughing, had turned away.

Devin stood and stepped forward. "So, leading up to the accusations, arrests and trials, you had dissension in town, with those who were close to town and didn't want to separate refusing to pay certain taxes—taxes that paid to build the new minister's house and on Samuel Parris's property. Now, I don't think that the young women in his house were horrible people. And why the elders let things go so far, we'll never know. Somehow a number of books on fortune-telling—prophesy— began to circulate among the young people in the community. I imagine they were greeted with the same enthusiasm as *Harry Potter*, *Twilight* or *The Hunger Games*. Remember, they weren't allowed to dance, and even hide-and-seek was considered a game for the idle.

"Parris happened to have two slaves, Tituba, and John Indian, her husband. Tituba was often in charge of the girls who lived in or visited the Parris household, among them Parris's daughter, Betty, and his orphaned niece, Abigail. They began to form secret little circles, reading their books, even going so far as to break eggs into water, then 'read' the patterns to tell the future.

Tituba was from Barbados, and she brought with her stories about spells and witchcraft. Betty and Abby undoubtedly got carried away.

"The two girls began shouting blasphemies, running around on the floor like dogs and scaring their parents. Dr. Grigsby was immediately called. He found nothing physically wrong with the girls and said it had to be a clerical matter. The community prayed, even fasted, but to no avail. The girls were pressured to name the witches who were tormenting them. They named Tituba and two local women, Sarah Good—who was a homeless beggar—and Sarah Osborne, who was very old and hadn't been to church in a long time—a grievous sin in the community. The three women—all of low social class—were formally accused of witchcraft. Magistrates Jonathan Corwin and John Hathorne—no *W* in the name, Nathaniel put that in to disassociate himself—came to investigate.

"The three women were arrested on March 1 of 1692. Tituba actually confessed to being a witch, though what they did to make her confess isn't known. Regardless, she told her examiners that she was visited by Satan, sometimes as a large dog, and that there was a coven of witches in Salem. By May, over two hundred people had been arrested on the charge of witchcraft. A court of Oyer and Terminer—from the old English version of the Latin "to hear and determine"—was called, and soon the frenzy had begun in earnest. Many more were accused and arrested, many of high-ranking status—and most of them those who opposed the Putnam family."

"So they had their own neighbors killed?" one lady said.

"Well, it wasn't that simple. Remember, the devil was very real to them. And they lived in a time when all of Europe believed in witchcraft. People really believed that witches could harm your livestock and kill your children. So what was really going on with those girls? Were they simply cruel? Deluded? Some think there was ergot, a hallucinogenic fungus, in the wheat, but then the whole town would have been having visions. Or was it something I think we're all capable of at times? You tell a lie so many times, it becomes the truth. You believe it yourself." She glanced over at Brent. He had taken a seat and was catching his breath.

"In June," she said, "one gentleman of the court, Nathaniel Saltonstall, resigned, horrified by the other members' reliance on the 'spectral evidence' that was being presented. But that didn't bring any rationality to the proceedings. On June 10, Bridget Bishop was the first to be hanged by order of the court. The hysteria had begun." She indicated Bridget's bench; Rocky was still sitting there.

He smiled at her and winked. For a moment, she

stared back at him blankly, thrown off and far too attracted to him and the way he smiled at her.

But Brent was still sitting down and drinking his water, so she gave herself a mental shake and kept going.

"One of the oddest things—the way we see it today, anyway—was that some of the accused confessed, then accused others, and none of them were hanged. Instead, they were left to rot in jail. Those who *were* hanged were, in fact, the true Christian believers, the ones who wouldn't confess to a lie and admit to being witches. That would be against God, and they were intent on saving their immortal souls.

"As time went on, some of the accusers became the accused themselves. A woman named Martha Corey was accused of witchcraft on March 12, and her husband, Giles, spoke against his own wife. Then he himself was accused on April 19. Today we see Giles Corey as a sad old man. But in fact, he was a strong old bugger. He knew that his property would stay in his family if he refused to plead either innocent or guilty, so Magistrate Corwin had him pressed in hopes of forcing him to either confess or claim innocence. Heavy stones were piled on his chest until finally he suffocated. A marker commemorating the event stands at the Howard Street Cemetery. But all Giles would say was . . ." She paused, smiling. "If you've spent time here in Salem, you know."

"More weight!" a kid called out.

"Exactly," Devin said. "He might not have been the kindest of men, but he did know the law, and by dying without giving a plea of guilty or not guilty, he kept his land. And in fact, his heirs are still there to this day."

As she finished speaking, she looked over toward Bridget's bench and frowned.

Rocky was gone.

He'd seen her standing slightly downhill by the entrance to the cemetery.

At first she had been nothing but a deeper shadow in the darkness. But then the shape of her shadow had resolved itself into a woman, and not a woman in regular summer tourist clothing. A long skirt had hugged her legs and moved in the breeze.

He'd quietly left the tour group and walked slowly in her direction. But by the time he reached the cemetery gate she had turned and was headed down to Derby Street.

He followed her, and when she reached the corner she turned back and saw him—and saw that he could see *her*.

He recognized her face. It was the face in the portrait Jane had drawn that afternoon. The face that Mina Lyle had seen in the window the night that Devin had heard the sobbing.

"Wait, please," he called softly.

Her face seemed to whiten; for a minute, he could see her clearly in the combination of moonlight and illumination from the well-lit main street.

Then she turned and fled around the corner. He raced after her, but there was a crowd of people walking along Derby Street in search of restaurants and bars, or heading home after a long day of exploring the city.

He moved through the crowd, searching, studying every group he passed. He even walked into the brewery and a few restaurants, looking for her, but after a good forty-five minutes of fruitless effort he gave up and slowly walked back to the cemetery.

A fine mist had crept in. The kind that made the cemetery ethereal and sad. He waited, watched and considered jumping the fence, but he knew there would be no point.

She was gone.

Of course, she could disappear at will. She hadn't even needed to turn that corner.

He could never catch her unless she allowed him to.

He could only speak to her if she wanted to speak to him.

The tour group had moved on. He wasn't worried. He had a pretty good idea of the route they would follow, so he would catch up to them eventually.

He walked down by the site of the old jail, by

the Anglican church, then on to a few of the other stops on most of the tours. They wouldn't have wandered too far; the tours didn't tend to go more than a few blocks in either direction off Essex Street.

He caught up with the tour in front of the Gardner-Pingree House. As he joined the crowd, he realized that Devin was still speaking.

"The house was built in 1804 by Samuel McIntire but was sold in 1814 to Captain Joseph White. Joseph White was the victim of a brutal murder—and his killer's trial was presided over by Daniel Webster himself. Parker Brothers, a Salem company, bought the American rights to a British game called Cluedo and marketed it as Clue. This house served as a real-life basis for the game. Captain White was bludgeoned in the bedroom with a candlestick, as well as stabbed with a knife. Nearby houses and people involved in the arrest and trial were added to the pieces and characters. In addition, many people believe that both Edgar Allan Poe and Nathaniel Hawthorne used the trial in their works— including Poe's classic tale of a guilty conscience, 'The Tell-Tale Heart,' since one of the men hired to carry out the murder hanged himself in his jail cell."

Brent Corbin stepped up to join her. "The trials and other grisly events in the history of Salem have been explored in numerous books, many of which I carry in my shop if you're interested, so let's move on and I'll tell you the last story of the evening."

Devin looked around as the group began to follow Brent, and Rocky knew the minute she'd spotted him. She walked over to where he stood, almost directly across the street from Crow Haven Corner, the city's oldest witch shop.

She didn't speak, but she did look at him questioningly.

"Good thing we came on the tour," he told her. "Or, I should say, good thing *you* did."

"Every time he tried to speak, he started coughing, poor guy," Devin said. "So . . . where did you run off to?"

He didn't get a chance to answer, because just then a woman ran up to her, trying to stuff a bill into her hands.

"Thanks! You were great. We learned so much."

"Oh, uh, no . . . um, please, give this to Brent."

But the woman was already gone, racing to rejoin the rest of the group. Devin winced and looked at him. For a moment, with her wry smile, the light in her eyes and the scent of her so powerful, he was tempted simply to touch her . . . to draw her into his arms.

Luckily she spoke, and the spell was broken.

"Looks like I got a twenty. Buy you a drink, Agent Rockwell?"

"Sure," he told her.

They walked across the street to a restaurant that was still open for a few hours. Luckily it wasn't very full, and they were given a curved table near the window to the street and no one seated near them. There were menus already lying on the table, and they both ordered shepherd's pie, as if they'd realized simultaneously that they were starving.

When the waitress had left them, Devin turned to him and demanded, "Where the hell did you go?"

"I saw her," he said.

"Who?"

"The woman your aunt saw at your window the night our Jane Doe was killed."

"You *saw* her?"

He nodded.

"And you chased her?"

He nodded again, then waited as the waitress delivered their drinks.

"And you . . . spoke with her?"

"No. She disappeared."

"Well, that's not really helpful. But . . . are you sure it was her?"

"I'm sure. I think I scared her, but she didn't disappear right away. She let me follow her down to Derby Street first, which makes me think she wants to talk."

Her eyes were on his, glinting like sapphires in

the light of the little candle that burned on their table.

"Then why did she disappear?" Devin asked.

"Because," he said softly, lifting his beer in a salute, "I think she wants to talk to *you.*"

7

Dinner was actually nice.

Almost like two people who liked each other being out on a . . .

A date.

They talked about things that had nothing to do with ghosts and murder. He told her he'd lost his dad, who he'd adored, and had always wanted to go into law enforcement because of him. His mom, who he saw as often as his schedule allowed, was happily remarried and living in Arizona.

"Doesn't she worry about you—about your job?" Devin asked.

"She married an ex-sheriff and then a retired cop. She's accustomed to it. She'd probably be more worried if I worked in a convenience store. What about you?"

So she told him about her parents, that they were happily retired and she saw them several times a year—sadly, the last time being not so long ago, for her aunt's funeral.

As they talked, Rocky said that there were times when he really missed the area. When she asked him if he would ever move back, he shook his head slowly. "Not in the near future. I've just gotten where I really want to be, and that's based in Virginia."

"Another state with a lot of interesting history," she said with a smile. "Jamestown, Williamsburg, revolutionaries, pirates, the Civil War . . ."

He laughed. "Yep."

Eventually they left the restaurant. She had a feeling they were both sorry to go.

"Are you still planning to meet up with your friends?" she asked him. "Now that your 'people' are here?"

He paused at that. Essex Street was quiet. Most of the ghost tour guests had headed back to their lodgings. A few late-night bars were still open, but at that hour Essex Street wasn't the hotbed of activity it was by day.

Until Haunted Happenings, of course, but that would come with the fall.

He nodded, looking around. "Not a creature is stirring," he murmured, then smiled at her. "But do you think they're watching?"

"Ghosts?" she asked.

"Uh-huh."

"Probably," she said softly.

"And yet most people never even know they exist—or think about it on a daily basis. Anyway, back to your question," he said, walking again in the direction of the car. "Yes. My 'people' are all nice, and two of them are from the area—assigned to the case for precisely that reason. They'll have fun with my old crowd. You liked Jane and Angela, didn't you?"

"Very much," she told him, getting into the car.

"Good. That's two people you'll already know," he said, and moved around to the driver's side. "And Jack, of course."

"Jack?"

"Detective Grail."

"Oh! That's right," she said, remembering. "You two are old friends."

"Yep. Never thought he'd be a cop. Another of our friends—the biggest slacker of us all—went to law school, and now he's a successful attorney."

Devin laughed. "All my friends, it seems, embraced the history of this town and opened stores or became guides. Or both."

"You could certainly be a guide if you wanted to."

"I love what I do, but who knows what the future will hold?"

As they drove back toward her cottage, Devin looked out at the streets of Salem. Yes, it was commercial. Yes, it was a tourist town. But people here also remembered their real history. And they honored it.

When they reached the house, he walked her up the path without asking.

Devin opened the door and looked in. "Auntie Mina?" she called.

There was no reply from her aunt, so she stepped in, and Rocky followed her.

"I'll do the check-out-the-house thing," he said.

As he'd done before, he went through every room, looking in closets and under the beds. When he finished and rejoined her by the door, he said, "I don't want to make you paranoid, but it's always a good idea to be careful. I just wish you weren't out here alone."

"I'm not alone. I have Poe and Aunt Mina," she told him.

He gave a halfhearted smile. "You were pretty amazing tonight."

"Pardon?"

"You know your history—the people, the victims, the accusers, the social climate of the time. And the more recent history, too, of course."

She stood in the doorway smiling. "There's so much about the people who lived here that's so fascinating. Take the gray house that borders the cemetery. Nathaniel Hawthorne's in-laws lived there, and he wrote a story about a house next to a cemetery that was filled with spiders. And wondering about his in-laws makes me wonder about *him*. What does our background have to do

160

with the way we live our lives? Do we embrace it? Run from it?"

He laughed softly. "I know. From the area, remember? Where the girls first became 'afflicted' is actually Danvers today, and where Giles Corey had his property is Peabody now. But it was all Salem back then."

Devin laughed. "Okay, so you did grow up around here. And I certainly don't want to escape the area. It's just that sometimes I feel I know it *too* well. Still, for better or worse, this is home." She hesitated, looking at him. "You really think that Salem's history is relevant to the case?"

"For some reason, yes. A hunch—maybe the way the victims' bodies were arranged. Definitely the pentagrams."

"I know I sound like a broken record, but the Wiccans here today have absolutely nothing to do with what happened in the past."

"No—and yes. Don't you think maybe the Wiccan community here has thrived because of history?"

"I suppose."

He exhaled thoughtfully. "Here's the thing—they used witchcraft in 1692 to spread terror and kill people. Whoever is doing this is using modern Wicca in some way, apparently for the same reason."

"And does that help you?"

"Right now it's about all we've got, even if it

doesn't lead anywhere yet. We have nothing physical. No trace evidence is almost unheard of. We have no hairs, no fibers, no blood from the attacker—nothing to go on forensically."

"They haven't found *anything?*"

"Not yet. But we *will* catch him—or her. This time."

"You think a woman could be doing this?"

"Yes. There's no reason a woman can't wield a knife."

"True."

"You all right?" he asked her. "I can . . . well, I can stay on the sofa or in your aunt's old room—I think she'd let me."

She smiled. "I'm fine," she told him.

They were standing so close together there in the doorway. For a moment she wondered how someone she found so seductive and attractive had come into her life—and why he'd had to enter as a consequence of a tragic murder. And yet, despite the circumstances, there was something chemical between them, she thought. Or maybe the bond was more cerebral.

Apparently they both spoke to the dead.

No, it wasn't that. She smiled slightly.

As in her *Auntie Pim* books, maybe it was slightly magical.

She thought they were going to touch. Their lips were close. . . . They would touch, and then . . .

He cleared his throat and stepped back.

"Please tell me that you have me on speed dial," he said.

She nodded and smiled, and stepped into the house. "Don't worry. I'm not taking any chances. I'm young. I like living."

"So do I," he said softly. "Lock—"

"The door."

He took another step back. "I'll be listening for the bolt."

She shut and locked the door, then leaned against it and closed her eyes, listening as his footsteps took him down the path to his car.

"Dearest girl, you should have kissed the boy."

Her eyes flew open. "Auntie Mina!"

Well, she thought dryly, she wouldn't be having any wild affairs in this house, that much was for certain.

Not when it came with a chaperone.

Aunt Mina wagged a finger at Devin.

"Men like him don't come along often in life, my girl. Trust me. I lived long, and saw much. You shouldn't throw away such a rare opportunity."

Rocky returned to the hotel room to find the rest of the Krewe already set up in the suite that Sam Hall had taken; it had two bedrooms, one for him and Jenna, and one for Angela and Jane to share. There was also a good-size kitchen/dining area.

There were papers all over the table.

163

"There's coffee in the pot," Sam told Rocky.

"And a bottle of Jack if you need something stronger," Angela offered dryly.

He poured himself coffee.

"All right, here's where we are," Jenna said when he'd taken a seat at the table. "First, still no answers on our Jane Doe in the morgue. I tried missing persons across the country and couldn't come up with our woman. I also showed her picture to everyone I could think of. No one remembers her."

"I went over the bulletins from agencies across the country. Came close a few times, but the best we had was a woman with horrible teeth," Jane told him. "Not our vic, I'm afraid."

"How does a woman just disappear and die—and no one even misses her?" Rocky asked.

"I don't know," Angela said. "Sad. But it happens all too often."

"Poor thing," Jane murmured. "But I was noticing, as I'm sure you did, that there are only a couple of general similarities between the dead women. Age doesn't seem to factor in—Melissa Wilson was seventeen, Carly Henderson was thirty-two and the M.E. says our Jane Doe was somewhere in between—but they all had the same approximate size and build." She paused and produced a copy of the drawing she had done earlier, only enhanced with color and shading. "Take a look. This is the woman Mina Lyle saw—

a spirit trying to help, though whether she was an actress or a genuine Puritan, who knows. But if you compare all four women, there's something similar in their faces. Not eye color, obviously, but the fine-boned structure. They all have a slightly fragile appearance—an innocent appearance."

She was right. They didn't look like sisters, but there was a similar quality about them.

"I saw her again tonight," Rocky said, nodding at the drawing.

"Where?" Sam asked. "Did she speak to you?"

Rocky shook his head. "She was watching the tour. Devin wound up giving most of it—her friend was sick. Kept coughing. I think she was watching Devin."

"If so," Sam said, "we just have to hope Devin will communicate with her."

"She will," Rocky said.

"And we'd better hope we're not putting her in danger," Angela said.

Rocky tensed, heat flushing through him.

He should have stayed away from her. He should have told her to call Jack Grail for reports, if she wanted updates. He shouldn't have gone to her house.

Or maybe he was berating himself for nothing. Maybe she wouldn't have been as careful if he hadn't insisted that she stay in, that she keep her doors locked. She might have gone off for a walk in the woods. . . .

Bur the killer wasn't just biding his time in the woods. He was going about his daily life; he was blending in with the crowd.

A crowd that just might include people Devin knew. People she considered friends.

"There are five of us. We'll keep an eye on her," Sam assured Rocky. "And if we need more manpower, you can call your buddy on the force."

"I've got those numbers you were looking for," Jenna told Rocky.

"And?"

"Dark SUVs? There are hundreds. People who own a dark SUV and fit the age range? Over half the group. But that dwindled down a lot when I looked for people who were here thirteen years ago and within the age range then as well as now. Then I took those names and looked into who we know has an athame."

"And?" he asked again.

She looked over at him. "Down to eighteen people."

Startled, Rocky got up to stand behind Jenna and look over her shoulder at the computer screen. Most of the names she pulled up meant nothing to him.

But there were several that did.

Jack Grail himself was on the list—along with their old buddy Vince Steward.

And Renee.

But they weren't the only ones.

Theo Hastings was also on the list.

As was Devin's old friend, the intrepid tour guide Brent Corbin.

"Ghosts appear in many different ways. There's no way to fight it. Sometimes ghosts are the remnants, the souls, of those who've passed on. Sometimes they're the remnants of knowledge in our minds. They're there, but we can't quite connect with them."

Aunt Mina was talking to Devin. Except she wasn't, not really—not even her ghost. She couldn't be, because Devin was asleep. She knew she was asleep, and she even knew she was dreaming. But the dream was so much like life. It flowed, and she was trapped within it, unable to stop time or step outside it.

They were standing on a hill. Gallows Hill. But it wasn't the Gallows Hill of the witchcraft trials, because no one knew exactly where the execu-tions had taken place. The town fathers had stipulated that the hangings were done out-side of Salem proper. It wasn't the Gallows Hill of today, either. What the city had designated as Gallows Hill was a recreational area.

But none of that mattered in the dream. She simply knew she was on Gallows Hill on a long ago day. There was a cart track that led to the hill, winding through heavy trees. She saw that a path had been created to lead the condemned to the heavy branch of a certain old oak.

Panic seized her. She was floating in the air and still some distance away, but she could see what was happening. And she didn't want to see. She didn't want to see people dying horribly by strangulation or a snapped neck. She didn't want to hear the tears—or the silence of those who had come to see their loved ones' passing and yet dared not protest.

People were arriving by cart. Five, she thought. She tried to turn away. And then she heard the whispers. She didn't know where they came from, couldn't tell if they were male or female. But there were two of them.

"She'll be the death of us all."

"We must do something. When one is accused, it seems all around them, all who support them, are accused, as well."

"You have children. Many children have been accused and now rot in jail."

"I know."

"What will we do?"

Devin heard something. A prayer . . . and then something like a choked-off sob. She turned and saw the body of a woman swinging beneath the heavy branch of the old oak. Head bowed, neck broken . . .

Or so Devin prayed.

But death was not so merciful and quick. The woman kicked and squirmed. It was horrible to see, until finally . . .

168

She was dead, strangled, and the deed was done. And in Devin's dream the clouds roiled overhead and darkness descended.

She awoke drenched in sweat, almost screaming aloud. A moment later, a worried Auntie Mina was there in her room, trying to comfort her.

"Just a nightmare, love. You had them when you were a child, too."

"I did?"

"You did, sweetheart. Don't worry. You're safe. I'm watching out for you."

A ghost was watching out for her.

She smiled. "Thank you, Auntie Mina," she said.

"I love you, dear. Now try to get some sleep," Aunt Mina said. And then she disappeared.

Devin stared at the ceiling for a moment. Just days ago she'd had a comfortable life, a good career, friends, and she'd been . . .

Normal.

And now a ghost was reassuring her after a nightmare.

Out in the parlor, Poe let out a sudden caw.

She could almost swear the bird had said, "Nevermore."

Rocky found James Jefferson, the second name on Jenna's list, living in Lynn and running a mom-and-pop grocery store.

He'd already been to see Mary McCafferty, first

on the list. Mary hadn't driven in ages—she'd broken her leg in several places three weeks ago on a hiking trip to Colorado.

James Jefferson was an affable man, and he recognized Rocky's name from years past. "I think you were the great white hope when you were here," he told Rocky. "You don't remember me—and you wouldn't. I was only a freshman. Boy, could you throw a football!"

As it turned out, Jefferson had been on vacation in Florida until two nights ago. No, he said in answer to Rocky's question, his children didn't use his car. They didn't even live in the state.

Just as Rocky left the grocery store, he got a call from Jenna and Angela, who had been interviewing the people who lived in Lynn. One, Cindy Marks, had been working a church school carnival the day their Jane Doe had been killed, and half the parish could attest to that. Another, Roger Garcia, was a salesman, and he'd been in Buffalo on the date of Carly Henderson's murder.

Fourteen. They were down to fourteen names. Then it was thirteen. His next call was from Sam, who had gone down to Boston where Jordan Michaels, a magician by trade, was playing at the convention center. Michaels, it seemed, had been playing to sold-out crowds around the country for the entire summer. Tens of thousands of people could attest to his whereabouts. He'd also been out of state until just a week ago.

"You sure about this list?" Sam asked him.

"No, I'm not sure at all. But we had to start somewhere." Rocky didn't like the fact that the parameters he had settled on to narrow down the suspect list involved people he knew. He paused for a moment. "I think I'm going to plan a get-together tonight."

"Pardon?" Sam said, an edge of disbelief in his voice.

"With three of the people on our list," Rocky added.

"Ah." Sam was quiet a minute. "Sorry I doubted you."

"Yeah. Thanks. Just be ready to party—and pay attention."

"How are you explaining us?" Sam asked.

"Using guile and a clever ruse—I'm going to tell the truth," Rocky told him.

When he hung up, he called Jack. He explained that due to simple process of elimination, they were "suspects" and needed to answer a few questions.

Jack sighed. "Well, let's try not to piss off Haley," he said. "I'd do anything to catch the killer, but don't forget—I have to live with Haley."

"Right," Rocky said. "I'll be careful. You want to call Vince and Renee, or should I?"

"You don't really think it could be one of them, do you?"

"No."

"Then—"

"I have to be sure," Rocky said.

He hung up and called Devin; he wondered if he had planned the get-together for that night because he didn't want her to be alone and needed an excuse to spend some more time with her.

Yeah, probably.

But it was also true that his friends were on his suspect list.

When Devin answered, she sounded pleased to hear his voice.

And a little uneasy, as well.

"Are you all right? Has anything happened?" he asked.

"No, nothing, but I've been reading all kinds of history books."

There was something she wasn't telling him.

"That's great, but aren't you supposed to be writing?"

"Not every minute of every day, and I love reading," she said. "And there are things I had forgotten, or at least not thought about in ages, things I never had a solid opinion on. But I'll tell you about it later. How about you? Have you come up with anything new?" she asked anxiously.

"No, but I'm having that get-together tonight. We're going to meet at Jack's house."

"Oh. Do you want me to drive myself there? I just need to know the address."

"No," he told her quickly. "I'll pick you up. About six. Is that all right?"

"Yes, definitely," she told him.

It was 5:45 p.m., and Devin was ready, armed with a number of books from the collection that she, her aunt and her parents had acquired over the years. She planned to share them with Rocky at the right time—and with others, if a question arose.

Auntie Mina had been around most of the day. Poe had gotten accustomed to the fact that Aunt Mina was there, yet not really there. He had grown fond of sitting on Devin's shoulder, which made her grateful that Aunt Mina had rescued the bird a long time ago, when he'd been very young, and trained him well.

In fact, Poe was far better trained than the puppy she'd rescued when she was four. Her parents had lovingly tended to the little mutt, but the poor thing had never really mastered control of his bladder. But then, he'd been riddled with worms and other parasites when she'd found him and spent his first weeks at the vet. Pup—she hadn't been even slightly creative with his name—had died the year before she left for college. She still missed him.

Even with Poe there, Devin felt alone in the cottage. Auntie Mina had recently faded out while sitting on the sofa and watching her beloved reruns of *Frasier.*

She'd spent most of the day reading, trying to make sense of her dream, which had continued to plague her throughout the day. Most of what she read was information she'd known—or at least known about. There was quite a dispute about the real location of Gallows Hill. Historian Sydney Perley had determined early in the twentieth century that it couldn't possibly be where it was "officially" located, the current recreational area. She was sure a copy of the map Perley had used or created for his thesis had to exist, but she couldn't find it online.

She'd called Brent to see if he knew where she could locate a copy. He'd been busy but had promised to see if he could come up with it. Of course, he'd wanted to know why.

"Your tour last night," she told him. "It got me intrigued with the city again."

"Now that I think about it, you were a little too good," he said. "Don't become my competition."

"Not a chance," she assured him.

The day had passed quickly, and having Aunt Mina there had been somehow reassuring.

But now Aunt Mina was gone and it felt as if time was crawling.

She glanced at her watch: 5:50 p.m. Rocky would be there soon. She picked up her keys, ready to lock the house.

And that was when she saw a face at the window. *The same face Auntie Mina had seen. The face of the woman Rocky had tried to catch up to the night before.*

The woman who wanted to speak . . .

To her.

The woman stared in at Devin.

Devin stared back at her.

Then the woman turned away.

"Wait!" Devin cried, having no idea if she could be heard or not.

She set down the pile of books and headed to the door, throwing it open and rushing out.

"Hello?"

The woman was nowhere to be seen. As Devin desperately looked around, she saw her.

A fleeting remnant of her in her dark Puritan garb and her white cap . . .

Disappearing. Disappearing into the canopy of the trees.

Devin hurried after her, trying to see through the green darkness under the canopy of the trees, the little clump of woods between her house and her neighbor.

"Hello? Please, I'm here—please, talk to me." Forgetting all about personal safety, she headed for the trees. "Hello?"

No response. She heard nothing. She saw nothing.

"Please, I'm trying to help you. And we need you. We need you, and I believe that you're trying to talk to me."

A strange shimmer shifted the air around her. It was almost as if the air itself had turned to forest green. And yet the sun hadn't fallen, and little dapples of light made their way through the leaves.

She realized she'd walked deeply into the stand of pines and oaks. Even as she called herself a fool and started back, she heard a rustling in the woods.

What, she asked herself, had she done?

Walked out like an idiot.

She winced, trying to swallow her fear and berating herself for her sheer stupidity in her eagerness to reach the disappearing specter.

She stood dead still, thinking maybe she'd imagined the sound.

But it came again. A rustling. Ghosts—in her experience—didn't rustle brush and leaves the way that the living did. Someone flesh and blood was out there—between her and her house.

Had she even shut the door? If she went back, was she in just as much danger?

It came again. The sound. Someone was moving closer to her.

The rustle again, and then . . .

The evening sunlight trickled weakly through the trees. It created shadows that moved and writhed as the soft breeze of near-dusk shifted branches and leaves.

But the dark form was real.

A man was standing there, clutching something tightly in his hand.

A knife?

Her heart seemed to stop.

And then slide back into action.

*What to do? She hadn't even brought out her
hockey stick!*

Slip back into the trees? Head for the road?

Run for your life! she warned herself.

She suddenly heard the sound of a car out on
the road, slowing. . . .

It was Rocky, coming to pick her up.

But would he arrive in time?

*All she had to do was scream and he would find
her. Save her.*

Too late!

He moved. The figure lurking in the green
shadows of the trees moved closer.

Coming toward her.

A scream rose in her throat.

8

---

*The beautifully wrought silver pentagrams had
to be a crucial clue,* Rocky thought.

But it hardly took a brilliant mind to know that.
The trick was in figuring out what they meant.
Were they a straightforward indication that

witchcraft was involved, or were they a cold-blooded attempt to cast suspicion on the innocent Wiccan community?

Jenna had looked at him with narrowed eyes when he'd asked her to cross-reference purchases of similar pentagrams with the remaining names on the suspect shortlist, then amended it to the entire list of dark-SUV owners, "Just in case."

"Do you know how hard it was to discover which of the people on that list had purchased athames?" she'd asked him. "First you have to do the credit search and get their card numbers. Then you have to search for places where athames are sold and break down their sales records item by item. And now you want pentagrams," she'd said, rolling her eyes. "Half the people who come to Salem buy a pentagram."

"But we're only looking for people who are already on our radar," Rocky told her. "Not every tourist who's come through in the past thirteen years."

Sam laughed and told Jenna, "Hey, I'll help." He looked at Rocky. "I understand what you're doing, but remember that some of the facts and figures we get may not mean anything."

Rocky nodded. He liked Sam, just as he really liked every one of the agents in Jackson Crow's Krewes. He liked the way they worked. They all had one another on speed dial and felt comfortable calling any time of day or night if a clue appeared, and when they were on an active case they got together at least once every twenty-four hours to discuss where they were so far and where to go next.

"In the end," Sam said, "sometimes it all comes down to instinct. And we're already running these searches based on your instinct, aren't we?"

They were. But they weren't relying just on instinct. They'd talked things through, and tomorrow Sam, Jenna and Angela were going back to the two recent crime scenes, while he and Jane revisited the place where Melissa had been killed, though that killing had been thirteen years ago and the odds of finding anything helpful were remote.

"But about tonight . . . why don't you fill us in on your friends?" Sam had asked him, before he and Jenna lost themselves in the data. "Tell us what to expect." Because of his legal career, he tended to approach things in a linear and straight-forward way.

Now, as he drove toward Devin's house, Rocky reflected on the plans for tomorrow. They would look for physical evidence. But more than that, they would search for clues that might not be physical.

Does it come down to me to solve this? he wondered. Was that really why he was back, all these years later?

It occurred to him that he should probably be

grateful that he was still in California working a set of drug-related murders when Carly Henderson was killed. If he hadn't been, he might be his own prime suspect.

Did this case really go back that far? Did it have something to do with events from thirteen years ago?

But how and why? It was unusual for a potential serial killer to just stop at one murder and not pick back up until years later.

Unless Melissa Wilson had been a separate case and whoever was killing now was simply taking his or her guidelines from the details of her murder to throw them off the track.

Not likely, he told himself. There were just too many unreleased details that had been exactly the same in all three murders. So if they *were* dealing with a copycat . . .

Then it was someone who had seen Melissa Wilson dead.

And that included his old friends, no matter how much he didn't want to believe that one of them could be guilty. Even Haley—she hadn't been with them, but they had all talked about it immediately after, probably describing far too graphically what they had seen.

He stopped trying to fathom the possible association between his own past and the recent murders, because he'd reached Devin's house.

Her door stood wide-open.

As he jerked the car into Park and jumped out, he heard a terrible, high-pitched scream rip through the air.

It didn't sound human!

"Devin!" he shouted, and ran to the front door. "Devin!"

He saw Mina, hovering just inside, her eyes enormous with fear.

He didn't waste time asking questions she probably couldn't answer, anyway; he just raced into the woods that bordered the house.

Devin never had the chance to scream, because a chilling sound tore through the air before a sound could burst from her lips.

It was a terrible shriek—as if some ancient god had let out a horrible cry.

For a split second she was stunned, unable to move or even to think.

Then she recognized the sound. She knew what it was.

The scream of a crow.

Suddenly she heard a man screaming. "Stop it! What the hell?"

She knew the voice—just as she had recognized the crow.

Devin stepped back onto the path. Just as she had suspected, the man standing in the green shadows of the path was Brent Corbin.

"Devin!" he cried. "Get him off me!"

"Brent!" she shouted. "What on earth—"

"Your raven! That stupid bird attacked me!"

Poe was about to dive-bomb Brent again. "Hey, mister—come here," Devin called.

"Sweet Jesus!" Brent cried. "He's a monster."

"Well, what the hell did you expect, sneaking around the woods?" she demanded.

"Sneaking? I was coming to see you, and then I saw you out here and followed you."

She looked and saw that he was holding a cardboard poster tube, and in her fear she had seen a knife. Okay, maybe she was getting just a little paranoid.

But a woman had recently died here. . . .

Just as Poe settled on her shoulder, Rocky came rushing through the trees. He had a gun out, ready to shoot.

"What the hell?" Brent demanded. "You people are crazy! Put that thing away, and get that wretched bird out of here, too."

"Brent, he's fine now," Devin said. "He's on my shoulder."

"What's going on here?" Rocky demanded harshly.

Poe cawed loudly, and Brent flinched. He didn't seem to know where to turn. He didn't want to take his eyes off Poe or Rocky.

Rocky looked at Devin. She widened her eyes and lifted her shoulder in a shrug. Poe squawked again.

"Get that monster away from me!" Brent said.

"Calm down," Devin said. "He only went after you because he was protecting me."

She almost smiled; she might not have a big dog, but she did have an attack bird.

"From me?" Brent demanded. "Rocky, please. Lower that gun."

"Tell me what the hell is going on here," Rocky snapped. "Why are you two out here in the woods?" He looked from one of them to the other. "Well?"

"I saw the—I thought I saw something, so I came out to investigate," Devin said. Rocky's eyes darkened, and he opened his mouth to speak. She quickly explained. "I know, I know, but I wasn't thinking. So anyway, I came out here, and everything was fine, but then I heard . . . I heard Brent." She turned to face him. "You should have said it was you instead of scaring me like that. Poe was just protecting me."

"From what?" Brent demanded.

"You. I thought you were coming after me."

"Coming after you? I came out to see you, so I was just following you," Brent said. "And now your boyfriend is here—and he's still aiming a gun at me."

"Why?" Rocky's question sounded like a gunshot. "Why did you come to see Devin?"

"I brought her a copy of a map she asked me

about. A map of Salem with the location of the real Gallows Hill according to Sydney Perley."

At last Rocky put away his gun. She noticed that beneath his casual denim jacket he had a shoulder holster.

At the moment she was glad that Agent Rockwell was armed.

This is a good thing, she told herself. When homicidal maniacs with knives were running around in the local woods, a fed with a gun was a good thing.

But Brent still looked terrified.

"Rocky?" she murmured.

"Your front door is wide-open," he told her.

She winced. "Let's go back so I can close it, then."

"I think I'd rather just go home," Brent said. "I know people are afraid because of the murders, but . . ." He looked at Rocky. "You've been away. We have pretty strict gun laws."

"I'm an FBI agent," Rocky informed him.

Brent looked stunned. "Agent?" he asked, and turned to Devin.

"Hey, everybody has to make a living," she said lightly. It didn't work. Brent still looked ready to collapse.

She set a hand on his arm. "It's all right. You just scared the hell out of me. Poe saw me come out here, and he followed me to protect me," Devin said.

"He scratched my cheek—practically gouged it," Brent said.

"It's not that bad. Come on—I'll get the first-aid kit."

"I might get rabies," Brent said.

"Birds don't get rabies," Rocky assured him. He was speaking to Brent, but he was staring at Devin.

His expression was filled with words he didn't speak.

What the hell were you doing out here? Are you mad?

"Let's go in," she repeated.

They walked back to the house. Rocky was on the alert, aware of everything—the perfect agent, Devin thought. He told them to wait at the door while he checked the house, but Devin could see Auntie Mina there and knew she would have told them about any intruder.

But Rocky went through the motions, anyway, because Brent would have been suspicious if he didn't. Devin set Poe back on his perch and ran to the kitchen for the first-aid kit, then dabbed antiseptic on Brent's scratches.

He grumbled through the whole procedure that the bird was a devil and should be put down.

"Stop being such a baby. Your scratches aren't even that bad," she said.

"It's going to be a long time before I come see you again," Brent said.

Devin saw Auntie Mina by the mantel and could tell she was amused by Brent's carrying on.

Devin glared at the ghost. *It's not that funny!*

Aunt Mina's smile faded, and she nodded in acknowledgment that the situation was genuinely serious.

After going through the entire house, Rocky joined them in the parlor where Devin was just finishing up.

"He could have put my eye out," Brent said.

"But he didn't," Devin pointed out.

Rocky was silent; Devin was certain he was waiting for Brent to leave before exploding and telling her that she had taken a stupid and dangerous chance.

"Good as new," she told Brent, stepping back. His scratches hadn't even bled.

Not much, at least, she thought, wincing inwardly.

"Where's the map?" she asked Brent.

He picked up the cardboard tube and produced a rolled-up map. "Obviously, this isn't original, but there's been an upswing of interest in Perley's theories. Larson Jones, who owns the shop next to me, ordered a bunch of these, so I ran over to get you one, and then I drove out here so your bird could attack me." He glared at her reproachfully.

It was going to be a long time before Brent forgave her—and Poe.

"That's so thoughtful of you. I wish you had

called, though. I'm truly sorry about Poe, Brent," she said.

He grunted.

"What do I owe you?" she asked him.

He waved a hand in the air. "Nothing. You took over on the tour for me. But next time you're looking for something, you can come in and get it."

"And here I was thinking of having a lovely Halloween party," she murmured.

He smiled. "By Halloween I'll be all right. And I'll get Beth or someone to stand in front of me and shield me from the monster."

"Can I get you something to drink? Coffee? Tea?" she asked.

"No, I'm heading home. Going to gargle salt water and try to get my voice back before my tour tonight."

"Well, thank you again."

Brent nodded and headed for the door.

Devin followed him, feeling Rocky right behind her. He made her uneasy. She felt his heat, breathed his scent. She was almost painfully aware of him as . . .

The opposite sex.

She closed the door and returned to the parlor, steeling herself for the anger she knew was coming.

But he didn't yell. She realized that he was breathing deeply. Finally he looked at her and simply asked, "Why?"

"Because I saw her."

He took that in, staring at her. At last he spoke. "The woman Mina saw at the window—the night you found our Jane Doe?"

"Yes. I saw her. You said that she was trying to talk to me, so I ran out after her."

Then he asked her, "Do you have any self-control at all? You couldn't stop yourself?"

"Hey!" she snapped.

But he had a point. She knew how stupidly she had acted.

Which, of course, was emphasized by the way he stood quietly.

Mina was still by the mantel, standing there quietly.

Rocky spun on her suddenly.

"And you just let her go?" he asked Mina.

"I couldn't stop her," Mina said. Now, of course, she was staring at Devin, too.

"She might have listened to you," Rocky said. "She obviously has no idea just what danger is out there."

"Hey! *She's* standing right here. And yes, I made a tremendous mistake, but you will recall that you were the one to tell me that she might be the key," Devin said.

"I never told you to run out into the woods after her!" he said. "And come on—you know it."

"I can't stay locked up forever," Devin said.

He shook his head. "It won't be forever."

"It's been thirteen years since the murder of Melissa Wilson," Devin said.

She wished she could take it back. She knew that fact had been like a thorn in his side— something that had haunted him terribly throughout the years.

"This time, it won't take so long," he said.

There was truth, conviction, and dead-set determination in his voice. And she felt something warm shoot through her.

He wouldn't stop. He wouldn't give up. They'd have to drag him away before he left here without finding the killer.

"What I did wasn't smart," she said. "But I won't do it again. I promise. I was just so eager to talk to her that I forgot everything else. I won't let it happen again."

"You could have followed her," Rocky said to Aunt Mina.

Aunt Mina was silent a minute. "No, I couldn't."

"Why not?"

"I . . . can't seem to leave the house."

"But other ghosts—" Rocky began.

"I don't know about other ghosts. I only know I can't do it. I try to leave and I disappear in my own mind . . . or soul, or whatever it is that remains. I—I can't leave the house."

That puzzled Rocky, and Devin was glad. It took his mind off her idiotic behavior in the woods.

"It's all right," Rocky reassured Aunt Mina. "It's not as if—Well, I don't have answers. I don't understand life and death any better than any man." He smiled. "You're here with Devin, and that's a good thing."

He was incredibly gentle with Aunt Mina, but when he turned to Devin again it was with a frown so fierce she was surprised she didn't incinerate on the spot.

"Look, Devin, I know I'm just the fed you flagged down in the road, but—"

"I understand. I really do," she said, exasperation growing in her voice. "I won't let it happen again."

"You had better not."

Apparently he was going to drop it there. He turned and stared quietly into the fireplace for a moment. She saw his hands and realized that he was shaking slightly.

Because he'd been afraid.

For her.

Well, of course. He'd arrived to screams and shrieking in the woods and . . .

He knew what it was like to find the dead.

There was nothing personal in his concern.

He turned suddenly, his entire demeanor changed. "Why did you want that particular map?"

"Oh, I had a strange dream, that's all," she said. "I dreamed I was on Gallows Hill. I was watching the executions and listening to people talk—afraid to protest, afraid to say anything. If they protested, they'd wind up accused, too."

"And the map?"

She laughed. "Well, no one knows the actual location of the historic Gallows Hill, but there's a growing belief that a historian named Sydney Perley, back around 1921, came up with a pretty good idea of where the real hill was. Everyone knows the sheriff had been ordered to ensure that the executions were carried out beyond the boundaries of the town proper. And there are documents that tell us Benjamin Nurse rowed a boat to secretly retrieve his mother's body after she had been hanged, so we know the real hill was near the water—and though it's been filled in, there was a pond at the base of what Perley identified as Gallows Hill. Anyway, after the dream I started reading and I got curious. I wanted to see the Sydney Perley map."

"May I see it?" Rocky asked her.

She unrolled the map.

"This is where he says it was. It's actually a residential section now. This street here—Proctor Street—was just a cart path at one time. A *cart* path. They took the victims to be hanged by cart."

"I've always thought Perley had it right," Aunt Mina said. "In fact, I've been there. It's just a little hill covered with a little patch of forest land, rather like the one that borders this house, and it has never been developed."

"You've really been there?" Devin asked her.

"Of course. My coven and I went often to pray," she told them.

"I know it's real police work, but I'd like to go there," Devin said to Rocky.

"Tomorrow," he promised her, then glanced at his watch. "We should get going. We're late."

"I'm sorry."

"It's not the end of the world. However, I did set this up, and it involves two groups of people who don't know each other, so . . ."

"Let's go," Devin said.

Rocky said goodbye to Aunt Mina, who Devin thought was looking a little wistful.

"We'll have a little dinner party here in a day or two, Auntie Mina," Devin said. "Rocky can bring his coworkers."

Aunt Mina seemed to perk up. "That would be lovely."

Rocky looked thoughtful as they got into the car.

"What is it?" she asked him.

He smiled. "I was thinking that wouldn't be a half-bad idea."

"What?"

"Having a get-together at your house. Mina would be delighted and . . ."

"And?"

"And our Puritan might make an appearance when we're all here and it's safe to go into the woods."

As they drove, she realized that they were heading to a residential section near the historic area favored by tourists.

She looked curiously at Rocky.

"Jack's always loved the old Victorians," he told her.

Jack's house was beautiful. They were greeted at the door by his wife, Haley, a lovely woman with brilliant hazel eyes, blond hair and a welcoming smile. She greeted Rocky with a big hug and a kiss on the cheek—she clearly knew him well—but was almost as enthusiastic to meet Devin. She said she had all the *Auntie Pim* books—she read them to her son—and had been thrilled to hear that Devin had moved back to town.

"Appetizers and drinks are all set up in the dining room already," she told them. "Go on in. But, please, if anyone starts singing our high school anthem, I'll beat them with a wooden spoon, I swear."

Rocky promised her that he would never do any such thing before they headed back to join the others in the large dining room. The beautiful cherry table, large enough to seat twelve, was covered with the promised array of food and drink. As they entered, Devin recognized Angela and Jane, and Rocky introduced her to Jenna and Sam Hall, the other members of his team, and his friends from "the old days," Vince Steward and

Renee Radcliff. Vince was a mammoth man—taller than both Rocky and Jack. Renee was a tiny, well-built brunette with manicured nails and a bubbly personality. She, too, said she enjoyed the *Auntie Pim* books. She didn't have children yet, but she loved babysitting for Jackie and read them to him before bed.

Conversation was casual. Sam and Jack talked about a mutual friend, Detective John Alden, who had held Jack's position a few years ago but had recently left the area to take a position in Colorado. John Alden had been involved in a case of a teen accused of butchering his parents; Jenna and Angela had also worked the case, and the four of them ended up discussing it, along with changes since the Krewe had last worked in the city.

It seemed an incredibly easy meshing of people, the makings of a charming evening.

It might have been any dinner party, except that there had been murders much like the one that had changed the lives of the hosts and many of the guests—and a number of them were suspects.

The two groups mingled nicely. Rocky belonged to both, and though she didn't belong to either, everyone included her in their conversations.

At one point, Jackie woke up crying; Jack went off to his bedroom and came back with him, and they all oohed and aahed over the little boy.

"Any of you have kids yet?" Jack asked the agents.

"Not us," Sam said. "Jenna and I haven't even made it official yet."

"Angela actually married the boss," Jenna teased. "So maybe the rest of us will follow their lead."

"Wait, I'm confused," Jack said. "You don't make it official and you don't act like you're together, but—"

"We're coworkers when we're working and we don't run around blasting out the information when we're a twosome," Jenna clarified. "But we're not discouraged from being together. We work well together. We just don't bring it into work."

"Ah, well, you are special people, huh?" Jack teased.

"For the good or the bad," Angela said lightly.

"What about you, Angela? Do you have children?" Renee asked her.

"Not yet. We work a lot," Angela said.

"Well, sometimes you just have to do things, you know?" Haley said.

"Haley!" Vince said. "All you wanted in life for as long as I can remember was marriage and that baby."

"She used to date Rocky," Renee put in. "But she finally decided he was a lost cause and gave up."

Devin turned to look at Jack. He shrugged good-humoredly. "They were the Barbie and Ken of our high school. But they were going different ways, and they knew it." He grinned at Rocky. "My gain."

"Absolutely," Rocky said, lifting his glass to Jack. "You two are perfect. And Jackie is a great kid."

Devin considered them curiously, but there didn't seem to be any ill will between them.

It wasn't until Jackie was back in bed and they'd all helped Haley bring out dinner—clam chowder and broiled scrod—that they sat down around the table and the conversation turned serious.

"I guess it's pretty obvious," Vince said, looking at Rocky. "You're not back to stay—or to vacation. You're back because of the murders."

"Yes," Rocky said simply.

Renee looked at the Krewe, then turned to Jack. "So they've taken over. What are the cops doing, then?"

"We haven't taken over," Rocky said. "It's a joint investigation. What we want is the murderer caught."

"This case is still wide-open," Angela said. "We have so few real clues that there's no limit to what we must investigate. We need a lot of man-power."

"Of course," Vince said. He drummed his fingers on the table. "God, I hope you get him."

"We intend to," Rocky said.

"Could it be the same person who killed Melissa?" Renee asked.

Vince leaned forward, staring at Rocky. "Could it be? That was so long ago."

"It's certainly possible," Rocky said.

"But how can you know that?" Renee demanded.

Vince was still staring hard at Rocky. "Because these murders were the same," Vince said quietly. "God help us all. You found them the same way as Melissa."

"Vince," Renee murmured uncomfortably, "you can't know that."

But Vince shook his head. "No, I was there. And what I saw has been imprinted in my mind all these years. You found them lying the same way . . . outstretched, like a pentagram. The blood on the throat . . ."

Renee shivered. "Stop it, Vince, please."

"I can't. Because they're thinking it was someone who was here at the time—and here now."

9

"Like one of us," Vince continued.

Silence fell for a brief second.

"Me?" Renee squeaked. "You think that it could have been me?"

"No," Rocky said.

"He's lying," Vince said, and laughed bitterly. "I'm an attorney. I can tell when a man is lying. Trust me—I've listened to liars for years."

"I'm not lying," Rocky said, looking at Renee. "It would have been almost impossible for you to have killed any of the women. You're too short." He looked back at Vince. "Could it have been one of the rest of us? Yes."

"So I could be a suspect?" Vince asked.

"Frankly, yes," Rocky said. "Have you taken up the Wiccan religion recently, Vince?" he asked.

"What?"

"Wiccan—did you become a Wiccan?" Rocky asked.

"No!"

"Then why on earth did you buy an athame?"

Vince stared at Rocky in openmouthed surprise. If the situation weren't so critical, Rocky would have been amused. Vince had come a long way— law school was no easy track—but right then he looked like the kid in class who had just been told there was going to be a pop quiz on the material he *hadn't* studied the night before.

"What?" Vince asked.

"Athame. It's a double-edged blade used in the Wiccan religion. It's normally ceremonial, but it's the closest match we've found for the weapon used to murder our victims."

Vince reddened. "I know what an athame is,"

he muttered. "You think you're the only one who knows anything?"

"You said, 'What?' " Rocky reminded him. "I thought you were asking what an athame was."

"Why are you attacking Vince?" Renee asked. She was sitting next to him, which made her look even tinier—and Vince look almost like an ogre.

"Guys, this is a dinner party, not an interrogation," Haley said.

Rocky didn't flinch. "I'm not attacking anyone," he assured her. He looked at Vince evenly. "I'm just asking questions."

"How the hell do you know so much?" Vince demanded. "Oh, that's right. You're a fed. Big Brother *is* watching."

"There's no conspiracy here," Angela assured him.

"Did you get a warrant to violate my privacy?" Vince asked.

"I didn't need one. If you use a credit card, the record of your purchases is on the internet and readily available to anyone, not just law enforcement. But you're stalling, Vince." He smiled to take the sting out of the words. "And you're good at it. I'm glad you got your law degree. I can only imagine how effective your arguments are in court. Back in school you already had the ability to convince half our teachers it was their fault you hadn't done your homework."

Vince's jaw tightened as he looked down and

shook his head. He looked back up at Rocky. "We all have our strengths. It was easy for you to get it done, and easy for me to talk my way out of it."

"Vince," Rocky said, "I'm not attacking you, but I need to know. Why did you buy it?"

Vince looked around at the agents. "I don't know which of you is the computer pro, but you can check this out. I was defending Midnight Mercantile. They had a shipment go overboard just outside Boston Harbor. They lost a lot of merchandise, including a large order of athames, which was recovered and the contents unsalable. I bought one made to the same specifications to demonstrate in court that if the contents had been made to the manufacturer's promised standards, the time they spent in the water wouldn't have ruined them to such a degree. We subjected my athame to salt water for an equal amount of time, and I proved my point. You want the athame? I'll get it to you."

"I see," Rocky said.

"That's it—you *see?*" Vince asked.

"I told you. I was never attacking you, I was asking you."

Vince laughed. "Rocky, come on. I'm a lawyer, remember? Asking questions . . . that's an attack."

"No, it's a request for information," Rocky told him.

Haley stood and walked around the table, setting her hands on Vince's shoulders. "Come on,

Vince. Give Rocky a break. We all remember when Melissa . . ." She trailed off and looked at Rocky. "I feel like all of us had a hand in her death. That's why we've all been so haunted ever since by what happened."

Renee let out a little choking sound. "No, Haley—we can't blame ourselves."

"We can," Haley said. She looked over at Rocky again. "She was crazy about you, and I encouraged it. I admit some of it was slightly sour grapes. You and I had called it quits. I knew she'd had a crush on you since we were kids, so I encouraged her to go after you—knowing darned well you were just counting the days till you could move on. I don't think I was trying to be mean— I was just a kid and jealous despite the fact that we were over. That night . . . Renee and I were in a rush to get to a sale at a vintage shop in Danvers. Melissa called, and I told her if she didn't make it to my place in thirty minutes, we were leaving without her because the shop would close if we didn't get going. She said okay, she understood, and if she didn't make it in time, just to go on without her. She didn't show up, so we left. And you guys . . ." she said, turning to look from Jack to Vince to Rocky. "She said she'd called you for a ride, Jack, and you said you had plans, you were busy. And what were you busy doing? Drinking beer in the back of Vince's pickup."

"We *are* guilty," Vince said softly. "We're guilty

because we were lousy friends. I'd had a few beers before I even went over to Rocky's place. She called me, too, but I was afraid to drive her— I didn't want to get stopped by the cops. Rocky's place was just down the street, but you lived farther away. If only I'd done it," he murmured.

There was silence in the room. Devin and the Krewe could only listen, Rocky thought, but as far as he and his old friends went, yes, they were all guilty in their own ways.

Speaking for himself, Rocky thought, he should have sat Melissa down. He should have told her that he'd always love her as a friend, but they were never going to be a couple.

He was surprised to hear Devin gently clear her throat. "Forgive me, I wasn't there, but listening to you . . . what you're all feeling is survivor's guilt. Melissa's death was a tragedy, but whoever killed her is guilty—and not any of you. I don't have a degree in psychology, but I interviewed a lot of people who'd lived through tragedy or lost someone to it when I was a reporter. And I've seen this so many times, even in cases of natural death. A relative or a friend dies and you realize they'd asked you for help with something or just to go to lunch, and you brushed them off. It's one of the best things about us—the way we feel remorse for hurting someone's feelings."

Jane spoke up. "Why don't you all run through the events of that night—no attacks on anyone.

Maybe one of you will remember something that can help us."

"We called him the Pentagram Killer," Haley murmured, then patted Vince's shoulder and returned to her chair.

"I thought the information about the pentagram necklaces never went out," Sam said, frowning as he leaned forward.

"It was never released to the press," Jack said, "but you have to remember we were just a bunch of high school kids, and we told one another pretty much everything. We grew up playing in mud puddles together." He paused, looking sheepish. "We played witchcraft trials."

And they made me play Magistrate Corwin," Vince said. "Because I was big and so was he."

"In middle school, Haley and Rocky became a couple," Renee said.

"There was a dance I wanted to go to," Haley said. "I needed an escort, so I asked him. After that, we just kind of paired up."

"The rest of us were always just friends," Jack said. "The kind of friends you told everything to—shared everything with."

"Were any of you into Wicca?" Angela asked.

"No, we're all from what they refer to as good old New England ancestry, with parents who were die-hard Episcopalians," Vince said. "If I'd said I thought being Wiccan was cool, I'd have been grounded for a week."

"Wait!" Haley exclaimed, leaning forward so suddenly she almost knocked over her wineglass and just managed to save it. "The week before, we all went down to the wharf at Salem, remember?" she asked excitedly. "There were so many wonderful stores. I bought a wand—and Melissa bought a bag of herbs for a love spell."

Rocky frowned, remembering.

He'd thought nothing of it at the time, and to be honest, he still wasn't sure it meant anything. They all went down to the shops in Salem sometimes. It was just what you did if you grew up around there.

Did it mean anything?

"Oh, great, we all went down to Essex Street," Vince said, his tone sarcastic. "We looked at Wiccan necklaces and bought spell bags. One of us must be guilty."

Devin spoke up then. "Vince, I don't think it's that at all. Maybe someone saw Melissa buy that spell bag. Maybe they thought she was Wiccan, or making fun of Wiccans—there are a thousand possibilities."

"And that's the problem, isn't it?" Haley asked.

"Yeah, but did the cops or *anyone* think it could have been any of us back then? We were kids, terrified kids," Renee said.

"But we found her," Vince said. He looked over at Rocky. "Or Rocky did. He knew right where to go. How the hell was that?"

Rocky shook his head and felt a self-mocking smile curve his lips. "I heard her," he told them.

That was greeted by silence.

"You know, you could be on top of the suspect list," Jack said.

"Oh, please," Haley said, waving a dismissive hand in the air. "It wasn't any of us. I know it wasn't any of us."

"And Rocky was in California when Carly Henderson was murdered," Jack said. He looked at Rocky a little sheepishly. "I checked that out."

"You wouldn't be a good cop if you hadn't," Rocky told him.

"What did Melissa's family say at the time?" Devin asked thoughtfully. "What did they think she was doing?"

"She told her mother she had a ride, and she walked out of the house to meet him. Or her," Haley said. "Her mother never got over it. She died about ten years ago. Heart failure. I'd say it was a broken heart."

"Does she have any siblings, especially any still living in the area?" Angela asked.

"She had three older brothers, and Joshua is still here. The cops talked to him at the time, of course, but you can interview him again," Jack said. "I talked to him myself after the latest murders, but you might come up with something I didn't."

"You've got to solve this, Rocky. None of us

will ever really be right if Melissa's killer gets away with it," Vince said. "If we can do anything to help—anything—just ask."

"Consider it a pact between old friends and new," Haley said.

Jack smiled. "We don't have to poke holes in our fingers and swear in blood or anything, do we?" he asked his wife.

"I hope not," she said, then looked at Rocky earnestly. "I'll do my best to think of anything that might help. Not that we didn't at the time, but . . ."

"But you're adults now. And you see the world a little differently with the passage of time," Sam told them.

"So . . . in the midst of this, a weird question, maybe," Haley said. "But I did work really hard on dessert, so who's still hungry?"

Everyone laughed, clearly relieved for a chance to leave the past behind for a few minutes, and agreed that dessert was a great idea.

Haley smiled, and Devin rose quickly. "Want some help?" she asked.

"Sure, thank you."

"Want me to get the coffee?" Jack asked her.

"That would be great," Haley said with a smile for him.

Dessert and coffee were served, and as if they'd made a silent agreement, everyone kept the conversation light. The locals all apologized to

Devin for thinking that her aunt had been a real witch—a real spell-casting, broom-riding witch—when they'd been kids.

"I'm actually surprised we never met," Haley told Devin. "My mom went to see your aunt often, but not about . . . you know, spells or anything. My dad said your aunt should have had a degree, because she was the best therapist he'd ever met. He said she had a way of putting things into perspective for people, and that she told stories that were like parables, helping them figure out what to do."

"Thank you, Haley. It's nice to hear she was thought of that way," Devin said.

"Unfortunately, the world is also full of idiots," Jack said. "You should see the old reports I found on your house, Devin."

"Oh?" she asked.

"People reporting weird lights and sounds—oh, and a ghost that walked in those woods next door. Some old guy—he's dead now—complained to the police about your aunt conjuring up the dead. People get really crazy ideas. Sometimes it's almost possible to understand how we hanged a pack of innocent people."

"It always seems sad to me that the ones who wouldn't stoop to lie were the ones who wound up dead," Haley said.

"Thankfully, those days are over," Devin murmured, then looked at Jack. "If they weren't,

Auntie Mina wouldn't have made it to her ripe old age—she'd definitely have been hanged."

Haley laughed. "Well, since the practice of witchcraft was illegal and punishable by death, they would have hanged half the people living in Salem right now."

Soon it was time to leave. Despite the heated exchange when Rocky had first mentioned the athame to Vince, everyone parted on the best of terms. When Rocky and Devin started out, Haley stopped them.

"Devin, even if this jerk goes away again, I hope you know you're always welcome here," Haley told her. "We'd love to see more of you."

Devin thanked her as Sam, getting into the rental with the others, called back to Rocky, "See you at the hotel."

"You got it," Rocky said.

Devin waved to them and then slipped into the passenger seat of Rocky's car. They'd gone a mile or two before she spoke. "You really go right for the jugular, don't you?"

He turned to look at her briefly before returning his attention to the road. "I don't actually see it that way. I see it as giving someone a chance to explain their actions before starting the whole pain-in-the-butt interrogation process."

"Interesting—and yet, with my friends, you're willing to take long walks and schmooze forever without getting to the point."

He glanced her way again. She was smiling—not attacking him. She was truly curious.

"Well, we all have our reasons," he said. "Most of the time we have physical evidence to work with. This case . . ."

"Apparently, what you did was right. You got your answer—and you got everyone to admit they feel the same as you about your friend Melissa's death."

"At least I can track down the truth about Vince's athame," he said. He looked over at her again and realized that he wanted to pretend they were driving home from a date, that they had met and liked each other and had been out tonight for the sheer pleasure of being together.

Instead, I met you over a dead body, he thought.

It hadn't taken him more than a few minutes earlier to appreciate the fact that she cleaned up nice, as the saying went. She was always stunning, but tonight she'd worn a blue halter dress with some kind of a wrap. The color emphasized the blue of her eyes, and the silky fabric clung to the curved length of her body. And her natural warmth had won everyone over. Whenever someone had complimented her books she had been modest and gracious, explaining that her aunt's stories had enthralled her back when she was a lonely child.

"So was he telling the truth?" Devin asked, breaking into his thoughts. "Vince said he can tell

209

when people are lying. Do you have some kind of radar for that, too?"

He laughed. "Yes, there are certain physical manifestations that go with lying," he told her. "But those who know them can hide them. I don't think Vince would have lied, though. He knows that even if I don't verify his story myself, one of the Krewe will."

She turned to look out the window. "It's strange. I knew some people talked about Auntie Mina, but I never realized just how . . . well, how ignorant and vicious they could be."

"Don't kid yourself," he said quietly. "The world is filled with wonderful people. But there are also a lot of people who are ruled by their bone-deep prejudices, and some of them think the laws of this country deserve lip service and nothing more."

When they reached her house, he walked with her to the door, as always. And though Auntie Mina was there—watching reruns of *Murder, She Wrote*—Rocky went through the place and checked things out, anyway.

Thoroughly.

Twice.

Because he didn't want to leave.

He'd finished his sweep of the house—not wanting to offend Mina, he'd told her that he'd wanted to make sure no one had tampered with the doors or windows from the outside—when his eyes lit on the pentagram Devin had purchased from Beth's store.

"Mind if I borrow this?" he asked her.

She looked at him with a slightly ironic smile. "You think a retired schoolteacher who works as a medium and creates jewelry might be a serial killer?"

"No need to get defensive," he said. "Although we all get defensive sometimes, don't we? No, I don't really see Gayle as a murderer. But if we can trace the medallions, at least we'll have something concrete to work with."

"But when she first started making them, they were sold in dozens of venues," Devin said.

"We follow leads," he told her. "That's what we do. Some of them go somewhere, some don't. If this turns out to be a lead, we'll follow it."

Devin lowered her head for a moment. "Of course, feel free to take it."

"Thank you. I'll get it back to you," he promised.

He really couldn't stay any longer.

When he finally bade Mina good-night and headed to the door, Devin followed to lock it behind him. "Tomorrow . . . well, I know you're busy with the case, but . . ."

"Yes?" he urged her.

"Did you mean it earlier when you talked about checking out Perley's theory on Gallows Hill?" she asked.

"Of course. I'm not the only one working the

murders, you know—it really is a task force."

Hell, yes, I meant it, he thought. *Anything to be with you.*

The thought of feeling that strongly about someone was disturbing. But he couldn't forget the fear that had raced through him like wildfire when he'd arrived earlier that evening and seen her door standing open.

When he'd rushed into the woods, following the shrieking cry of the raven carried on the wind.

"And," he added a little too harshly, "no running into the woods by night. I don't care if you see our Puritan ghost and she asks you out to tea. No leaving the house like that."

"No, I think I'll stay in. Sorry," she said when she saw the thunderous look on his face. "I was teasing. I promise."

They were close again. So close he could feel her heartbeat, feel her breath. The compulsion to simply reach out and pull her to him, press his mouth to hers, was almost overwhelming.

He really needed to leave; he didn't know her feelings for him. He needed time himself—away from the temptation of being with her.

He stepped back. "I'll get here around nine-ish, okay?"

"Perfect. Thank you," she told him.

She closed the door between them. He waited until he heard the bolt slide, and then he headed to his car.

• • •

That night, sleeping—though perhaps not exactly sleeping—Devin found herself on Gallows Hill again.

She was part of the air, there in her mind but not in the flesh. It was the end of summer, she thought. Right when the nip of autumn hinted now and then that fall would be brief and the warm days of summer would quickly give way to winter's bitter chill.

She heard the sound of the death cart that brought the condemned to the hanging tree.

As the cart drew closer she heard sobbing. Any conversation was whispered, but sobbing was allowed. One could cry for the fact that the devil had come to Massachusetts and targeted the vulnerable among them.

This time she caught only fragments of conversation.

". . . must be done."

"She'll be the death of all of us."

"What difference . . . legal or illegal?"

"If she is gone . . . no mockery in court."

Devin couldn't see the speakers, couldn't even tell their sex, though she thought there were only two of them. She tried to hear more than the brief snatches of conversation that hung on the air, but she couldn't.

The sound of the cart grew louder.

That . . . and the weeping.

She awoke with a start.

This time she was shaking, though she didn't feel frightened. She ran out to the parlor. The television was still on, showing reruns of *Perry Mason*.

"Devin! What is it, dear?" Auntie Mina asked.

Devin was already busy at the bookcase, searching through all the titles. Auntie Mina had loved a good mystery. There were shelves of fiction. There were also numerous books on herbs, on witchcraft, on the history of religion and on just about every other topic that dealt with spirituality.

There were also history books. She was looking for one that Aunt Mina had purchased forever ago—a reprint of a work that had first been published in the early 1800s, as she recalled. It had been written by an author named Michael Smith, who'd claimed to be a descendant of Hattie Smith, who had been arrested for witchcraft, confessed and then rotted in jail for almost a year after the last hangings. His conclusions had been hotly disputed, if she remembered correctly.

"Devin?" Aunt Mina said worriedly.

"I'm all right, Auntie Mina. I'm looking for the Smith book on Salem."

Aunt Mina looked at her curiously. "The Smith book? Really? It's never been considered one of the better histories of the area. Why that book in particular?"

"He wrote about a young woman from Salem Village who had been accused. She was never arrested because she simply disappeared."

"Yes," Auntie Mina said. "I remember reading about her."

Devin found the book at last. She looked at the copyright page and saw that the first printing had been in 1804. It had been reprinted once in 1886 and then again in 1964.

"You found it," Auntie Mina said. "You're going to want the last few chapters. The first half deals with the situation here in Salem in the context of the witchcraft panic across the Christian world at the time. But the second half is specifically about the people here in Salem. I was particularly touched by the story of little Dorcas Good. Only four and half years old when she was arrested. Poor thing. She confessed to the magistrates that her own mother was a witch, and that she must have been, too. But who knows what those so-called 'examiners' put into her head. She was in jail for over ten months and came out of it completely insane."

Devin took the book to the sofa and sat down. Her ghostly aunt followed her. Somewhat disturbed by the very late—or very early—hour, Poe let out a few squawks of protest to let Devin know that they should both still be sleeping.

But she had found what she wanted and ignored his complaints.

" 'Chapter thirty-three,' " she read aloud. " 'Margaret Nottingham, nee Myles, was young, just nineteen, lovely and well-liked within the community. Shy and sweet, she was married just a year and had an infant daughter the year the winter of discontent came upon Salem. Despite her humility and kindness, she answered truthfully when spoken to. She felt strongly that they were overpaying Reverend Parris and that they would be a more closely knit community if they were to maintain only one house of worship. She was equally vocal against the first arrests and was heard to say the girls themselves were witches to accuse one as goodly and pious as Rebecca Nurse. A day before she was to be arrested and taken to her own examination, Margaret disappeared. It is to be hoped that Margaret escaped the area entirely and perhaps made her way to New York, but letters and diaries of the time suggest that she met with a different end, possibly murdered by a member of her own family lest others should be accused due to their association with her.' "

"You believe she's the woman at our window," Auntie Mina said.

"When I was a little girl, you told me that dreams can be memories. Maybe, in my dreams, I remembered that I'd read about Margaret," Devin said, smiling. "The woman who comes here is obviously a ghost—and I believe she's a ghost from the time of the trials, not a reenactor. Yes. I believe that we've found the identity of our mystery woman. I think that Margaret Nottingham comes to our window in hopes that we'll discover her truth."

"And what does that have to do with the recent murders?" her aunt asked. "While a killer might have been in the neighborhood now and thirteen years ago, he couldn't possibly have been here in 1692. So what is the connection?"

Devin smiled grimly. "That, Auntie Mina, is what we must find out."

10

When Rocky arrived in the morning, Devin had the parlor strewn with books and papers and maps. Auntie Mina was nowhere to be seen. Devin explained that she didn't yet have the necessary strength to remain visible at all times.

"What is all this?" he asked, gesturing at the mess.

"Research. Did you know that the last witch to be executed was a woman named Temperance Lloyd, killed in England in 1682? Lord Chief Justice Sir Francis North was disgusted by the proceedings, saying that the poor woman was condemned on 'fancy and imagination.' She confessed, but of course you can get anyone to say anything if you torture them."

"I'm sure the confessions here in Salem were coerced, as well," Rocky said.

"Well, naturally. Tituba must have been scared out of her wits with everything going on—ready to say anything to make the men 'examining' her happy. But they were only falling back on a long history of torture and interrogation in Europe, where tens of thousands of supposed witches were burned on the Continent and in Scotland, and hanged in England."

"You've certainly been busy," Rocky said, looking around at the amount of material surrounding her. "What brought this on?"

"Another dream," she admitted, then hesitated, looking at him. "The ghost of our Puritan woman has been around awhile. And we know that," she added quickly, "because I found reports that people have claimed for years that they've seen her at this house. Think about it. Less than thirty years ago people—including your friends—thought my aunt was scary just because she was Wiccan. Even though a lot of things started changing in the sixties and seventies, when Laurie Cabot arrived and was declared the Official Witch of Salem by the governor, and tourists started coming in droves, some people are still afraid, and people who are afraid strike out at others."

"You've lost me," Rocky said. At the same time,

he realized that if he had a cause, a passion in life, he would certainly want her on his side. Feeling off balance, he moved away to say hello to the bird.

He wanted to touch her.

He couldn't let himself.

"Okay, I think this murderer is killing because of whatever happened to a Puritan woman named Margaret Nottingham all those years ago."

"Why?" Rocky asked her.

"I don't know, exactly. But somehow, I feel like it has to do with old practices and the past."

"You think that somehow this woman was a practicing witch in the middle of a Puritan colony in 1692?"

"No, I think she was murdered because her family were afraid she was going to accuse them to save her own life. I think Margaret Nottingham was murdered by someone close to her."

"Why didn't you just ask her about it when you talked to her?"

"I never talked to her."

"Then how do you know her name?" he asked.

Devin shook her head. "I found a book that talked about her. It's mostly theory and conjecture, of course, but his argument that she was murdered makes sense. And since so many ghosts are murder victims condemned to walk the earth until justice is done, it makes sense that she's the Puritan woman."

"Okay, let's say you're right, and that's her and she was murdered. So are you saying someone wants to avenge her death now—over three hundred years later? And they're trying to do so by pinning the murders on today's Wiccans?"

Devin stared back at him, obviously frustrated. "No, I just think there's a connection. Maybe some rite was going on when she was killed. Maybe someone is just picking up again where her murder began because they're crazy or something. I don't know. But . . ." She hesitated momentarily. "What happened when you—how did you find Melissa Wilson that night?"

He stared back at her and let out a long breath. "She called me."

"On the phone?"

"No."

They were both quiet in tacit understanding.

"How did you explain that to the others?" she asked him.

"It wasn't easy, and as you saw last night, they didn't exactly believe me."

"I noticed."

He shrugged. "I said pretty much the same thing you said to me—that I'd heard something coming from the woods. Everyone assumed that the killer had hung around and then when Jack, Vince and I burst into the woods, he ran away. We were only seventeen, but the three of us were pretty big. He wouldn't have wanted to take on all of us."

"No one ever suspected you?"

"Yes, actually, the police grilled me for hours," he admitted. "Helped me get an edge on interrogation techniques before I even started in criminology."

Her eyes were on his, and he knew she understood exactly how he had felt.

"I bet it was rough," she murmured.

"Explaining that I thought I had heard a dead girl? 'Rough' doesn't begin to cover it." He smiled dryly. "That's what's so great about the Krewe. You don't have to go through a song and dance, don't have to lie. You don't have to pretend that trees were rustling when you really heard a voice. But . . . back to the point. We need to figure out if the past really does have anything to do with the present."

"Well," Devin said, "there's a way to do almost anything. We just have to figure out what it is."

His tone was far harsher than he had intended when he said, "You don't really have to do anything, you know. Except keep your doors and windows locked, don't go wandering off alone if you're out . . . and be careful as all hell."

She smiled grimly. "Really? I don't think so. If I'm in danger, I'm in danger wherever I am and whoever I'm with. I found the body. I introduced you to Beth, Theo, Gayle and Brent. And I went with you to Jack's house, so . . . I'm in. Now, are we going to check out Perley's theory on Gallows

Hill? Because whether you're coming or not, I'm going. Oh, and since you're so worried about me, what about that pepper spray? I'd ask for a gun, but I don't know how to use one."

"Guns are easy at point-blank range," he told her. "Point and shoot."

"You're giving me a gun?"

"No, but I do have pepper spray in the car for you. And I'll be damned if you're going off investigating anything alone."

She smiled in satisfaction, and he realized that she'd been waiting for him to say exactly that.

Her smile was a killer. She wasn't just unusually beautiful, with her vivid coloring. It was her energy, her *life* and her passion that were so arresting.

He knew he needed to take an emotional and physical step back—again.

Somehow he took a step forward instead. And she didn't move away. It was as if she waited, both hesitant and anxious. And if he touched her . . .

"Ah, Agent Rockwell," Mina said suddenly.

And there she was, peeking out through the kitchen doorway.

There went that moment, Rocky thought ruefully.

"I feel so much better when you're here. I can watch the house, of course, and warn Devin if I see someone, but I can't always be here, and I can't actually *do* anything to an intruder. I'm not really much of a protector, all in all."

"You do a fine job," Rocky said reassuringly. "But actually, Devin and I were just on our way out, so we really should get going."

"Where are you headed?" Mina asked.

"To check out Sydney Perley's theory on the location of Gallows Hill," he said, turning to Devin. "Shall we?"

Before they got in the car, he showed her how to use the pepper spray, which didn't take long.

He'd brought her three containers: one normal spray can to keep in the house—particularly by her bed at night—one small enough to go on a key chain and one disguised as a lipstick tube. Same basic principle as a gun, he explained. Point and shoot, but aim for the eyes.

"Don't forget, this doesn't bring down an opponent, it just blinds him and gives you time—up to half an hour or forty-five minutes—to get away."

"I got it," she told him. "Point, spray, aim for the eyes."

"Exactly."

"Pink," she said.

"Pardon?"

"*Pink.* The other two are black, but the one for my key ring is pink."

"You don't like pink?"

"I just didn't see it as a color you would choose, Mr. Man in Black," she said, smiling.

Devin found herself near him during his pepper-spray demo, and she couldn't help noticing all kinds of ridiculous little things. The soft feel of his corduroy jacket, the crisp look of the shirt he wore beneath, his clean-shaven cheeks and, of course, his eyes. He smelled clean—soap and shampoo and some kind of masculine shaving cream or cologne. There was something intriguingly intimate about the way they stood so close.

"Actually, I don't use lipstick, either," he told her, humor in his eyes.

"They'll have to come up with lip balm pepper spray," she said.

"I'm sure they already have."

His fingers brushed hers as he warned her to spray in the right direction—nothing worse than blinding yourself when you were already under attack.

"Got it," she assured him. Their faces were inches apart. She thought he was going to lean forward just another inch and . . .

But his eyes were on the house, and he backed away.

Nothing like having a chaperone at her age, Devin thought—and a dead one, at that.

But she didn't speak and neither did he. Instead, they got in the car and she dug her copy of Perley's map out of her shoulder bag.

"Okay, in 1692 Peter Street was Prison Lane. And Essex Street led to Bridge Street and on to Boston Street—and the only way in or out of town was over the bridge the street was named for. We know from many sources that the condemned were taken by cart to the execution site. Most historians think it's unlikely that Magistrate Corwin would have chosen a site too far outside the town limit. Which leads us right here."

"There's a drugstore on the corner," Rocky said.

"And houses all around, yes, but all of that development, even the houses, is from the past hundred years or so. I've read some blogs by people who were doing the same research. There's still a patch of woods here, though, on a rocky little rise behind someone's backyard. I wonder why . . ."

"Why it hasn't been developed?" Rocky asked. He cast her a glance and a grin. "Imagine a house built on a killing field like that. I see horror movie written all over it."

She gave him a warning stare. "I haven't had a chance to look up the county records yet, but Perley had a letter written by a Dr. Holyoke in 1791. Holyoke talked to a man who had lived to be a hundred and whose mother had often spoken about the hangings. She said she could see Gallows Hill from her house and had hated the days of the executions. She'd stood at her window with her baby in her arms and prayed that they wouldn't come for her. What I need to do is see if I can find genealogical records to figure out who the woman was and a deed of ownership to tell me what house she lived in. Obviously it won't be easy or someone would have done it by now, but if I can track down that information, I bet we'll have proof that her house was right around here somewhere."

A few minutes later he parked along the street and they got out of the car. After a bit of walking around they spotted the little hill with its patch of trees.

The terrain had probably changed a bit, of course. Three-hundred-plus years of snow and rain led to erosion and reshaping.

But she could still see it.

She could narrow her eyes and see the hill rising higher than it did now, could imagine that the pond still existed, and she could even visualize the well-known story of Benjamin Nurse, his mother's youngest son, though a man of twenty-six, rowing his boat silently in the night to find his mother's body where it had been discarded and take it away for burial.

The air stirred, but it was a warm breeze. The world around Devin seemed to grow distant, and she saw the lonely hill higher and scattered with rocks, along with a few strong trees. Someone whispered about the heat in July, and soon she heard the sound of horses, footsteps and a cart being trundled down the rocky path.

She wanted to cry out that they were wrong. That fear led only to hatred and prejudice, and that one day they would regret what they had done.

There were half a dozen women in the cart, and it was surrounded by others who had come on foot to watch the hangings, as well as those who were required by law to witness the executions.

Some were there only because they were afraid to stay away, as if refusing to watch as the ungodly were removed from the world might brand them as ungodly themselves.

She watched as the rope was thrown over the tree branch. She heard it rasp over the limb.

And she heard sobbing . . .

From the victims, from the crowd—maybe from both.

Suddenly she felt a presence beside her. She looked and saw that it was Margaret Nottingham.

"Walk with me," Margaret said softly.

Together they started toward the hill. The women huddled in the cart, eyes turned away from the ropes dangling from the tree, nooses tied and at the ready. The Reverend Stoughton began to speak to the condemned, demanding that they confess and save their immortal souls.

The cart was drawn up beneath the hanging tree and the condemned women were made to stand. A noose was slipped over each woman's head, and together they began to pray, finally fading into silence. All but one. Someone in the crowd demanded that Rebecca Nurse be allowed to finish her prayer.

And next to Devin, the specter of Margaret spoke. "It was all a mockery. A mockery of all that is just and good. Rebecca . . . how could any fault her? She lived a life of piety. The others . . . poor, often begging, or perhaps of different beliefs." She turned to look at Devin. "You must understand. When even such a woman as Rebecca can be brought to the gallows, people are terrified. When one member of a family is taken, more follow. If you give testimony on behalf of one you love, you risk the hangman's noose yourself. A four-year-old child resides in prison and did give testimony against her mother. And yet how do these confessions come to be heard? The weak are tortured, oppressed by fear and the demands of their oppressors and the examinations. They are so afraid they will say anything. When Governor Phipps demanded corroboration, goodwoman Rebecca Nurse was stripped before the crowd to find her witch's teat, and she suffered humiliation beyond bearing. The prison itself is rank with disease and sickness, and food is scarce, and several died there with no hope. And so—"

There was a gasp and a cry from the crowd as the horse was whipped and the cart was dragged from beneath the women. They struggled, kicking and jerking as they slowly strangled to death. Devin had to look away, and she turned to the specter at her side.

Would she have died in this same way had she lived to be accused?

As if she read Devin's mind, Margaret turned to her with a soft smile. "They saw suffering, and they were terrified of the woods and the Indians, and so they saw the devil's work in anything bad that happened around them. Fear made them believe in the devil, and I think they did indeed become demented. The sins of hatred and greed within their elders—one group wanting Salem to stay as it was, and another desiring separate villages—festered in their hearts. The children cried out against those they heard their parents ridicule, until it went wild and no one was safe anymore."

Margaret's expression was sorrowful, her face marked by the pain and guilt of everything that had happened here so long ago.

Devin could hear the ropes still swinging from the tree.

Then a storm rushed in and the sky turned dark. But it wasn't dark from the black clouds of a common storm; it was covered in a wash of red, like blood sweeping across the sky and covering the world. Or was it only in her mind that the world was changing? The red began to deepen to black. The darkness overwhelmed her, until there was no past or present, only a blackness deeper than any night.

Rocky caught her just as she began to fall.

He'd seen the apparition, but the ghost had ignored him and walked straight to Devin. Together they had walked forward toward a rise with a little stand of trees, but as he followed, he knew from Devin's eyes that she was seeing something more than the small deserted hill.

He didn't know how much time passed, but certainly no more than a few seconds. He had eyes only for Devin, who seemed hypnotized by something only she could see.

Only his well-honed reflexes allowed him to catch her before she hit the ground.

She blinked and looked up at him. "Is it over?" she asked.

"Is what over?" he asked. And then he knew. She had indeed witnessed something he'd been unable to see, and he was suddenly certain that it had been a scene from the past. An execution. "It's over," he told her gently.

She didn't struggle to get out of his arms but let him help her to stand, and she didn't object when he kept an arm around her for support. She looked around at their surroundings, looked to the trees, the rocky slope and the small crevice at the base of the hill.

"That's where they threw them," she said,

pointing. "They threw them into that crevice and covered them with dirt, burying them in unhallowed ground." Once again, she seemed to be looking at something only she could see.

"Let's go," he said, worried. He felt as if he was losing her. He understood seeing the dead, listening to the dead, learning from the dead. But something more was going on here. This place did not seem to be good for her. "Devin?" he asked.

She straightened, clearly able to stand on her own, and he dropped his arm as she looked at him. "She's here somewhere."

"Who? Our apparition?"

"Yes—and no. I'm certain Margaret is our ghost, and I believe her killer buried her somewhere around here. She seemed so sad. But I don't think she blamed her killer, because she didn't even talk about her own death. All her concern was for the condemned. She said if Rebecca Nurse, who was pretty much considered a saint in the community, could be condemned and executed, anyone could be. Everyone, especially the families of the condemned, was in danger of being accused and tortured into confessing. I was sure her family murdered her to avoid being accused themselves, but maybe it was a mercy killing to save her from hanging. I don't know—yet. But she's here. I know it. And we have to find her."

"We can't just start digging. For all we know this is private property," he said.

"I don't know where to start, anyway." She looked at him, disheartened.

Despite her words, he knew this mission to help Margaret meant something to her. After all, she'd found one dead woman. Why not another?

And yet, what good was it going to do—digging up a long-dead woman?

"Even if we did find bones, they might not be hers," he pointed out.

"I know. People believe that Benjamin Nurse wasn't the only one to recover the body of a loved one by night," Devin said. "But I don't think she's buried with the others. I don't know exactly where she is, I just feel I need to find her."

"It's too bad she didn't show you where to look," he said dryly.

"Are you mocking me?" Devin asked him, frowning.

"No," he assured her. "I meant what I said. It's too bad that Margaret isn't just a little bit more straightforward." He smiled. She was so . . . *possessed* by her determination to find the dead woman's body. "We can use portable ground penetrating radar. If there are bones here, we'll find them." He hesitated. "I just have to get Jack's approval, so I need to figure out what to say."

She threw her arms around him. "Thank you!" She held her breath for a moment, looking at him as if she was searching for words to explain her feelings. Finally she said, "She deserves to be found, and her story should be known. And she should receive a real burial—a Christian burial."

Her body was pressed to his, and he couldn't stop himself from holding her in return as they stood there on that windswept rise. Once again he felt the heated urge to hold her, to kiss her at last, to . . .

Yep. A house with a resident ghost and a public hill. His timing sucked.

Then Devin pulled away, and he realized that in her mind, they stood upon sacred ground.

"I'll call Jack," he told her.

"What are you going to say?" she asked.

"I'm working on it."

In the end he told Jack that he'd been looking deeper into local history and stumbled across Perley's theories, and he had a hunch the man was right and they might find something if they did some digging. Whether it would relate to the witch trials or to their current killer, he didn't know, but he felt strongly they needed to find out.

Jack thought he was crazy, but—since the feds would cover the expense—said they were welcome to dig, and he would take care of any paperwork.

Rocky asked Jack to keep things to himself so the dig site didn't become a media circus, then made a call to Angela. She promised to locate the necessary equipment and the Krewe, and be there in two hours.

"Happy?" he asked Devin when he got off the phone.

"Relieved," she said. "I don't think any of this can actually make me *happy.*"

They headed off to grab lunch at a small local café while they waited for the others. Once their food had been served, he started talking. "Let's try to figure this out. Why would someone now—say, a descendant of Margaret Nottingham or one of the condemned—kill other innocent women to avenge her death? Wouldn't they go after law enforcement or judges?"

She smiled. "Yes, well, some think the condemned already had their revenge." She quoted, " 'I am no more a witch than you are a wizard. If you take my life away, God will give you blood to drink.' "

"Sarah Good to Nicholas Noyes, her last words before her execution," Rocky said. "Of course, it was twenty-five years later, but Noyes did die of a hemorrhage—choking on his own blood."

Devin shook her head. "Margaret isn't after revenge. She's showing us what can happen if hatred and fear lead to persecution so we can stop it from happening again. Maybe our killer is driven by prejudice and fear, or maybe he has some sick, twisted reason for wanting to drive others to feel that way."

"Maybe. But we still need to figure out how the pentagrams fit in. If they were created by—

and perhaps bought by—the same person . . .”

“You really think a schoolteacher—”

“I think she might have sold them to a store that sold them to the killer.”

“Thirteen years ago, she was still teaching.”

He nodded. “Yes, she was—right here in the area.”

Devin sat back, frustrated. “You do realize that Boston is only twenty miles away.”

“This is local,” he said.

“How do you know?”

“Because something about it is personal. What happened in the past, what’s happening now . . . there’s a personal dimension to both of them.”

His phone rang just as he and Devin were finishing their lunch. It was Sam, telling him the rest of them were five minutes from the site. They all met up by the hill, and he helped Sam drag the equipment out of their SUV, then explained how to use everything. Then they paired up— Sam and Jenna, Jane and Angela, and he and Devin—and began the search.

“Shall we try over there?” he asked Devin, pointing toward the crevice.

“No,” she said softly. “If we find someone there . . . well, we might prove that this is Gallows Hill, but for now we’re looking for Margaret’s grave. For some reason I think it’s over that way, beyond the trees.”

She led them to the area she had in mind, and

they created a primitive grid and then worked in silence for about an hour.

Suddenly Angela cried out, "Over here! We've got something."

Everyone ran over to look at the radar screen. He could see the shapes of bones—badly disarticulated but unmistakable—with something else in the center.

Human bones.

Devin had been right.

He looked up and realized she wasn't with them. He turned back and saw that she was standing in the center of a group of trees with a field of last year's fallen leaves beneath them.

"I'll get shovels," Sam said.

Angela pointed at the screen. "It's amazing. Rocky—there, that looks like the skull. And the bones . . . some are missing, I think, but those look like ribs."

"How sad," Jane murmured.

"Devin?" Rocky called, turning back toward her again.

She hadn't moved.

She didn't seem to hear him.

He remembered her earlier entranced state and, worried, hurried over to her.

She spoke at last, just before he reached her.

"Slow down," she told him.

He did, moving carefully. "Devin," he asked, "what is it?"

She turned to him. Her blue eyes seemed enormous, her expression one of incredible sadness.

"I've found someone else," she said.

And she had.

The woman was laid out like the others, with arms and legs outstretched, her head forming the top of the star. Bracken and fallen leaves still hid most of her, and she hadn't yet begun to decay, so they hadn't detected the scent of death.

She had been young, with dark hair. She was wearing jeans and a sweater, and she looked almost as if she'd lain down to make angels in the leaves.

But the thread of blood around her neck gave the lie to that story.

As did the pentagram lying on her chest, glinting through the leaves.

11

Devin was certain that Jack Grail was looking at her with suspicion, even though Rocky had explained to Jack that they had been searching for a long-dead woman, not another recent victim.

The day had become filled with crime scene technicians, the Boston M.E. and his crew and a multitude of police—state and local—along with representatives from the museum to assist in the investigation of the bones and, of course, the FBI team. Officers from a number of the small area towns kept crowd control running smoothly.

Rocky and the rest of the Krewe had focused on the latest murder victim until Jack and his men had arrived to join them.

Now, though Jack was being polite and hadn't even suggested that he intended to take her down to the station for questioning, much less arrest her, he seemed to be asking the same questions over and over again.

"Devin, I still don't understand—why this sudden interest in quite literally digging up a woman who's been all but lost to history? And what made you think someone would kill her and bury her here, where, if you're right, they were hanging the condemned witches? And, *you,* Rocky! What the hell were you doing focusing a full FBI team on a woman who died hundreds of years ago just because Devin got caught up in some historical wild-goose chase, when we have our own murders to solve?"

"Why the hell shouldn't I?" Rocky demanded, his tone irritated. "It's not like we've been getting anywhere with the current case, and the whole witchcraft-Wiccan connection seems to tie the present to the past, don't you think? And the fact that we found another victim here on what may very well be the real Gallows Hill seems like a pretty strong indication I'm right."

"But you were looking for a victim murdered three hundred years ago!" Jack said. "It was pure luck that you—that *Devin*—stumbled on another body. Not to mention that there were no witches in 1692," Jack said. "No real witches, anyway."

"No, but we wouldn't have the Wiccan community we have here now if it hadn't been for the witch trials," Devin said. "There's a connection here, we just don't know what it is yet. Maybe revenge."

"You think someone is killing people over a three-hundred-year-old grudge?" Jack said incredulously. "Come on, you grew up here. What have the descendants of the victims done? They've demanded that their ancestors be pardoned—that's what they've done. They haven't gone running around killing other innocent people."

"Jack, I don't know. I don't have any answers—not yet. But I was researching, and—"

"Stop researching," Jack snapped.

"Dammit, Jack!" Rocky told him. She could see that Rocky was becoming heated in her defense, and despite everything, it filled her with warmth.

"Hey," she said softly. "I know you guys are both the pros and I'm just a writer, but I can't help thinking that if you can find the motive, it will help you find the killer."

"I hope so," Jack said. "Because now we have a third body on our hands."

239

"Fourth body," Rocky said.

Jack looked at him.

"Whoever is doing this killed Melissa Wilson," Rocky said flatly.

Jack stared at him, then nodded slowly. "Four," he agreed. "No ID on her, either. I hope to hell we don't have another Jane Doe," he said, shaking his head and walking away.

Rocky looked at Devin. For a moment she thought even he was looking at her with suspicion. But then he said, "Don't let him get to you. He's just being a good cop." He tried a smile. "Problem is, he's a cop who doesn't see ghosts."

"I was thinking earlier that we'd be the first ones hanged."

He offered her a wry grin. "I'm sure the Puritans would have seen our ability as witchcraft, so I guess you're right."

"I did have a great-great-great-whatever-grandmother who was arrested as a witch. She survived until Governor Phipps's wife was accused and he outlawed the use of spectral evidence." She smiled. "Remember? They believed that witches could send themselves out as specters to harm others."

She heard excited murmurings coming from the people clustered around the old grave and walked over to see what they had discovered, only half-aware that Rocky was right behind her. She saw that they had abandoned their shovels and were using delicate brushes to uncover the bones them-selves.

Others might debate her identity, but Devin knew it was Margaret Nottingham in that grave.

She had been buried deeply. Whoever had dug her grave hadn't wanted her to be found, not by the residents of Salem and not by any roving animals that might have disturbed her rest.

"It appears that she was buried on her back," one of the anthropologists said, his tone excited, while another of the group began snapping pictures. "From the way the bones have been arranged—see the wrist there, and the phalanges, the fingers—her arms were crossed over her chest, as they would have been in a good Christian burial. And there's something there on her chest. Maybe a cross?"

Rocky reached into his back pocket for a plastic evidence bag. Without a word, he pushed through the group around the grave and jumped down into the spacious hole they had dug around the corpse. Before anyone had a chance to protest he used the evidence bag like a glove and reached for the object. Like the bones themselves, it was encrusted in dirt, but he studied it carefully before inverting the evidence bag around it.

He hoisted himself up out of the hole, his expression unreadable.

"What is it?" Devin asked.

"A pentagram," he said quietly.

•••

The dead woman was Barbara Benton, from Ohio. She had come to Salem on vacation with several friends. She was twenty-seven years old, single and the manager of a chain clothing store.

The two friends she had come to town with— Juliet Manson and Gail Billet—had seen her picture on the news and had come forward to identify her.

Jack was calling her parents.

Rocky took the job of meeting with the two friends to find out what he could about Barbara's activities once she'd arrived in Salem. Because he was afraid for her to be alone, he left Devin with Jane and Angela. She was going to go back to the hotel with them, so they could do further research into Margaret Nottingham and her family. Rocky had kept the medallion and sent it to the lab so it could be cleaned and compared with the others for style, chemical makeup and historical context. Jenna and Sam were waiting at the lab to reclaim it as soon as it was ready.

Rocky met Juliet and Gail at their hotel, a small historic building right in town. They were both nearly hysterical, and getting them to calm down enough to answer questions wasn't easy. How could they answer questions? She was dead. Barbara was dead.

"And we owe it to her, her parents and you to bring her killer to justice," he told them.

Juliet was dark haired with red-rimmed brown eyes, and she fought to hold back her tears. "She was—she was the best."

"This whole trip was her idea. She wanted to explore her roots," Gail said. She was a redhead with freckles that were nearly lost against the red blotches crying had left on her skin.

"Her roots?" Rocky asked.

Juliet nodded. "Her family moved to the Midwest sometime in the 1900s. But she could trace her dad's family all the way back here. She said she had a great-great-whatever who'd lived here during the witch trials."

"One of the condemned?" Rocky asked.

"No, no, just someone who lived here. But Barbara always wanted to come here. We'd planned this trip for years," Juliet said.

"It was her dream trip," Gail told him. And then she began to sob again, and Juliet put her arms around her and they sobbed together.

Rocky waited. When their crying eased again he asked, "When did you last see her?"

"Last night—on Essex Street," Gail said. "We were at the bar on the corner . . . almost directly across from the hotel." She winced. "This was a bad time for her. Her fiancé was killed overseas a few months ago. He was in the service. But being here, taking a trip she'd dreamed of . . . she finally seemed to be having a good time again. She was talking about how she wanted to go and see where her family had lived."

"Somewhere in Danvers," Juliet added.

"And then what? Did you all go back to the hotel together?"

He looked at the two of them as they both went pale, stared at each other and burst into tears again.

"We did. But then she went back to the bar for her phone," Juliet said.

"She thought she'd left it on the table," Gail explained.

"And that's the last time you saw her? Didn't you worry when she didn't come back to the room?" he asked.

"She was next door—she had her own room," Juliet said. "This place is historic and cool, but the rooms are small, and the bathroom . . . She thought that we should have two bathrooms between us."

"When she wasn't there this morning, we just thought she'd gone out early," Juliet said.

"She wanted to explore the archives," Gail said. "Do some research into her family."

"And she was afraid we'd be bored. We were going to spend the morning on our own today, shop, do what we wanted, then meet up for dinner," Juliet said.

"And then we saw her picture on TV!" Gail said with a sob.

"What time was it?" Rocky asked them.

"Not that long ago . . . I guess about four this afternoon," Juliet said.

"I mean last night. What time did you leave the bar?"

"Oh. Late," Gail said. "We had such a great day, so we were just relaxing over a beer, you know, and—"

"What time did you leave the bar?" Rocky persisted gently.

Juliet turned to Gail. "What do you think? Maybe near midnight?"

"That sounds right. We'd been on a ghost tour," Gail explained.

"We had *such* a great guide," Juliet said, tears welling in her eyes again.

"Barbara loved him," Gail agreed.

"Do you remember his name?" Rocky asked.

"Oh yes, Brent. His name was Brent," Gail said. "Brent Corbin."

"I know that we work in mysterious ways," Angela said, sitting across the table from Devin in the suite the agents had taken, "but it's going to be difficult to solve a three-hundred-year-old murder."

Jane and Angela were at their computers; Devin had a book open in front of her, having gotten them to stop at one of her favorite shops to pick up a few books, this one on the symbology and use of the pentagram through history.

"Very difficult. And we're not doing so well

on finding the current killer, either," Jane said.

"And maybe the two cases have nothing to do with each other," Devin murmured dejectedly. "I don't know. I heard Margaret Nottingham—the woman whose grave we found today, I'm certain of it—the night I found the victim near my house. And then I kept dreaming about Gallows Hill— if that even *is* Gallows Hill. Maybe I was just being influenced by the things I'd heard all my life, stories I'd read and stored in the back of my memory, or . . ."

"Let's assume that it *does* mean something," Angela said. "The ghost came to your house and found you. She somehow knew that she could reach you, and she led you to our Jane Doe. And whatever formed the impetus for your dreams, I think we have to accept those as true, as well, given what we—you—found today. So now we know that your ghost, Margaret, was killed, then buried—with a pentagram, just like our recent victims—on what seems to be Gallows Hill, where our newest victim was also found. So, yes, that does suggest that the current murders are related in some way to what happened to her during the witch trials."

Devin looked over at Angela and Jane. "Their friend—Rocky and Jack's friend—who was murdered thirteen years ago, she was from here, right? Did her family go back to the days of the witch trials?"

The other two women looked at each other, then shook their heads. "We've read the reports, of course," Angela said. "But there was nothing in them about her family history."

"I guess we can wait and ask Rocky," Devin said.

"Or we can look it up online," Jane said.

"Do you have a deep, dark, secret federal way to find information?" Devin teased.

"Sometimes," Jane said, laughing, "and sometimes I just go to the same ancestry sites everyone else uses."

She took Melissa's file from the stack in front of her on the table, consulted it, then started typing information into her computer. Several minutes went by. Both Angela and Devin watched her without speaking.

"Melissa Wilson's mother was a Harte," Jane said at last. "The first Harte arrived in Boston in 1630. His son moved to Salem Village in 1660. The male line came to a halt with Melissa Wilson's mother's father," Jane said.

"I don't remember anyone named Harte being associated with the trials," Devin said.

"I don't know the history like you do," Jane said, "but neither do I. Of course, there were plenty of families who weren't accused and didn't take part in the persecutions."

"Let's look up Carly Henderson," Angela suggested.

"All right, good idea," Jane murmured.

She leafed through the files on the table for the right one and started typing again.

Again, they were silent as they waited. Then Jane let out a long breath and looked over at the two of them.

"This one is more complicated. Carly's grandmother was from Los Angeles. Her father was from Providence. But *his* mother was from Andover, Massachusetts, and . . ." She looked up and nodded grimly. "Yes, her family dates back to the time of the trials, as well. Their family name was Manchester."

"Manchester," Devin murmured.

"Mean anything to you?" Jane asked.

Devin shook her head.

"Well, these two are related if only because of their family histories," Jane said.

"We need an ID on our Jane Doe," Angela said. "Then we can see if she has family ties to the area, too. If she herself was from the area, someone should have noticed by now that she's missing."

"What about the new victim?" Devin asked.

"We don't have much of a file on her yet. I could be spinning my wheels and not come up with anything useful," Jane said. "Then again, I spend half my life spinning my wheels, because searching for the truth is almost always like hunting for a needle in a haystack." She pulled over another file and started typing again.

Devin turned to Angela. "They'll give Margaret a real burial, won't they? I mean, they won't stick her in a museum somewhere, will they?"

"Adam would never let them," Angela told her. "Adam Harrison. He's our director."

"What's he like?" Devin asked, curious to know more about Rocky's ultimate boss.

"He came from family money, then multiplied it and became a philanthropist. His son, Josh, died young, but Josh had been—"

"Special," Jane said. "The same way we're special."

"After Josh's death, one of his best friends—the girl he was with when he was killed—somehow acquired his abilities," Angela said. "She could see Josh."

"And she could use her ability to help people," Jane said.

"Adam didn't have the ability to see ghosts himself, but he recognized the talent in others, so he began to collect people like us to work for him as private investigators," Jane said.

"The government started calling him in to help with cases no one else could solve," Angela said.

"And then he was offered the position with the FBI and officially allowed to recruit the Krewes," Jane explained.

"Special units, officially," Angela said with a smile.

"And so here we all are," Jane murmured, but

she was frowning, her attention back on her work.

"My husband, Jackson, is our field director," Angela said. "He was Adam's first hire. Jane is from the Texas Krewe, and like a lot of us, she has a law enforcement background."

Conversation faded after that, as the three women lost themselves in their work.

"Hey, listen to this!" Devin said a few minutes later. "I suppose I shouldn't be surprised, but it turns out people have been using pentagrams as jewelry for a very long time," she said. "This is from the grimoire called the *Key of Solomon*, though it's generally accepted that Solomon had nothing to do with it and it's really a fourteenth or fifteenth century Italian study of the magic arts. Anyway, listen to what it says about pentagrams. 'Thou shalt preserve them to suspend from thy neck, whichever thou wilt,' and then there's a long translation on what to do, things like using your name, turning to the east, and then, 'Thou mayest be assured that no enchantment or any other danger shall have power to harm thee.' "

"So does that mean our killer thinks that they're a protection against evil, then murders the people he's trying to protect?" Angela asked. "It doesn't make any sense."

Devin was thoughtful. "The Age of Enlightenment might have been dawning in Europe as the witch trials began, but that didn't mean much enlightenment had reached the colonies. Back then, most people were deeply devout. God was everything because life was so dangerous. Infant mortality was high, women died in childbirth, men died early, as well, from disease and the hardships of making a living from the land. Maybe Margaret's killer thought the flesh was nothing—that murder was all right because only the soul mattered. The pentagram has been used in Christian designs—it can represent the crown of thorns and the nails in Christ's hands and feet."

"That's possible," Jane murmured. "I mean, maybe in the mind of a very sick puppy."

"Well, if you look at the things that were happening across the Christian world at the time, there were a lot of sick puppies out there. I'm not sure that someone who killed a loved one to save them from being tortured, publicly stripped and humiliated, then hanged, was any sicker than the rest."

"In an odd and convoluted way, that makes sense," Angela said. "So you think Margaret's death was a mercy killing, basically?"

Devin closed her book. "I don't know. It's all so frustrating. And Margaret's death may be completely unrelated."

"And it may mean everything," Angela said.

"Yes, it just might," Jane said, looking up at them. "I'll have to verify my findings, but—"

Just then the door opened and they heard

Rocky call out, "It's me!" He walked into the room, his eyes going immediately to Devin. "I found out something interesting. I don't know if it means anything, but Barbara Benton had family in this area at the time of the trials."

"We know," Jane said, turning the computer toward him. "We looked her up online, along with Carly and Melissa, and they had family here at the time, too."

Rocky smiled. "You've been busy. In all the things you find in a file, three-hundred-year-old background checks aren't usually included."

"Devin found some interesting things, too," Angela told him.

"About pentagrams," she said. "There's a long history of people wearing them for protection from evil."

"Does that include the Puritans?" he asked.

She shook her head. "I don't know, but it's possible. At times the pentagram has actually been associated with Christ."

"So while some people might have thought anything that wasn't traditionally a part of their belief was evil, others might have seen it as a protective symbol—even in Puritan New England?"

She nodded.

Rocky nodded. "Thank you. Excellent work all the way around. You've given us some interesting angles to follow. Now if we can just get a name for our Jane Doe. Jane?"

"Yes, I'm still trying to find out. We'll ID her eventually, Rocky. I promise."

He nodded. Then he looked at Devin. "I need you," he told her.

"Uh, okay," she said.

"We have to talk to your friend."

"Which friend?" She frowned. "Do you mean Gayle Alden? To see what else she can tell us?"

"Yes, well, we will need to see her. But later."

"Then?"

"Your friend who took Barbara on a ghost tour last night, not long before she ended up dead. Brent Corbin."

"You can't be serious, Rocky. Brent Corbin? He'd just turned fourteen, I think, when your friend Melissa was killed. And he's—he's a nerd!" Devin said.

Rocky glanced at her. They were speaking as they walked. "Nerds don't kill?"

She shook her head. "You don't know Brent."

He stared straight ahead and let out a long breath. "Devin—he followed you into the woods the other day."

"Because he'd brought me the map I was looking for and saw me go into the woods."

"Devin, I'm not going to see Brent to arrest him, but I need to talk to him. He was one of the last people to see Barbara Benton alive."

"What about people at the bar where she was drinking before she disappeared? It would make more sense to ask the bartender if she really did come back or if he saw anyone paying special attention to her."

"Brent was at the bar, too."

"What?"

"Her friend Juliet saw him there drinking a beer at the bar before they left. And no one remembers seeing her come back," Rocky said quietly.

"So she told them she was going back—and then she just disappeared?" Devin demanded.

"Yes."

They'd reached Brent's shop—Which Witch Is Which.

Brent was behind the counter, selling tickets for his eight o'clock tour.

"Hey!" he said, looking up. He was smiling, but his smile quickly disappeared when he saw their faces.

"Oh, God, sorry. I heard you found another victim. I'm so sorry," Brent said earnestly. "It's weird, though. It hasn't affected business. Don't see many young women walking around alone, but the streets are still busy enough. I just filled my tour—I'm going to have to send people over to my competition tonight."

"That's why we're here, Brent," Devin told him.

"You want to take another tour?" he asked her, frowning.

"No, we're here because of your tour last night," she said.

"Why?" Brent asked, his confusion apparently genuine.

"Haven't you heard? They have an ID," Rocky said, watching Brent's face.

Brent still looked baffled. "I've been working all day."

"Barbara Benton, the victim, was on your tour last night," Rocky said, his eyes narrowed on Brent.

Brent gasped. His surprise seemed real. "Oh, no," he murmured. He looked at Rocky. "Who . . . which . . . ?"

"She was one of three women who came together—they were from Ohio," Rocky said.

Brent's hands, still holding money from his last transaction, began to shake. "Which one?"

"Dark-haired," Rocky began.

"Two of them had dark hair."

"She was about five-six. Medium build," Rocky told him.

"In a sweater and jeans," Devin said.

Brent paled. "I remember her," he said. "She was having a great time. It was her first trip here. When we weren't stopped somewhere, she was keeping up with me and talking. She told me she'd had family in the area. She was going to look them up and find out where they'd lived— see if she had any distant relatives still here. My God. She was so . . . alive," he finished lamely.

"She *was* alive—until one or two this morning," Rocky said.

"I feel sick," Brent murmured. The money fell from his grasp and slipped to the floor behind the counter. He didn't even seem to notice.

"Brent, her friends saw you at the same bar they were at after the tour," Rocky said.

"What?" Brent said, blinking as he looked at Rocky. He didn't look away—*he didn't look guilty.*

He looked perplexed.

"Yeah, I had a beer at that place on the corner before heading home."

"Did you see Barbara and her friends there?" Rocky asked.

Brent shook his head.

"She couldn't stop talking to you, and you remember her clearly now. But you didn't even see them?" Rocky persisted.

"No. I told you, I didn't see them," Brent said, flashing a glance at Devin. Anger was overtaking his shock. "I was thirsty after talking for a couple of hours, so I went and had a beer. I suggested the bar to people on the tour, but I came back here at the end of the tour. I sold a few things and hung out to answer some questions for a family that was still wandering around the shop after everyone else left. Then I went to the bar and had my beer, and then I went home. Period. I didn't see them. You can't honestly think I killed someone, can you?"

"Right now I don't think anything except that I need more information," Rocky said.

"We're just trying to catch a killer, Brent," Devin added.

"We?" he asked, staring at her with a hard smile. "We? When did you join the feds, Devin?"

" 'We' as in the whole community," she said.

Brent stared at her and shook his head. "So you found a body right by your house, and then today you found another one. You look a lot guiltier than I do, Devin."

"Did anyone say you looked guilty?" she asked him. "Come on, Brent, please just help us. Someone had to have seen her."

"Someone, maybe, but not me," Brent said.

As he spoke, they heard a cell phone ringing. Brent's lay on the counter, so he picked it up and then frowned. "Not mine," he said.

"It's definitely not mine," Devin said. "Different ringtone."

"And it's not mine, either," Rocky said.

Rocky pointed to Brent's jacket, which was hanging off the back of the chair behind the counter. "May I?" he asked.

"What?"

"Your jacket is ringing," Rocky said.

"Can't be," Brent muttered.

Rocky had already reached over and picked up the jacket; the sound was definitely coming from a pocket. He reached in and carefully, using only two fingers, pulled out the ringing phone. The caller I.D. said Bro.

The phone was in a pink Hello Kitty case.

Rocky looked from the phone to Brent. "I think we *are* going to have a talk down at the station."

12

Rocky, with Sam Hall standing at his side, watched through the one-way mirror as Jack Grail questioned Brent Corbin.

He'd especially wanted Sam with him, since Sam was an attorney and was more knowledgeable on the inclusion of circumstantial evidence.

Because that was all they had so far.

Brent still looked as dazed as he had back at his store.

Jack was good at questioning a suspect. He knew how to keep the subject off balance, leaning forward to attack one minute, then sitting back, sympathetic. Right now he was asking if Brent needed anything—coffee, water, a soda?

Barbara Benton's cell phone was with the lab techs, who were analyzing her call log. So far, from what he'd been able to gather himself before turning the cell over, there had been no unusual activity since she'd arrived in Salem. She'd contacted the archives of several local museums, and she'd called her work, her parents and her friends. Nothing jumped out.

Except, of course, Brent Corbin's number.

But that had probably been to make reservations for the tour.

Meanwhile, Brent's own calls were being traced even as he sat there being interrogated. They had twenty-four hours before they had to charge him or let him go, but in Rocky's opinion they didn't need the time. They had the evidence. They were just trying to get him to talk before he was arraigned or asked for an attorney, which so far he hadn't done.

He just looked lost.

He could be playing them. If he were a sociopath, his own interests would be paramount and the deaths he had caused as meaningless to him as swatting flies.

He was a nerd, Devin had said. Smart. A historian.

So smart he could act this innocent while smiling on the inside?

"Look, I don't know what else to tell you!" Brent said to Jack, and he sounded desperate. "The woman was on my tour, yes. I had a beer, yes. But I never saw her at the bar. And then I went home."

"And yet you just happen to have her cell phone. The cell phone the restaurant staff never found—and Barbara never came back to retrieve," Jack said, not for the first time.

"I'm telling you—I don't know how it got into my pocket," Brent insisted.

"You're going to be charged with murder," Jack said quietly. "Maybe you have a grudge against the local Wiccan community for some reason. Do they look down on you because you run a witchcraft shop but you're not a Wiccan? You carry pentagrams, herbs, wands, chalices—"

"Yes, and T-shirts, and souvenirs, and books," Brent said.

"And yet you've only ever ordered one athame."

"Big Brother *is* watching," Brent said bitterly. "I just never bothered to carry athames, because they're available all over town."

"So why the one athame, Brent? Obviously you didn't intend it for sale. Not just one. It had to be for your personal use," Jack said. "Why?"

"I liked it! It's a handsome knife. I planned to use it in a Halloween display," Brent said. "Hell—half the people in this city own an athame."

"You had her cell phone."

"What does that have to do with me owning an athame?"

"Because an athame is a double-edged blade—and our murder weapon was a double-edged blade," Jack said. "But you already know that."

"I *don't* know that!" Brent protested. "Take my athame—test it for blood. Do whatever you want."

"We will. But it will go easier on you if you just talk to us now."

"I don't have anything to say."

Jack stood up suddenly, excusing himself.

"What do you think?" Sam asked Rocky.

Rocky shook his head. "He had the woman's cell phone, but he swears he didn't put it in his pocket. And there were no prints on it at all."

"It *is* possible that the killer—assuming that's not him—put the phone in his pocket," Sam said.

Rocky nodded. "But don't forget, I found him in the woods by Devin's house. Her bird attacked him right before I showed up."

"They *are* friends, although that may make him look more guilty rather than less so. Based on the evidence, the women are taken by surprise. He gets them to the murder sites on some pretense, and since they're not suspicious he easily manages to get behind them and slit their throats. It was the same this time, right?" Sam asked quietly. "No defensive wounds?"

Rocky shook his head. "Of course, the autopsy report isn't in, but I saw the body. The report won't be any different."

Just then Jack entered the room and joined Rocky and Sam. "You brought him in, maybe you can do better with him," he said to Rocky.

Rocky was thoughtful for a minute. "Maybe he didn't do it," he said.

Jack let out a snort. "He had her cell phone! This is the first break we've had, Rocky. He had to have done it."

"Sam?" Rocky asked.

"They'll never convict him on what you've got so far—if a D.A. will even take him to court. Circumstantial and nothing more," Sam said. "And you haven't even tried to connect him to the other murders yet."

"That's true. I'm missing a piece of the puzzle. But when I find it, everything will fall into place. What's your gut feeling?" Rocky asked.

Sam shook his head thoughtfully as he stared at Brent, who was just sitting at the table and waiting, looking around as if he'd woken up in a box and had no idea why. "Don't know yet."

"All right, I'll give it a try," Rocky said.

He left Sam and Jack to watch and walked into the interrogation room. Brent looked up hopefully. "Rocky! I know you had to call the cops because of the cell phone, but . . . you have to get me out of here. This is ridiculous—you know me. Okay, you just met me, but you know Devin, and Devin has known me since we were kids. She'll tell you. I didn't kill anyone. I couldn't. I don't know how the phone got in my pocket. I had a beer and I went home. That's it."

"Did you have your jacket with you?"

"Yes, slung over the back of my chair," Brent said. He looked suddenly hopeful. "That's it, Rocky. That has to be it. Someone put the phone in my pocket. They wanted to make me look guilty."

Rocky said. "Look, I want to help you."

Brent leaned back, staring at him. "All I can do is keep telling you that I didn't do it. I'm not a killer—I could never be a killer. You have to prove I didn't do it and get me out of here."

"Let's see what else we can find out," Rocky said.

"You promise you'll look for the truth?" Brent asked him.

"I promise I'll look for the truth—wherever it leads," Rocky told him. He stood and walked out of the room, pausing at the door. "For your own safety, stay here. If someone really is trying to frame you, you're better off staying out of their reach."

Sam and Jack came out to the hall to meet him. "That's it?" Jack asked.

"We need more," Rocky said.

"More? What the damned hell more do you need? Barbara Benton, alive and well, says good night to her friends and goes back for her phone, only she never makes it. The phone turns up in Brent Corbin's pocket, and the woman turns up dead," Jack said.

Sam was silent but he looked at Rocky, and Rocky knew what he was thinking. Brent Corbin had been living in Salem when Melissa Wilson was killed; he had a dark SUV; he had recently purchased an athame, even though he ran a store that carried Wiccan supplies—except for athames.

"It's not enough," Rocky said. "We have to find something more, not to mention we need to compare his whereabouts to the times of the other murders. Have we gotten the search warrants for his home and business yet?"

"Should be through any minute," Jack said. "But it's got to be him."

"We don't know that for sure. And if we let ourselves believe he's guilty without checking every possibility . . . well, that could make us convict an innocent man and leave the real killer to strike again," Rocky said.

It was 3:00 a.m. but while Devin had dozed on and off, she hadn't really fallen asleep.

She was too restless and too upset. It just couldn't be Brent. She was anxious to talk to Rocky again and tell him all the reasons why Brent couldn't be the killer. She'd already explained everything to Jane, Jenna and Angela, who had driven her home from the station. Angela, she thought, had been open-minded. Jenna and Jane—well, they hadn't argued. They'd humored her at least.

It had been surreal, Rocky calmly explaining to Brent that he would have to come in for questioning, Brent protesting, Jack Grail arriving to take Brent to the station, Rocky trying to make her understand as they followed, while she argued with him the whole way, still in shock herself.

The rest of the Krewe had met them there. Sam had stayed, and the women had convinced Devin to let them take her home, since there was nothing for her to do there.

They hadn't wanted to leave her alone, but even though she knew Rocky would be furious, she'd insisted they leave, promising that she'd lock herself in and not open the door to anyone who came by. She'd said that she was drained and tired and just needed to be alone to rest. Reluctantly, after making sure the house was clear and everything locked up tight, they'd gone. But now, even though she was exhausted, she couldn't stop her mind from spinning.

It didn't seem possible that Brent had killed Barbara Benton and all those other women.

Of course, having a murdered woman's cell phone in his pocket was pretty damning, she knew. But what if he was being framed and someone had slipped it into his pocket to make him look guilty?

She remembered that Auntie Mina had warned her once that she always needed to think things through; she couldn't just rely on her heart. Too many people over too many years had been fooled by those they cared about. How well did she really know Brent?

"It just—it just can't be," she said to herself.

But when she woke up from another restless doze at 3:00 a.m., she knew she was wide-awake and there was no point trying to fight it. She got up and went out to the parlor.

Poe ruffled his feathers and cawed in protest when she turned on a light.

"Sorry, boy, can't sleep," she told him. "But I'll get you an apple."

She chopped an apple into pieces for him and brewed a pot of coffee for herself.

Brent had barely been fourteen at the time of the first murder. She simply couldn't believe that the boy she'd known could have been a cold-blooded killer.

She gave Poe his apple and left the cage open in case he wanted to come visit, then sat down at her computer and pulled up her latest manuscript. She was at the point where Auntie Pim had invited the gnome into her kitchen and was giving him hot chocolate and sugar cookies—and a lesson in morality.

She tried to write, but she just wasn't in the right frame of mind to think about magic and sugar cookies and happy children.

Instead, she went online and began researching murders that had been committed by children.

She was upset to discover just how many there had been.

Far too many.

The cases she found went well back in history. Often, older boys attacked younger girls, even toddlers. Some started out with a penchant for

266

tormenting animals. Others were bullied and then turned around and became violent themselves.

As she sat there, Poe suddenly let out a long caw.

That startled Devin. She almost jumped out of her chair.

Poe was clearly distressed. He flapped his wings and cawed loudly again.

"What? I gave you an apple," she said.

He flew out of his cage, but he didn't light on her shoulder or on the old secretary where she worked. First he landed on the curtain rod, but after flapping around he finally settled on the back of the sofa.

His behavior was unsettling.

"Auntie Mina?" Devin said.

But the ghost of her aunt was nowhere to be seen.

Suddenly something banged against the rear of the house. She jumped up from the desk, her heart in her throat.

It was nothing, she told herself. *Maybe a tree branch had fallen. Maybe there was a coyote prowling around.*

Or maybe a man was out there, intent on murder.

But they had Brent in custody.

Except she didn't believe he was a murderer.

For long moments she stood, terrified and frozen, listening to the thunder of her heart.

She heard nothing more.

Maybe it had all been her imagination. Maybe it wasn't such a good thing to wake up at 3:00 a.m. and start reading about homicidal children.

She looked at the clock. Now it was almost 4:00 a.m. Soon it would start getting light.

Not soon enough.

"Okay, Poe, maybe there's a lost dog out there or something. Rambunctious squirrels. A cat in heat. Who knows? I'll go grab the pepper spray."

As she walked into her bedroom to get the pepper spray and her cell phone, she heard another noise—out front this time.

She swore softly, her fingers curling around the spray can. She slipped back into the parlor and turned off the light. No point broadcasting her whereabouts. She walked to the door and looked out through the peephole, but she didn't see a thing.

Backing into the corner between the door and the wall, she called Rocky, glad she'd decided to put him on speed dial earlier.

Despite the time, he picked up almost immediately. "Devin?" he said anxiously.

"Rocky, I think there's someone outside my house," she whispered.

"I'm almost there," he told her.

"What?" *He was almost at her house at 4:00 a.m.?*

"I just left the station," he said briefly. "Stay inside and don't hang up. I can be there before the cops. I'll keep the line open," he told her. "All right?"

"All right," she murmured.

She kept her back to the wall, staring into the darkened house.

There was someone out there.

She heard movement all around the house now. Or was she only imagining the rustling, the furtive noises?

Someone was out there in the night.

Stalking her.

It could be the breeze, she told herself. The rustle of crisp leaves as the wind moved through ancient and gnarled trees.

It could be her mind, betraying her.

Then she heard someone twisting the back door knob and caught her breath.

It was real.

Her fingers curled tightly around her pepper spray. She didn't know whether to freeze or run back and look, but at least her pepper spray was aimed and ready.

There were two locks, she reminded herself: the lock on the knob and a dead bolt above. No one was getting in that way.

But there was a small glass-paned window in the rear door, too. If the intruder smashed it in, then reached through for the knob and the dead bolt . . .

"Devin, you there? Devin?"

She jumped at the sound of Rocky's voice on

her phone. "Yes," she whispered. "He's at the back door."

"It's locked, right?"

"Yes. But . . ."

"But what?"

"I don't hear anything. I think he moved," she said.

She was shaking, she realized, but then something snapped inside her and she realized she was angry even more than she was afraid. She moved quickly across the room, phone in one hand, pepper spray in the other. She wasn't going to crouch like a cornered rabbit by the wall. If someone came in, she was going to get them first.

Light suddenly flared out front, quickly growing until it sent an amber glow through the drapes and into the parlor.

"He's out front and something . . . something's happening," she whispered.

"I'm on your street. Stay where you are."

Devin hugged the wall, silent, watching the mysterious glow.

And then she smelled the smoke.

"Fire," she said. "He's trying to burn me out."

Rocky jerked his car onto Devin's lawn, shocked to see that the lawn on the left side of the house was ablaze.

He slammed the car into Park and jumped out, pulling his gun. Racing to the front door, he shouted her name. He could feel the heat of the fire ripping through the slight chill of the night, but despite his fear for Devin he realized that it hadn't been set where it would ignite the house.

The front door flew open. Devin was there, a fierce light in her eyes along with the fear, her dark hair spilling over the long white T-shirt she wore. *Unharmed and well, pepper spray clutched tightly in her fingers.*

Not a typical damsel in distress, he thought wryly. *She might welcome help, but she was also ready to fight to her dying breath.* "It's all right," he told her, reaching her and lowering her hand. "It's me."

"The yard's on fire."

"Yes," he said. He had his phone out as he scanned the yard and dialed 9-1-1—and then Jack Grail.

"A fire?" Jack demanded. "Someone set a fire in her yard?"

"Yes, it seems to be in a circular pattern," Rocky said, then turned to Devin.

"Get back inside and lock the door," he told her.

"Like hell! Everyone knows not to split up," she said.

"Devin—get in and lock the door. No one's in there, and you'll be safer inside."

And there wasn't going to be anyone in back, either. Whoever had been here had escaped into the woods and was probably long gone by now.

They'd come to torment Devin, not to hurt her. *But why?*

Even though he knew he wouldn't find anyone, he wasn't about to take chances with Devin's safety. He moved carefully around the house, circling toward the back.

As he suspected, he didn't find anyone. And though he scanned for footprints, he didn't find any of those, either, because the ground was too hard.

By the time he circled back to the front door, he could hear the sirens of the fire truck and police cars that were on the way.

The fire had already died down, though, which meant that with the moonlight, he could see the pattern burned into the lawn.

It was a pentagram—a pentacle, actually. A five-pointed star surrounded by a circle.

He headed back to the front door, where she'd been watching for him, and she opened it as he reached it.

"Gone?" she asked.

"Yes, we'll get men searching the woods, but . . . yeah, long gone. I'm betting he took off the minute he lit the fire."

A fire engine arrived then. Men started working on what remained of the blaze, and the chief approached Devin and Rocky.

"Chief Lindy," he said. "Anyone hurt?"

"No, we're fine," Rocky said.

"What happened?" the chief asked.

Rocky presented his ID and told Lindy, "Someone was walking around her house—apparently trying to break in. But I believe his real intent was to set that fire."

Devin looked at him, then to the place where the firemen had already put out the blaze.

Chief Lindy followed her gaze. "Looks like he used an accelerant to draw a pattern. We'll get our experts on it," he said grimly.

"Thank you," Rocky told him.

Police cars were already pulling onto the grass. Several officers got out, but Jack was the first one to reach them. He looked haggard.

"You all right?" he asked. Frowning, he, too, studied the burned pattern on the lawn. He turned to Rocky. "So . . . someone came here to burn a pentagram into Devin's lawn?"

"Looks that way," Rocky said.

"Why?" Devin murmured.

"I don't know," Rocky said. "Jack, can you get your men searching the woods for anything they can find? And maybe try to get some prints off her back door—that's where he was trying to get in, right?" he asked Devin.

She nodded.

"Of course," Jack said.

While Jack gave his men directions, Rocky put a call through to the Krewe. Sam answered on the first ring; he sounded damned sharp for someone who, like Rocky himself, had been up all night.

"We'll be right there," Sam promised.

Jack returned, and he, Rocky and Devin went inside to talk.

Her raven cawed in protest and instantly flew over to settle on her shoulder. She apologized to Jack, who told her not to worry—he liked birds.

Devin "wore" the bird well, Rocky thought. Her hair was as shimmering and dark as Poe's blue-black feathers.

"I have coffee on," she said.

They headed to the kitchen. Neither of them asked her anything; she simply began calmly relating what had happened in chronological order.

"I wasn't sleeping well," she said, almost apologetically. "I decided to get up and try to work. And then . . . well, honestly, first Poe started acting strangely. And I realized I was hearing something move outside the house. But it's an old house and old houses creak. So do the trees, and there are a couple of old oaks growing very close to the house, so I thought maybe it was just the branches scraping against the walls. But then I distinctly heard someone trying the back door," she said.

"What did you do?" Jack asked.

"I grabbed my pepper spray and called Rocky," she said. "And as we were talking, I saw the glow of the fire behind the drapes and started smelling smoke."

"You got here quickly," Jack told Rocky.

"I was on my way, anyway," Rocky said.

"Why?" Jack asked him, then looked at Devin. "Have you been getting threats?"

"No, no, not at all," she told him.

"Are you Wiccan?" he asked her.

"No," she said.

"And we haven't released the detail about the pentagrams on the bodies," Rocky said.

"Yeah, but stuff leaks. Cops talk," Jack said, shaking his head. "You know, you tell your wife, she tells her sister . . . no matter how hard we try, information gets out there." He looked at Devin again. "Do you think this was an actual threat or just a warning to get out?"

Devin shook her head. "Jack, I swear, I have no idea."

"I don't think you're safe here," he said.

"Where can I go?" she asked. "Besides, you don't know any more than I do whether this guy wanted to hurt me or just scare me. At least you know Brent Corbin wasn't the one trying to break into my house tonight."

"True, and also true—though not likely—that this might just be some kid getting up to mischief and not connected to the murders at all," Jack said. He cleared his throat. "Your great-aunt was Wiccan, right?"

"Yes."

Jack looked at Rocky. "The Witch in the Woods," he said softly.

"What?" Devin demanded.

Jack said, "I'm sorry, Devin. I know she was a really nice woman. When we were kids, though . . . she was the Witch in the Woods. A lot of our moms came to see her."

Devin's jaw tightened. "She read palms, tea leaves and the tarot," she said. "Mostly she read people. She didn't tell them their fortunes—she made them think about their situations and what they could do to change them."

"I understand that," Jack said. "Once we grew up, most of us got that. I'm just telling you what we thought as kids. And now here you are, living in her house and writing stories about witches. Maybe someone thinks you're Wiccan, too, and that somehow your return caused Melissa's killer to start up again."

Or even that you're *the murderer, Devin.*

Jack didn't say the words out loud. They were there nonetheless.

Rocky felt his muscles tighten. "Jack—"

"Hell, Rocky," Jack cut in. "Don't go getting mad at me. I'm just throwing out theories."

Rocky knew that; he might have come up with the same theory himself.

"Let's just get to the real point," Devin said accusingly. "You think *I* could be the murderer, don't you?"

"Just calm down," Jack said. "I know you're not, it's just that right now none of us have any real idea what tonight's events mean."

"I just—I just can't understand why anyone would come after me," she said.

"Give it some time, and then, if you think of anything that might help us . . ." Jack said.

She smiled dryly. "I know the drill. I'll call you. And I'll think," she promised.

Jack let out a sigh. "All right. I'm going to go home and get a few hours of sleep. But if anything comes up, call me."

"I think we should try to get some sleep, too," Rocky said.

"Sleep?" Devin asked skeptically.

Rocky smiled. "You're coming with me."

"To sleep?" she asked.

Jack coughed, grinned and turned away.

"I'm getting you a room at the hotel," Rocky said.

She opened her mouth to protest, but he spoke before she could.

"Please, I'm begging you," he said, knowing his exhaustion was clear in his voice. "I've been up all night talking to your friend Brent, so no protests, okay? At least for today, you can't stay here alone. Not after what just happened."

She let out a sigh. "What about Poe?"

"He's a bird," Rocky reminded her.

"Yes, but I can't just leave him."

"He'll be all right for now. We'll come back and get him later if it looks like you're going to be away for long," he promised. "Hey, Poe and I— we're close, you know. I'll make sure he's not neglected, I promise you."

It was as if Poe understood. He let out a caw and flew to his cage.

He was ready to do his part in solving the crimes, even if that meant staying there alone— and standing sentinel over the cottage in the woods.

13

Rocky thought that he was dreaming when he first heard the knock on his door. It felt as if he had barely fallen asleep, and he knew he wasn't thinking clearly.

It was still early in the morning, but at least it was daylight. By the time Devin had gathered a few things and they'd gotten to the hotel, Angela had already seen to it that Devin had a room on their floor—one between the suite the Krewe had taken and Rocky's own. They meant to keep her close.

They'd all been exhausted. When his head had finally hit the pillow, it was past six. Many guests were already waking up to begin their days.

He knew he'd left the Do Not Disturb sign on the door, so it couldn't be a maid.

And if it were an emergency, his phone would have rung.

He jumped up, grabbed his Glock and walked to the door in his briefs. Looking through the keyhole, he saw that it was Devin.

He threw open the door.

She stepped back in surprise, and he realized she wouldn't have been expecting him to open the door with a gun in his hand.

"Are you all right? Did something happen?" he asked her quickly.

"No. Nothing happened. I'm fine. And I'm sorry." She indicated the Glock. "I guess that actually *is* a gun and you're *not* so happy to see me."

He leaned out through the doorway, frowning, and scanned the hallway in both directions.

"What is it, then?" he asked.

"May I come in?"

He opened the door and let her in. Backing away, he wished he'd taken a moment to grab one of the hotel robes, even though she herself was wearing nothing but a theme-park nightshirt.

He was definitely glad to see her.

"Hang on," he said quickly. He slid his gun back

into the small holster by the bed and pulled on the hotel robe.

"What's wrong?" he asked, belting the robe. "You can't be here just to say good morning."

She lowered her eyes for a long moment. "Wow, you're making this kind of difficult."

"I'm making things difficult?" he asked.

Difficult? He couldn't even seem to belt the damned robe.

Her eyes met his. "Yes. I guess I was having a fantasy thing going on in my head," she said huskily. "I knock on your door. You open it. I step closer to you, and . . . and you whisk me into your arms. I thought you'd felt the same way at my place, except Auntie Mina always seems to appear at the most inappropriate times. I can't stop thinking about you, and I just wanted—"

She didn't get any further, because he stopped attempting to belt the robe and pulled her into his arms.

"Is this what you had in mind?" he whispered.

Talk about a fantasy . . .

"Yes . . . this," she said.

He let his hands fall to the hem of her cotton nightshirt and slowly drew it over her head. Then he shrugged off the robe; no sense hiding anything now.

Her fingers slid along the waistband of his briefs, hovering lightly in front, a smile curving her lips.

"The gun is gone—and I *am* happy to see you," he said. Then he slipped easily out of the briefs and drew her to him again.

"In fact, you'll never know *how* happy," he said huskily, tightening his arms around her, feeling the length of her against him, breathing in the perfume that was all her.

For a brief moment he just held her in his arms, felt the silk of her skin, and thought that, yes, there were moments when he had to believe a greater power was smiling down on them. He remembered seeing her on the road when she'd flagged him down, how she had appeared almost mythical, black hair streaming in the breeze, shimmering in sleek darkness. He remembered her eyes, so blue, as if they contained all the colors of the sea and the sky. He had been almost mesmerized when he had first seen her.

But then, of course, reality had intruded in the form of a body in the woods.

But now there was a different reality. And he thought they both deserved the luxury of enjoying this moment in all its beauty.

She was real, not some mythical apparition, and her hair was dark and rich and like velvet where it touched his naked flesh. Her eyes were a more magnificent blue, and the way she moved against him was raw and carnal, but still as elegant as a whisper of silk. The mere touch of her fingers as she stroked his face was arousing; the pressure of her lips against his shoulder awoke a storm of fire that shot through him, flesh and blood and bone.

He threaded his fingers through her hair, tilting her head so that she was looking up at him again, and he smiled slowly.

"I think this is witchcraft," he told her.

"What?"

"Magic," he said, and kissed her, feeling her lips part beneath his and sensing her hunger in the way her mouth moved, welcoming his.

The kiss grew fevered, then he broke it off, gasping for air, and slid his hands down her back, along her arms, to her spine again, pressing her closer and closer to him. He needed to taste her flesh, and he let his lips and tongue taste her throat, her breasts. He felt the catch in her breath, felt the way she seemed to melt against him, and then he gasped at the way she touched him in return, every touch of her fingertips . . . lips . . . tongue more erotic than the last.

He wasn't sure how they reached the bed, but somehow they were there, and he lifted her, kissing her all the while and reveling in her answering hunger, her passion.

In the delirium he somehow made himself pause; he hadn't come prepared. She understood his hesitation and smiled, and whispered softly that she was on birth control.

Then they were together again, on his bed,

naked and entwined, touching each other, seeking each other's most sensuous secrets. Their bodies twisted and turned; they couldn't seem to get enough of each other. Urgency filled him, the need to touch her, to give to her, to be certain that she felt the same blaze that seemed to rule his every movement. His mouth teased down her abdomen to her inner thighs. She was liquid beneath him, arching, writhing, whispering, though he couldn't make out the words. When he rose and straddled her at last, she wound her legs around him, and he thrust into her slowly, reveling in the way her tight flesh gloved his sex and in the look in her eyes as he leaned low against her, caught her lips in a kiss and began to move.

They made love. . . .

And made love and made love.

Finally they lay together, exhausted, spent, damp, still striving for breath and feeling the slowing thunder of their hearts.

She curled against him. "You were right," she whispered. "Magic."

He stroked her hair and lay there savoring the moment, just being there with her, lying naked together.

He turned to speak.

She was sleeping. Sweetly, at peace, her body still entwined with his.

He closed his own eyes and found the mercy of sleep himself.

● ● ●

Devin could hear the shower running when she woke up and realized Rocky was in there, getting ready to face the day.

She smiled, thinking she could just slip in with him. . . .

But a glance at the bedside clock told her it was already noon. Half a day gone—and he undoubtedly had things he needed to do. If she joined him, with the steam and the soap and . . .

One day, she thought, she would be accustomed to him in the way all lovers inevitably became accustomed to each other. They might take showers just to get clean. They might see each other naked or dressing and not instantly feel the urgent need for sex. . . .

One day?

Last night—or rather, early this morning—she'd walked in on the man and thrown herself at him. That didn't mean there would be a next time or that they would ever be longtime lovers or spend enough time together to stop feeling the urgency of last night.

Would he think that she was desperate, pressuring him?

Did he do this often?

Had she ever done anything remotely like this before? No!

Suddenly she didn't want to face him. Not here, not naked, not in his bed.

She hopped up quickly and retrieved her nightshirt, slipped it back on and hurried to the door.

Then she realized that, given the intruder last night, he would worry if she simply disappeared, so she scribbled a note and left it on the bed. It read simply "Thanks. Gone to get dressed for the day."

She heard him turn off the water and she ran to the door, threw it open and looked out into the hall. Luckily, none of the other agents was out there. There *was* a housekeeper with her cart moving down the hall.

She stopped Devin just outside her door. "Miss?"

"Yes?" Devin panicked and nearly snapped out the word.

"Will you have service today?" the woman asked.

Devin smiled. "Yes, I'm sorry. Later today, I think," she said. And then she realized that in her mad "I'm going to play out a fantasy" mode, she hadn't brought a room key.

She looked back at the maid. "Can you open my room for me, please?" she asked.

The maid looked at her. "You have ID?"

Devin didn't even have shoes—there were certainly no pockets in her nightgown.

"I don't. I—I swear this is my room. I went to . . . to tell my friend something and forgot to take a key. Please, can you help me?"

Devin had a horrible picture of having to go down to the lobby in her nightshirt with her hair . . .

Messed up as it could only be after a night of sex. No, she would buck up, go back to Rocky's room and ask him to help her.

She didn't have to. The maid evidently decided she looked honest and took pity on her.

"You bring me ID, please, to the door when I let you in," the woman said nervously. "This, it is against the rules."

"Thank you, thank you, I understand. I'll get my ID right away," Devin promised.

The maid let her in. She rushed to get her purse and ran back to hand her identification to the maid. "And my key—see, my key. And my name. And . . . thank you."

The maid smiled at her and nodded.

Devin thought that she would be leaving the woman a very nice tip when she checked out.

Once the maid was gone, Devin locked the door, sighed and hurried into the bathroom, grabbing clean clothes on the way, to hop into the shower. She hurried, seeing as the day was already half over, drying her hair and dressing as quickly as she could. The minute she left the bathroom she stopped and stood dead still.

On the table, along with the room service menu, was a medallion attached to a silver chain.

A pentagram.

She didn't touch it, only stared, wondering in horror if someone had put it there during the night or while she was with Rocky, and she just hadn't noticed it till now . . .

Or if someone had come in and left it while she was in the shower.

Rocky called the station and found out that Brent Corbin had spent what had remained of the night before in lockup, still denying that he had even seen Barbara Benton at the bar, much less murdered her.

He was just hanging up when he heard a fierce pounding at his door. He hurried and looked through the peephole. It was Devin, and she looked as upset as she'd been last night. The minute he opened it, she burst into the room. She'd showered and dressed, and he couldn't help but appreciate how nice she looked in jeans and a light sweater. What struck him most, though, was that her eyes were huge.

"Someone was in my room!" she gasped.

"What?" he demanded.

"Come on." Without waiting for an answer, she rushed back into the hall.

Rocky followed quickly, letting his door lock behind him, glad his wallet was in his pocket and his Glock was in the shoulder holster beneath his jacket.

Devin unlocked her door and hurried the few

feet to the table. Then she pointed. "This was here when I got out of the shower."

Rocky stared at the pentagram necklace, then turned to her. "Where did it come from?"

"I sure as hell don't know!"

"When?"

"I—I don't know that, either. I didn't even glance at the table when I . . . when I went to your room this morning or when I came back a little while ago. I went straight in to take a shower, then saw it when I got out. I don't know if it was here before or if someone was in here when I was showering. Rocky, the killer might have been in here *with me!*"

He walked over to her and pulled her into his arms. "We'll find out," he said harshly. "I'll pull every piece of video this place has—we'll find who did this."

She was shaking. "My house . . . my room. Why?" she asked.

"I don't know," he promised.

"But at least this means it's not Brent, right?"

"It certainly improves his odds. Meanwhile, hopefully we can trace this." As he spoke, he pulled his cell phone from his pocket. He called Sam first, then Jack Grail, hanging the Do Not Disturb sign on her door while he talked.

He was supposed to be on his way to the station to take another crack at Brent Corbin, but that could wait.

Taking Devin by the hand, he headed down the hall to the elevator.

"Where are we going? What are we doing?"

"Jack and Sam are on the way to meet us. We're going to get the hotel surveillance footage and go through it. He pointed to the camera lens aimed discreetly at the elevator. "Most hotels this size have cameras in their elevators and hallways. Not because crooks leave things in the guests' rooms, of course, but because they take them, and because there are cases of rape and murder in even the best hotels."

At the desk he showed the clerk his badge and, flustered, she went to retrieve the manager. He was a small man named Mr. Hogan, who listened gravely, nodding the whole while.

After that Mr. Hogan led them to a back office where there was a bank of cameras, several for each of the hotel's five floors. An elderly security guard was at the desk watching the screens. There were, the manager assured them, always two security guards on duty. One roamed the hotel while the other watched the office.

"So there's someone in this room at all times?" Rocky asked.

"Yes, sir," the manager assured him. "And if he blinks, we're still covered, because everything's recorded. We cover all three elevators and every hallway, along with the lobby and the entryway."

"What about the side entry?" Rocky asked.

Hogan pointed to another screen.

"We'll need all the footage from 4:00 a.m. till five minutes ago," Rocky told him.

"Yes, sir," Hogan assured him. "Bobby," he told the guard, "set up a computer station for the agent, please."

Bobby jumped on it, glad to show them the system. But when he went to play back the surveillance video, the screen came up empty.

Hogan was baffled and had Bobby run diagnostics that revealed every bit of the footage from 3:00 a.m. on was nonexistent.

"It's impossible," Hogan said.

"We'll get the police computer expert on it," Rocky said.

Within the hour, not only had Jack and Sam arrived, the department's computer technicians were working, crime scene techs were at work in Devin's room and both staff and guests were being questioned.

But despite all their efforts, they ended up with nothing. Whoever had hacked the surveillance system had known what he was doing and so far they hadn't found a thing to lead them to him. No one remembered seeing anyone enter Devin's room, and there were no suspicious fingerprints in the room or on the pendant. And all Bobby could tell them was that he hadn't seen anything unusual; everyone who'd entered a room had used a key, though if their intruder was good enough to remotely erase security footage, hacking a key card was probably child's play to him.

Rocky was frustrated, but he tried to keep his feelings in check.

"We'll leave someone working on the computer system," Jack told them. "Jonah Smith is the best man I've seen with a computer, so fingers crossed he can come up with something."

Just then Rocky heard Devin gasp and turned to see what had upset her.

She was looking at a local late-edition newspaper, which someone had brought in earlier and left lying around.

He saw the headline that had disturbed her. The Devil's Afoot in Massachusetts Again.

Devin picked up the paper, scanned it quickly and looked at Rocky. "Facts and just the facts with a sensational headline."

He took the paper from her. The ridiculous headline went with a report on the fire that had been set in Devin's yard. It mentioned that the house had belonged to Mina Lyle, a Wiccan, card reader and practicing medium in Salem from the days long before modern witchcraft had come to the city, and a woman descended from the original settlers of the town. The article went on to state that the house was now owned by Devin Lyle, author of the popular *Auntie Pim* series of children's books. Police, the article read, suspected a prankster or perhaps someone frightened by the current murders into drawing parallels with the witchcraft trials.

"What does any of that have to do with the devil?" Devin asked, clearly irritated.

"Nothing, but headlines sell papers," Rocky said.

"Freedom of the press," Jack said. "Don't let it frighten you, Devin."

She turned to look at Jack. "I'm not frightened, I'm angry. It's almost as if someone is starting a war against anyone who's Wiccan."

"But you're not Wiccan," Jack said.

"My aunt was," she said. "And she was the most giving person I ever knew. She never did one nasty thing to anyone. I just feel she's being maligned."

Jack looked over at Rocky. "These attacks on Devin—if they actually are attacks and not just sick pranks of some sort—may have nothing at all to do with the murders."

"How can that be?" Devin demanded. "I thought no one knew about the pentagrams the killer leaves on the victims' bodies?"

"It's not as simple as that, Devin," Jack said. "For one thing, we don't know that the killer works alone, for another, leaks happen. Someone could have heard about the pentagrams, someone with a grudge against you for whatever reason, and now he's using that knowledge to freak you out."

"But—" She started to protest, but he cut her off.

"But that said, I'm inclined—for a number of reasons—to think your friend Brent isn't our guy, even if I can't rule him out entirely."

"So . . . what?" Rocky asked. "Do we cut him loose and just keep an eye on him?"

Jack was thoughtful for a moment, then he said, "Yeah. We cut him loose."

Rocky nodded, but he couldn't help asking himself, *what if Brent was guilty but working with someone else?*

"Task force meeting," he suggested quietly. "I want all the crime scene techs, forensic people, everyone involved—my people, your people, everyone. There has to be something out there that we've missed."

Jack nodded. "I'm heading over to Corbin's shop now to see what the crime scene techs have found—if anything. We went over his home earlier—figured if there was anything at all, I'd wake you."

"Thanks. And?"

"Nothing." Jack looked at his watch. "I'll have everyone convene in an hour at the station. Because we've damn well got to come up with something." He turned to Devin. "It may not be your friend, but someone is out there killing, and I want him stopped."

"An hour," Rocky agreed.

• • •

Devin was grateful that Rocky had pulled strings to get her into the meeting. She sat and listened, impressed by the collected expertise gathered in one room. As a group, they were carefully analyzing every piece of information on the three recent murders in an attempt to create a trail of evidence leading to one specific person. Rocky reported on Barbara Benton's movements on the day of her murder. Angela did the same for Carly Henderson, who had closed the salon for the day and then done some shopping on her way home. She'd purchased candles at two different Wiccan shops, and soda and cheese at a deli. But she'd never retrieved her car and never made it home. Her roommate had been out late with friends and hadn't noticed her disappearance until the following morning.

"What all the named victims have in common, going back to Melissa Wilson," Rocky pointed out, "is that the women were all attractive, all young—only Carly was over thirty—and had been, at some time during the day, at one of the shops in Salem that sold Wiccan supplies.

"None of the victims was sexually molested. According to the M.E., the killer was of medium to tall height, and he came up behind the women and took them by surprise. I believe they all knew or trusted their killer, which is why they had their backs to him. The throats were slit left to right, indicating a right-handed killer. After death they were placed on their backs, their arms and legs arranged, and the silver pentagrams placed on their chests."

He paused and looked across the room at Devin. "As you know, a fire was lit in Miss Lyle's yard last night, with accelerant poured in the shape of a pentacle. At some point after five this morning and before 1:00 p.m., someone slipped into her hotel room and placed a similar medallion on her table. Whether these were the separate actions of someone with a grudge against Miss Lyle or are related to the case, we have yet to find out. How-ever, this person was able to hack into and erase the hotel's video surveillance system."

When Rocky finished, one of Jack's men reported on the medallions that had been found on the victims. They were all similar, but the composition of the silver and artistic techniques suggested different artisans.

Jack spoke next. He stood before the group and said, "We executed search warrants on Mr. Corbin's place of work and home this morning, but we found nothing to tie him to the murders, and the cell phone found in the pocket of his jacket had been wiped clean of prints, making it impossible to confirm or disprove his contention that it was placed in his pocket without his knowledge in an attempt to frame him. In the absence of any new evidence, Mr. Corbin will be released later today. At this point, we have to assume we still have a killer on the streets."

Then the lab technicians got up and began reporting on facts and figures, and Devin zoned out. She did notice when a young officer came in and approached Rocky, who listened to him gravely and nodded.

The officer left, and Devin felt Rocky's eyes on her. She looked at him questioningly. The meeting was finishing up, and he motioned to her to join him, and then he and the rest of the Krewe adjourned to the room Jack had set aside for their use.

"They have a fingerprint," Rocky said.

"From where?" Sam asked.

"Devin's back door. Whoever set the fire wasn't wearing gloves," Rocky told them.

"Did they find a match?" Angela asked.

"No, whoever's print it is, he's not in the system," Rocky said.

"So no career criminal?" Devin asked.

"No, and no one in the legal system, no one who has ever been printed for work purposes," Rocky said.

"So . . . we're nowhere," Devin said.

"No, we're somewhere. We just have to start collecting prints," Rocky said.

"Is that legal?"

"It is if we do it legally," Sam said.

"How do we do that?" Devin asked.

"We buy everyone drinks," Angela told her. "And then we hang on to the glasses."

"I think it's time to host a get-together," Rocky said.

"Where?" Devin asked.

"Your house." Rocky looked at his watch. "Brent will be free by then. I'm going to ask Jack to expedite his release. Because he needs to be there."

"And you think he'll come to any party you're at after being jailed and grilled?" Devin asked.

As if on cue, there was a tap at the door. Jack.

"Rocky, Brent's lawyered up, but we still have a few hours left if you want us to hold on to him," Jack said, "but I think we're still agreed on releasing him, yes?"

Rocky nodded. "Let him go, but, of course—"

"Yes, I'll put a tail on him," Jack said.

"Jack, you doing anything tonight?" Rocky asked him.

Jack's brows arched with surprise. "I was hoping to have dinner with my wife and kid, because this case is driving me crazy, but I gather you have something in mind?"

"I was thinking about a small get-together," Rocky said. "That will take care of dinner and hopefully avoid some of the going crazy."

Jack's expression turned to a frown. "A get-together? Tonight? Hell, Rocky, this isn't the time for a party."

"Devin's place," Rocky said. "Just friends."

"Friends like . . . ?" Jack said, waiting for some kind of an explanation.

"I'm asking Vince and Renee, too. And Beth Fullway, Theo Hastings, Gayle Alden and, of course, Brent Corbin."

"Corbin?" Jack said, stunned. "The same Brent Corbin we're holding in a cell right now?"

"Yep."

"I already told him Brent won't come," Devin said.

"A party. Oh, yeah. I can just see it. He's going to want to party with us, for sure," Jack said.

"Trust me, he's going to want to speak his mind and get sympathy from his friends," Rocky said. He smiled. "Devin, just make sure he feels it's our way of saying we're sorry. He'll come."

14

The one thing the warrants had produced was Brent's athame. It was in a leather case nestled on a fabric bed; the covered elastic bands that secured it in place hadn't even been broken.

"The guy could be a pro at getting rid of evidence," Jack began, "or—"

"Or he's innocent," Rocky finished.

Jack looked at his watch. It was going on four,

time to shut things down for the day. "You sure you don't want to cancel this party tonight?"

"No way. It's not a big party. Just dinner and conversation with friends," Rocky said. "I'm going to take off and pick up Devin. She's with Jane and Angela at the hotel. On the way back to her place, I want to stop by the bar where Barbara and her friends were drinking. If Corbin is innocent, then someone who was there that night slipped that phone into his pocket."

"I had men question everyone who was working there that night. None of them could contribute anything useful. They remember Corbin and the women, but no one saw them together," Jack told him. "And no one remembers seeing anyone messing around with Corbin's jacket, either."

"Sometimes a second go-around helps," Rocky said. "People keep thinking and end up remembering something else, maybe something small, but sometimes that's all it takes."

"It was a busy night. I already talked to the police. I'm sure you have the report."

The bartender seemed weary, Rocky thought—not uncooperative, simply weary. His name was Judah Baker; he seemed to be about thirty and, unusually for "wicked" Massachusetts, he had a rich Southern accent.

Rocky was glad he'd decided to do more of the

interviews himself. Not that he didn't have faith in Jack's cops, they just weren't . . .

They just weren't as invested, because they hadn't had a vision the night Melissa died, and they didn't speak to the dead. They might never know when a clue appeared right in front of them.

"I know you've been over this already," Rocky said. "But three young women have been brutally murdered, and more women's lives depend on what you can remember. We really need your help."

Judah looked past Rocky to Devin. "Hey," he said, frowning, "you've been in here with Brent. Aren't the two of you friends?"

"Yes," Devin said. "Good friends."

"But he was arrested, huh?" Judah said.

"He wasn't arrested, he was questioned," Rocky corrected. "Are you sure you can't remember anything else from that night?"

Judah shook his head. "I wish I could say, yeah, there was a creepy guy hanging around all night —musta been him. But if there was, I didn't notice him. I was moving a mile a minute."

"Did Brent stay at the bar the whole time he was in here?" Rocky asked.

"I can't swear to it, but *I* never saw him get up," Judah said. "We talked a little. He'd just finished his tour and wanted a beer before heading home, like he usually does. He seemed pleased, said he'd had a good tour. I told the cops all this yesterday," Judah said.

"I know," Rocky said.

He was surprised when Devin added, "Sometimes, once you take a little time and think about things again, you see more."

Judah paused, running his fingers over his clean-shaven head. "I barely even glanced at the tables. But if you're asking me who was hanging around the bar . . . people I know . . . let's see. Molly from the wax museum, Darryl who works at the playhouse down the way . . ." He paused, studying Devin again. "You're that author, right? You do the kids' storybooks."

Devin nodded. Judah picked up a glass and idly started drying it while he concentrated. "Another friend of yours was in here. Cute little thing. I've seen you all in here together before. I meant to mention it to Brent—I don't think he saw her. I'm trying to think of her name. . . ."

"The young woman who owns a shop farther down on Essex?" Rocky asked sharply.

"Beth Fullway?" Devin suggested.

"Yeah! Her shop's pretty cool. This Wicca stuff is all kind of new to me. I'm from Arkansas, not a local," Judah told them.

Rocky nodded and refrained from telling him that it was pretty obvious. He liked the guy's accent; he didn't want to say something that would make it sound as if he didn't.

"Was Beth alone?" Rocky asked.

"No, she was with the two other people from the store. An older woman and a guy."

"And Brent never saw them?" Rocky asked.

Judah let out a deep sigh. "I told you—it was really busy. All the tables were taken, people were three-deep at the bar. The three of them weren't here very long." He called to one of the women working the floor. "Gina, can you help these people?" He looked back at Rocky and Devin. "Gina was handling the tables that night—she might be able to tell you if anyone was trying to hook up with the women or anything like that."

Gina came over carrying her cocktail tray. She was wearing jeans and a T-shirt that advertised the bar. "Hey, you more cops?"

Rocky produced ID again.

"The local cops were crawling all over the place yesterday," she said.

Rocky nodded. "Do you remember the dead woman and her friends being in here?"

"I do—They were at that corner table." She pointed. "Nice kids. I couldn't believe it when I heard about what happened. They weren't blotto or anything. They didn't get carried away. They were very polite, kept to themselves all night, and they tipped well," Gina said. "I shake when I think about it. How horrible."

"You don't go home alone when you finish here, do you?" Devin asked, concerned.

Gina shook her head. "Not after what happened."

"No one will be leaving alone," Judah assured them.

"Barbara never came back in to ask about her phone?" Rocky asked.

Gina shook her head. "When the three of them left, that's the last time I saw them. There were other customers leaving at the same time, but . . . I don't know who they were. We get plenty of locals, but like most of Salem and certainly this area of town, we get a lot of tourists, too."

"I sent over the receipts from that night," Judah told them. "The cops have them, if that will help you any."

"We'll go through them," Rocky said.

And they would, but . . .

"A lot of people pay cash in a bar. Some don't want it on record how much they've spent, some are only buying a drink or two—not worth putting on a card," Judah said.

"Yeah," Rocky said. "Well, thank you."

Gina said, "Holly and Brenda were on last night. I'll send them over. But if you'll excuse me, the couple in the corner are looking at me like I'm the worst waitress known to man."

Holly and Brenda came over to talk with them.

Brenda was older, a slim, harried woman, but she only stared at them blankly. "Faces just blur together. They're one big cocktail order. I wish I could help you."

Holly was just as unhelpful. "I'm new—I just moved from Cape Cod. I wouldn't know a regular from the man in the moon."

Right before they left, Rocky went back to the bar and told Judah, "I'm going to bring you some pictures. You remember faces, right?"

Gina was back at the bar, giving him an order. "Pictures are a great idea. I'd know faces if I saw them."

"Me, too," Judah assured him.

"Thanks," Rocky said. Devin echoed him, and they left the bar.

"What now?" she asked.

"Back to the house. It's almost party time."

"As you wish," she murmured, pausing and stopping him, a hand on his arm. "Do you think this will get us anywhere? I still can't believe that anyone either of us knows—someone we grew up with!—could have done this."

Rocky wished he could say the same.

He'd been an agent too long; he knew better.

"Look at it this way. If we can eliminate them, that will help," he told her.

"And what about when the party is over?" she asked. "The hotel . . . someone was in my room."

"Jack has had the best video people over there all day—trust me, the cameras will be back up. And besides," he said, allowing himself a smile, "I won't be leaving you in a room alone. I mean,

304

if that's all right with you. You did run off this morning."

She flushed. "It seemed . . . prudent."

"Prudent?" He laughed. "You really are a New Englander, Miss Lyle. But seriously, you'll be with me. And my Glock. And I'm a very light sleeper."

"Nothing like feeling . . . secure," she said.

"Come on, then. For now, we have to get to a cottage in the woods."

It was, Devin thought, amazing just how easy it had been to set up the get-together Rocky wanted. When she'd called Beth, Theo and Gayle, not one of them had refused.

Vince, Renee, Jack and Haley had easily agreed, as well.

But when it came to one thing, it looked as though she was right. Brent Corbin hadn't called her back.

Maybe he would never call her back.

They were alone at her house; the other agents were out purchasing food and beverages for the party. Auntie Mina was on the sofa, half listening to one of her TV shows.

Aunt Mina was deeply upset that Devin had been in such danger the night before and she hadn't been there to help in whatever way she could. At the very least, she'd said, she could have been another set of eyes.

Calmed down at last—everything had turned out all right, Devin was fine—Aunt Mina had agreed that an episode of *Perry Mason* just might help.

Despite that, she was obviously paying attention to the two of them, since she piped in with an opinion now and then.

"I don't understand why you're so focused on the killer being someone we know," Devin said.

Rocky hesitated. "Obviously I don't want it to be a friend, but there's already a personal component to this, and I'm not just saying that because you were attacked, and you and I . . . I was there. I was the one who found Melissa's body. You found the third victim and the fourth. Whatever's going on seems to involve us."

"That's reaching, isn't it?"

"But reaching based on logic."

"My friends were just kids, thirteen . . . fourteen."

He looked at her. "You were the one who researched kids who kill," he reminded her. He took her hands. His touch was electric. Memory suddenly became physical, and she flushed.

"Somehow all this goes back to Margaret Nottingham," Aunt Mina said, interrupting the moment. "I know because she tried to reach Devin. That's why she came here, and the only explanation I can see for her coming now is because these murders are connected to her somehow."

Rocky looked at Devin. "She could be right," he said.

"Have you heard anything from the anthropologists?" Devin asked Rocky, backing away slightly.

"Not yet."

"But she was murdered."

"That's our assumption, yes."

"Maybe by someone who loved her and didn't want her thrown in a horrible, rat-infested cell, stripped and humiliated, then hanged," Aunt Mina said.

"Maybe, or maybe by someone who was afraid that she'd be putting them in danger if she were accused," Rocky said. "The answer is there, we just have to put the pieces together."

Her day had been overfilled with a dizzying roller coaster of emotions. First, there had been absolute fear of what had happened at her house. And then there had been . . . acting on instinct. Acting on what she wanted. Then astonishment that she had actually gone to him and asked for sex; sex that had seemed like the nova-burst of a new world.

Then she'd discovered that someone—almost certainly the same person who'd set the fire at her house—had been in her room. Someone was stalking her, and once again she'd been almost paralyzed with fear.

And then fear had become anger. Whatever it took, she was going to find the truth; she was not going to live this way. She wouldn't accept it.

"Maybe she decided she was going to fight what was going on. Maybe someone wanted to silence her," Devin said.

"Jealousy, hatred, fear . . . any one of them can fester in the mind," Aunt Mina said, "and drive seemingly sane people to all manner of evil acts."

Rocky walked over to the sofa and smiled at Auntie Mina. "I'd love to have known you," he told her.

She grinned at that, pleased. "Then just be thankful that you are special, young man, and you can get to know me now."

Rocky smiled again, then grew serious. "If our murders are based in contemporary hatreds, what would the specter of Margaret Nottingham have to do with them?"

"You're the agent," she reminded him.

He nodded. "I'm not sure that I have more knowledge on this score than you do, though, Mina. You were Wiccan, and there's definitely a connection of some sort between Wicca and the murders, and that makes you more of an expert than I am, at least on that aspect."

Aunt Mina looked at him, nodding slowly. "I'll think about it and see what I can come up with."

Then she turned to Devin. "You have my blessing to see him, you know."

"Auntie Mina," Devin murmured. She could feel herself blushing.

"Good heavens, child," Aunt Mina said, rising and walking toward Devin. "I was old when I passed, not blind." She turned and winked at Rocky, then looked back at Devin. "He's a keeper. Don't go playing too hard to get," she warned.

Devin shot a glance at Rocky, who had lowered his head, trying unsuccessfully to hide his smile.

Hard to get? Not her. She'd brazenly knocked on his door and basically asked if he wanted sex.

"Oh, no, not again. I hate this," Auntie Mina said, her voice fading along with her image. "I can't believe I'm going to miss the party."

And then she was gone.

There was a knock at the door; Sam, Jenna, Jane and Angela had returned bearing grocery bags filled to the brim. "Everything is easy to set up," Angela said.

"We brought grapes and apples, too," Jane said. "For you, Poe!" she called.

The bird cawed happily.

Devin led them to the kitchen to start setting up. "I'm still not sure how this is going to help," she admitted to Angela.

"Rocky's throwing everything in a pot to see what bubbles to the surface," Angela said. "If he's right, and this killer is somehow related to one or both of you, we just might learn something new tonight."

As she spoke, there was a knock at the door.

"Got it," Rocky said.

Devin noticed that as he went to see who it was, the other agents instantly went on alert. Sam shifted slightly, and she realized he was wearing a shoulder holster beneath his jacket. Angela straightened from setting a tray of cheese in place, and Devin saw the bulge of a gun tucked into the waistband of her jeans and hidden under the back of her shirt.

Everyone relaxed when it turned out to be Jack and Haley.

"We're out like big people tonight," Haley said. "My mom has Jackie. And I would be delighted to have a glass of the lovely Cabernet I see sitting there."

"Of course," Devin said, stepping up to join them. "Welcome, and by all means come and have a glass of wine."

"Just what are we doing here tonight, Devin?" Haley asked. "Trying to figure out if one of *your* friends is the homicidal maniac this time?"

"Haley!" Jack said in horror.

"Sorry. That was rude," Haley said, accepting the wine Devin had poured for her. "I guess I'm more upset than I realized about the other night." She smiled self-deprecatingly. "So, can I help in any way?"

"I think we're all set," Devin said, glancing toward the kitchen. "We took the easy route, I'm afraid. Pre-made pasta and salad."

"Have a seat. Enjoy your wine," Jane said, joining them.

As Haley took a seat on the couch, there was another knock at the door. Vince Steward had arrived, greeting everyone jovially. He didn't want wine; he wanted Scotch. Devin poured him one and he thanked her, then said to Rocky and Jack, "I heard you had one on the hook but lost him."

"You're referring to Brent Corbin?" Rocky asked.

"We didn't lose him, but we don't make a habit of holding people without evidence," Jack said, bristling slightly.

"And he's a friend," Devin said quietly.

"Hey, I'm just telling you what I heard," Vince said, perching by Haley. "Ivy Donatello, down the hall from me, has taken him on as a client."

"I thought you were in maritime law?" Rocky asked.

"I am. But it's a big firm and my colleagues have specialties of their own. Anyway, I think Ivy was a little surprised you let him go so easily. I heard he had a dead woman's phone in his pocket, and yet you cut him loose." Vince looked at Sam. "Still, nothing but circumstantial evidence when you get right down to it, so no jury could convict him. Don't you agree, Sam?"

"I can't imagine a jury that wouldn't find reasonable doubt."

"I'm assuming you obtained search warrants for his home and office?" Vince asked.

"We did," Rocky said. "And you know we can't discuss an ongoing case with you, Vince—especially when he's retained your colleague to represent him."

"I'm actually hoping Brent will be joining us tonight," Devin said, even though she knew her hope was unlikely to be rewarded.

Vince looked genuinely startled. "Really? You invited a possible murderer to have dinner with us?"

"Oh, I believe in his innocence completely," Devin said. "He's been one of my best friends since we were kids."

"Oh," Vince said. "Well, then, I look forward to meeting him."

On cue, they heard a knock at the front door again. It wasn't Brent, however, but Beth, Theo and Gayle, who had come together, probably direct from the shop.

Beth seemed surprised to meet Rocky's group and quickly dragged Devin off to the kitchen. "Are you all right? You sounded okay on the phone earlier, but what happened was just terrifying. And you're not even Wiccan. What do you think that they're trying to say? And Brent! They arrested Brent. Devin, did—"

She stopped speaking as Rocky walked into the kitchen and grabbed a bag of chips.

"We should eat soon—everyone is probably hungry," he said, smiling at Beth. "We'll give Renee and Brent another minute or two to get here, and then we'll sit down."

As soon as Rocky left, Beth looked at Devin. "Aren't you terrified?"

"No," Devin said, almost surprised to realize it was the truth.

"No? I would be."

"I hang with the FBI," Devin reminded her.

"You'd better hang with them all the time. Whoever this guy is—"

"He'll get sloppy," Rocky said, coming back into the kitchen. "Plates, Devin?" he asked.

"Over there," she said, pointing.

There was another knock at the door. Jack went to answer it, greeting Renee and introducing her to Devin's friends as Devin and Beth went back to join the group.

Devin watched Rocky but she couldn't fathom what was in his mind. He walked toward the door, and she followed him. Behind them, things seemed to be going well. Beth was talking with Haley. Theo, Gayle, Renee and Vince were debating animatedly about tarot cards—real or pure bull?—but they all seemed to be getting along well enough.

Suddenly there was another knock at the door.

Rocky looked at her with a grim smile and nodded. She walked to the door and opened it.

Brent Corbin had come, after all.

From the safety of his cage, Poe let out a long, mournful caw.

15

"I told you, I didn't do it," Brent said, accepting a beer from Devin. He turned and looked at Jack and Rocky. "And I should be pissed at the two of you bastards, but this beer tastes so damned good, I'm just going to bask in the fact that I'm here, I'm out and you two are assholes."

Beth slipped an arm around his shoulders. "They didn't really have a choice. They had to do what they did."

"Hold me in some scummy little room like a criminal? Tear up my store and my house? Yeah, no choice." Brent lifted his beer to Rocky and Jack. "Nice friends you have, Devin." Then he sighed heavily. "Just kidding. I understand. I guess. Wow, that sounds bitter. I really *do* understand. Of course, you cost me a couple of days' income and my neighbors are all looking at me like they think I'm about to attack them. But I'm cool, honest."

Beth laughed. "Oh, poor Brent! You sound like

you're not sure yourself if you're really all right or not."

"I'm not," Brent admitted. He took a deep breath and then a long swallow of beer. "It was awful." He looked pleadingly at Rocky and Jack. "You guys have to find out the truth. I can't keep going like this, with everyone looking at me like . . . like . . ." He shook his head and gave up trying to explain.

"Why were they questioning you in the first place?" Beth asked.

He explained about the cell phone—"I swear, someone must have put it there!"—then said, "Look, I'm out, and even if I'm here with the inquisitors from hell, I'm ready to have a good time."

Devin smiled and gestured for him to go get some food, but as she did she noticed that Rocky had his cell phone out, and she wondered why.

He saw her looking at him and smiled.

She suddenly realized he'd been nursing the same beer all night. He was acting like a normal party guest, but "acting" was the operative word. In reality he was watching. Watching closely.

"The thing is, Brent," Rocky said as they all moved toward the food, "if the phone was slipped into your pock—"

"There's no *if!*" Brent protested. "It *was* slipped into my pocket."

"Then whoever did it had to be at the bar, too," Rocky said.

"I . . . Let's see . . ."

"You were in the bar," Rocky said, turning to Beth. "Did you see anything?"

"What?" Beth asked, startled. "What bar?"

"The bar the other night, remember?" Gayle said. She smiled and shook her head. "We were there—you, me and Theo." She looked at Rocky. "I didn't see Brent there, but the place was such a zoo, that's not surprising."

"Oh! You mean the night we were doing inventory," Beth said.

"Night before last," Theo said. "We didn't stay. It was too crowded."

"That's what we hear," Jack said.

"Well, I, for one, wasn't there," Haley said. "*This* is *my* big night out."

"I wasn't there, either," Renee said.

"Because you were with me," Haley said.

Renee smiled. "Haley and Jack are letting me stay with them, because I was worried about living on my own."

"That's safe and smart," Beth said.

"Definitely—with everything going on, women should stay together," Gayle said, nodding.

"You can come stay with me if you want," Beth told Gayle.

"I have the big house—you could come stay with me," Gayle said.

"Maybe I will," Beth agreed.

"Hey, this is a party, right?" Vince said. "Maybe we could talk about something a little more cheerful?"

"Absolutely!" Jack said. "You asked for it. Here come the pictures of Jackie."

As he and Haley whipped out their cell phones, Devin found herself looking around the room. She'd known Beth and Brent most of her life, and Gayle for a long time, too, but differently, since she was older than they were. Theo was a newbie, but he'd worked for Beth for quite a while now.

His friends, she thought. It had to be one of *his* friends. They'd all been there when Melissa Wilson was killed, plus they'd known her, and that connection had to mean something.

As people took their food and moved to sit comfortably around the parlor, Vince and Sam Hall wound up in conversation, their shared profession providing an easy link. After his initial bout of anger, Brent seemed to be happy to relax and have a good time. At one point she noticed Rocky deep in conversation with Gayle.

She took a seat on the sofa near them and started eavesdropping. They were talking about the area.

"I love how this state is always changing," Gayle said. "Immigrants are always arriving, and most people welcome them. Of course, people do like to tease that Bostonians can be a bit snobby, but you can't really blame them, since a lot of them can trace their roots back to the earliest days of the colony."

"Me for one," Rocky said. "On my mother's side."

"Me, too," Beth said, walking over in time to catch the end of the conversation. "Gayle and Brent, too. Theo, you came from the Midwest, right?"

Theo laughed. "Most recently, yup."

Sitting in the wingback chair across from the sofa, Haley sighed softly. "I guess Jackie is destined to be a snob, because he got a double dose. Both Jack and I can trace our families back to when this area was first settled."

"Vince's family goes way back," Jack noted, lifting his glass in a mock toast.

"Dear God, we're more inbred than a pack of poodles!" Renee laughed. "And don't forget Devin." She turned to Devin and asked, "Didn't one of your eighteen-million-greats come here with Roger Conant, the founder of Salem?"

"Yes, he did," Devin said. "Both my parents are from Salem."

"We're all probably related to one another somewhere back in the dim mists of time," Beth said cheerfully.

"It would be fun to find out if any of us really are related," Vince said. "Except for poor Theo— you're practically a tourist," he teased.

"Hey, that's the way it goes," Theo said, laughing. "At least I'm not inbred."

The gathering had grown easy, relaxed—comfortable, Devin thought.

Except that Rocky seemed to think one of the guests was a murderer.

Eventually it was time for everyone to leave. Haley urged Beth and Gayle to stay together, and they agreed that Beth would stay at Gayle's place, at least for that night. Jack said that the chief and the mayor had decided to put out a news alert warning women not to go anywhere alone at night and to stay away from any wooded areas.

Then everyone was gone but Devin and the Krewe.

For a moment they were all silent.

"Well?" Rocky asked quietly.

"Theo was interesting," Angela said. "How well do you know him, Devin? There's something about him—he just makes me feel a little uneasy."

"He's worked for Beth for a while. Where he really came from, I don't know," Devin said. "I have no idea where he was living when Melissa was killed."

"Tomorrow," Rocky said, "we continue the archives. There's more information out there somewhere. We figure out what this all has to do with our Puritan woman—but we make a new effort, as well. We'll research Theo's movements over the last thirteen years." He turned to Angela. "We have fingerprints?"

She nodded. "I have a glass from everyone here—labeled by name and in a paper bag under the sink."

Devin stared at her—she'd been picking up all night, and she'd never seen Angela even take the glasses, much less label and hide them.

"You're good," she murmured admiringly.

"You learn," Angela said dryly. "At least now we can find out if one of our guests went to your house and set fire to your lawn."

"And now we know for sure that most of us did have ancestors here," Devin said.

"Yes. What we don't know is where they stood regarding the trials—and whether they had a connection with the Nottingham family." Rocky smiled grimly and said, "I did learn that Gayle's family was nearly banished. They pretended to be religious so they weren't thrown into the wilderness. But, according to her, they were never good Puritans."

"So . . . more research," Jane said.

"Better than finding more bodies," Rocky countered.

Devin couldn't understand why the evening—which had actually ended up feeling like a real get-together—had left her so wrung out. But once they reached the hotel, she didn't want to think about it.

And neither did Rocky.

He didn't even speak once they got to his room. He quickly shed his jacket and holster, and then she was in his arms. They kissed and stripped until their clothing was strewn along a path to the bed. She pushed him down on the bed, then straddled him and began to ease down his body, her hair fluttering over his skin, her lips teasing his flesh and every erotic zone. He rose against her, pulling her into his arms, pulling her down and locking them together. They stared into each other's eyes and began to move, until sheer physical pleasure swept away the events of the day and everything that had ever come between them.

He lay against her and whispered in her ear—teasing, sexual things—and his breath was hot and damp and it felt as if they had barely finished before they began again. She caressed his face as they moved together, loving its lines and planes. She writhed against him and wondered if it was possible to hang on to this world where they were one, or if the best she could do was to cling tightly to this feeling while it lasted. His body was slick and hard, and the way he whispered to her was arousing all by itself, and when they climaxed together in an explosion of heat, it was as if they were the only two people in the world.

After that they just lay together. She heard the beat of his heart and reveled in the security she felt as he held her and she held him in return.

She had never in her life slept so well as she did that night.

In the morning Devin found a note on the table next to a large pot of coffee. It told her to come to the suite next door. "Went into your room already —no new 'gifts' today. Cameras are working in the elevators and hallways. No visitors during the night—oh, and the maids are around, so dress to be seen."

She smiled, but she didn't need to go to her room. Rocky had brought back her things; she just had to shower and dress.

Before she did so, to be safe, she dead-bolted the door.

When she knocked on the door of the Krewe suite, a cup of coffee in hand, she was let in by Angela. Rocky was bent over a computer, watching as Jane worked. A printer was busily spewing out pictures.

They were, she realized, of everyone who had attended their party the night before.

Rocky looked up at her. "Good morning."

"Good morning," she said.

"Are you any good at research?" Angela asked her.

"Not too bad," Devin said. "I used to be a reporter."

Rocky straightened. "Jenna and I are heading out. I want to stop by the bar to speak with the staff again. They should be around even if they don't open till lunch. She's going to join Sam at the courthouse, where he's checking on Vince's records and activities over the past few years, especially in relation to his work as an attorney. On his way he dropped off the glasses at the lab for fingerprint analysis. I want the three of you to do some genealogical research, see what you can find online, check out some of the local archives."

Devin nodded and took a sip of her coffee. "Sure." She turned to Angela. "So what are we researching exactly?"

"We're going to find out who might have been related to Margaret Nottingham, the Myles family, and who the someone might have been who killed her. Then, we're going to try and figure out if she was killed because someone loved her, was afraid because of her—or, perhaps, afraid of her."

"Big order for the day!" Devin said.

"Yes," Angela agreed. "So. . . ." She stood up. "Jane?"

"Last of the pictures coming off now," Jane said.

"Okay, Jenna and I are out of here, then," Rocky said, collecting the pictures.

Rocky waved to Devin and then they were

gone. She noticed that he hadn't specifically warned her to stay with Angela and Jane.

Trained agents.

Who carried guns.

He seemed to have faith in her intelligence.

That or her natural instinct to survive.

Because she had no intention of going anywhere alone.

The bar staff were indeed getting ready for lunch, but the same crew wasn't on and Rocky could have kicked himself. He should have known that.

But the day manager, Tilda Merton, was a pleasant and cooperative woman who immediately understood his need. She was clearly rattled that the last victim had been in the bar shortly before her death, and that her phone had disappeared there.

She had taken Rocky back to the office to obtain the phone numbers he needed of the employees who had been on the night of Barbara Benton's death, so he could call and make arrangements to show them his stack of photographs.

"It must have been planned, don't you think?" Tilda asked. "I mean . . . someone must have taken her phone so she'd have to come back for it. It's scary, knowing that guy—that killer—is still out there. It's still daylight when I get off, but my husband comes to get me."

"That's good. Keep it up until we get the guy," Rocky told her.

When he left the bar, he made a quick call, looked down Essex in the direction he needed to go, then started walking.

Things changed, and yet they didn't. In some parts of Salem, as the clouds roiled overhead, you could narrow your eyes and think you'd gone back hundreds of years.

But then you looked again and the world was filled with cars and tourists, and the concept of hanging anyone as a witch was so foreign it was difficult to imagine that anyone could ever have done so.

And yet, some men still found a way to indulge the need to kill.

Instinct? he wondered, not at all proud of his species at that moment.

Or an aberration? The latter. Had to be.

Most people lived to protect the ones they loved, enjoy their friends and even make the world a better place.

He thought about Devin and realized that for the first time in thirteen years—since he'd found Melissa's body, in fact—he felt that there was light at the end of the tunnel. He hadn't realized that he was going through life without the least expectation of ever finding anything—*anyone*—permanent in his life.

But Devin somehow changed the world. She

was life at its best, its most vivid, its most passionate. Though to all intents and purposes they'd just met, she knew him, understood him. In the midst of all this horror and tragedy, there seemed to be something bright in his soul again. He'd just been waiting, he thought. Marking time. And now the time was here.

And this killer wasn't going to get away with murder, not any longer. Not with Devin in his life and very possibly in the crosshairs.

He quickened his steps. Judah Baker, the bartender who'd been on duty the night of the murder, didn't live far, just down on Derby Street.

He reached the address quickly. His thoughts hadn't kept him from walking like a man with a purpose.

The bartender lived in a duplex with a little yard. The building looked to have been built around 1850 and updated over the years.

Judah was at the door, waiting for him. "Hey," he said.

"Thanks for seeing me," Rocky said.

Baker grinned. "I'm not sure I have a choice, but not a problem. I want to help—Hell, anyone would want to help. Come on in."

He opened the door wider for Rocky to enter. The living room had been furnished cheaply, and there were posters all over the walls of swimsuit models and rock bands. It was pretty much the perfect low-rent bachelor pad.

Rocky sat on the sofa and pulled out the sheaf of pictures, then spread them out on the coffee table.

"I realize you're behind the bar and Holly and Brenda are on the floor, but you were closest to me, so I came here first," Rocky told him.

Judah nodded, staring at the pictures. He pointed at the picture of Beth—Rocky had managed to get a phone shot of her just before she popped a cracker in her mouth. "That's Beth—she owns a shop, but I already told you I know her and the people she works with. That's the guy—Theo something or other. And Gayle. I think her last name is Alden."

"Right," Rocky said. "But you said they didn't see that Brent was there, too?"

"Not that I could tell. People were piled up at the bar, like I told you. I think they had a drink and left," Judah said, taking a seat next to Rocky and looking at the other pictures.

He went through them all, a serious expression on his face. "This is a cop—I know him, too. He was in to ask questions afterward," Judah said. "After the murder, I mean."

Rocky nodded. "Jack Grail."

Judah picked up the picture of Renee and put it back down. "Tiny little thing?" he asked.

"Very."

Judah grinned. "If she was there, I didn't see her. But she looks like she's barely taller than the bar."

"What about this woman?" Rocky asked, showing him a picture of Haley.

"Oh, I've see her, too."

"That night?"

"No . . . several weeks back, I think. Early. Like when I first came on shift. It looked like she'd been doing some shopping."

"But not that night?" Rocky asked.

Judah shook his head, but he stared at another picture and then tapped it, looking at Rocky. "This guy. I think I saw this guy that night."

Rocky picked up the picture of Vince Steward and asked Judah, "That night—the night Barbara Benton was killed."

"Yeah, I mean, I've seen him before. I think he's an attorney or something. I don't know his name—but, yeah, I've seen him before."

"And you saw him that night?"

"Yes," Judah said firmly. "Scotch on the rocks. Same drink he always gets. He was definitely there."

Devin had been to most of the local museums before in the course of her life, but she had never been in the room she found herself in now with Angela and Jane.

When she asked Angela why they'd been allowed to enter this inner sanctum of records and learning without so much as a question, Angela had just waved a hand in the air. "Adam

Harrison can make one phone call and open doors you would never believe could be opened."

"I would love to meet him somewhere along the line," Devin said. "He sounds amazing."

"Who knows? You might. You never know when Adam will show up," Angela said, then went back to work.

The room they were in was climate controlled and filled with municipal records, ledgers, diaries, family Bibles and assorted other materials from the area's earliest days.

A scholarly woman with a slightly stooped back and horn-rimmed glasses—exactly the kind of woman you would expect to find holding sway over such a valuable trove—helped them at first. But then an assistant—a beautiful young blonde —came in to help, as well.

A lot of information had been programmed into computer files, so they were able to get a good start without going to the primary sources. But still, going back generation after generation wasn't easy.

Devin had been assigned to look up her own genealogy. Since both her parents had come from Salem, it was time-consuming and complicated. Then she got back to 1668 and discovered her parents had a mutual many-many-times-great set of grandparents.

"I *am* inbred," she said.

Angela laughed. "Well, at least no one married a first cousin, right?"

"No, it's about a fiftieth cousin or something like that." But even as she spoke, she gasped. She'd just discovered something a lot more crucial than a distant relationship between her parents.

"What?" Angela asked.

"Maybe I shouldn't be surprised," Devin murmured.

"*What?* Spit it out."

"I'm related to Margaret Nottingham!" Devin said. "Through my mom. Her however-many-greats-grandmother married Archer Myles, father of Margaret Myles Nottingham. Apparently the baby she had just before she died was a woman named Mary Elizabeth Nottingham who in turn married Andrew Barclay and had a daughter named Anne who married a Douglass—and the long line of Douglasses my mom comes from sprang from that marriage."

"Ah," Angela murmured. "That explains why Margaret comes to you."

"She's probably worried about you," Jane said.

"She should be careful," Angela said. "Twice, she's led Devin to a body, and that could actually be putting her into danger."

"I'm not sure she had a choice," Jane argued. "She wanted those bodies found, *and* she wanted Devin to know how she herself had died."

"Why didn't she just tell me what she wanted me to know?" Devin asked.

"She seems to be very shy and not all that good at communicating. We've seen ghosts like that before," Jane said.

"And," Angela said, "she may not know what happened. There's no reason to believe she was there when the women were killed. And since none of us has seen the murdered women, they were probably able to move on, so they weren't able to tell her."

"Maybe, or maybe they just haven't found one of us yet," Jane said, leafing through the old family Bible she was studying. "Hmm. Here's a name I wasn't expecting."

"Oh? What is it?" Devin asked.

"Hastings," Jane said, brushing back a lock of dark hair. "*Theodore* Hastings."

"There must be hundreds of thousands of people named Hastings in the United States," Devin said. "Well, a lot, at any rate." She grimaced. "Math isn't my forte."

"Yes, it's a common enough name," Angela said, getting up to look over Jane's shoulder. "But Theodore Hastings? At the very least, it's an interesting coincidence. When is the entry from?"

"Theodore Hastings was born to John and Mildred Hastings in 1677 in Salem Village," Jane said.

"Let's trace him and see where that takes us," Angela said.

Jane looked over at Devin. "I didn't think your friend Theo was from Salem?"

"He isn't—at least, not as far as I know. I sure as heck didn't know him until he showed up a few years ago and started working for Beth," Devin said. "Theo might not be any relation to those Hastings."

"True—but then again, he might be related and not even know it. We're talking about three hundred years and at least fifteen generations," Angela said.

Jane leaned back, stretching. "With everyone we're researching, this could take hours."

"At least there are three of us," Angela said.

They went back to work.

An hour later Angela sighed. "This could take days. Going back over three hundred years is beyond time-consuming."

"Yes," Devin agreed. "And you've got to figure that in three hundred years, someone must have fooled around and had an illegitimate child or two, or passed off her lover's child as her husband's. I mean, back then, there was no DNA."

Jane laughed softly. "You mean we don't know who was messing around with who when, and getting away with it."

"More or less," Devin said.

"But," Jane pointed out, "I'm not sure that matters. Perception and belief are what count."

A few minutes later, Jane let out a little cry. "Aha!"

"What?" Devin and Angela asked together.

"Actually, this one is kind of sweet," Jane said. "Two of your friends can trace their ancestry back to one of your long-ago relations, in a round-about way."

"Who? And how?" Devin asked.

"Your old teacher, Gayle Alden, maker of penta-grams, can trace her mother's lineage back to Mary Nottingham Beckett—sister of Margaret's husband. And your BFF, Beth, can trace *her* ancestry back to Rebecca Beckett Masters, sister-in-law of Mary."

"Hey! My turn for an 'aha,' " Angela said.

"What did you find?" Jane asked.

Angela looked up. "I found another connection —and you'll never guess who."

"Who is it?" Jane asked.

"Brent Corbin and Vince Steward."

"They didn't even know each other until recently," Devin said. "What's the connection?"

"I can trace them back to a woman named Elizabeth Blackmire," Angela said.

Devin and Jane looked at each other, and then back at Angela.

"And she was . . . ?" Jane asked.

"She would have been the first accuser of a young woman named Margaret Myles Nottingham. Devin, the two of them had an ancestor who cried 'Witch!' against *your* ancestor. After she accused Margaret, the 'afflicted' girls started screaming her name, too. Elizabeth Blackmire would have sent Margaret Nottingham to Gallows Hill—if she'd lived long enough to get there."

16

Rocky finished showing the photos to the bar staff, though he didn't learn anything from the two waitresses that Judah hadn't already told him, and headed to the station to meet up with Jack Grail.

"What do you think?" Rocky asked, leaning back in his chair in front of Jack's desk. "I keep remembering the night Melissa died. He came to my house, and he was being Vince—you know, kind of a teenage jerk. But I don't know where he was before he showed up."

"I showed up at your house, too," Jack reminded him.

"Yeah, you did," Rocky agreed, meeting his eyes with a level stare.

"You were there alone till we got there," Jack said.

"Yeah, I was."

"I was having dinner with my parents. You can ask them," Jack said.

"And I know *I* didn't do it, so . . ."

"God, Rocky, do we really suspect Vince?" Jack asked.

Before he had a chance to respond, Rocky's phone rang. It was Devin. He answered it quickly.

She was fine, she said. The three of them were still together, digging through the archives. She told him about the discoveries they had made, and he asked her if he could put their call on speaker so Jack could listen, too.

When they hung up a few minutes later, Jack looked at Rocky. "So, that's interesting. Vince and Brent Corbin. And yet it really does look like someone was trying to set Corbin up. We searched his home, his business, his vehicle—no evidence anywhere, and not a drop of blood on his athame, so that clearly wasn't the murder weapon. Can it really be Vince?" He looked sick. "If this three-hundred-year-old connection means anything, why would Vince set up some-one he's related to? Although I doubt he even knows he's related to Corbin."

"I'll talk to him and see what I can find out," Rocky said. "According to a bartender who has no reason to lie, Vince was there that night—and it was busy enough that he could have taken Barbara's cell phone off her table and dropped it into Brent's pocket without anyone noticing."

Jack shook his head. "When we were kids, I wouldn't have thought Vince was smart enough for anything like this, but then he went through law school, so maybe we were all taken in. . . . No. Can't believe it."

Rocky stood. "I'm going to talk to him."

When they left the archives, Jane, Angela and Devin headed to her cottage. While neither agent drew a gun when they got out of the car, Devin noticed that they were alert and ready.

She sincerely doubted that anyone was just waiting around her house to attack her when she showed up, but there was still something reassuring about having two FBI agents keeping her company.

They'd been talking in the car, and she'd been interested to discover that neither woman had intended to be a "ghost hunter" or even enter law enforcement.

As they headed in so she could feed Poe, they talked about some of the other Krewe members, assuring Devin that she'd like them all.

"They're just regular people," Jane said.

"Who can see ghosts the same way you do," Angela added.

Auntie Mina was at the house, and she was happy to see them. While the other two women talked to her and got to know Poe, Devin straightened up the cottage, although it was in pretty good shape considering she'd hosted a party less than twenty-four hours earlier.

Devin had just put on a pot of tea when her cell

phone rang. She expected it to be Rocky, but it turned out to be Sam, who had just left the lab with Jenna.

"We have a match on the fingerprints," he said. "We know who was trying to get into your house."

Her heart seemed to skip a beat. "Who was it?" she asked.

Rocky arranged to meet Vince for a late lunch at the hotel. Vince clearly had no idea that he was under suspicion. As they walked into the restaurant, he told Rocky how much he liked his fellow agents after getting to know them better last night. Then he lifted a hand for the waitress and ordered a Scotch.

Rocky opted for coffee. When Vince raised his eyebrows in surprise, Rocky said, "I'm kind of permanently on duty at the moment."

"Yeah, I guess. Jack, too. Hey, he doesn't resent you for being here, does he?"

Rocky shook his head. "We all want to catch this murderer—no one cares who the hell gets him as long as someone does."

"Yeah, I guess," Vince said, then joked with the waitress when she brought their drinks.

Rocky remembered that Vince was here at least once a month, probably more than that, for meetings.

"It's kind of hard to be second best all the time," Vince went on once the waitress was gone.

"Or, in my case, third best, but back in the day, we all had to get used to that whenever you were around."

"I don't think Jack ever thought of himself as second best—or that anyone else thought of us that way, either," Rocky said. "We were different, that's all."

"Yeah, I guess. Jack is a happy man these days, that's for sure. He got his shield, and he got the girl. And he's got a great kid."

"True enough," Rocky said, but he wondered. Was Vince just speaking casually, or was he making an effort to get under Rocky's skin—even stir up trouble between him and Jack?

Could Vince really be guilty? He'd proven he was no slouch intellectually, getting his law degree and going on to practice successfully.

"What made you opt for maritime law?" Rocky asked.

Vince grinned. "I tried personal injury for a while. I was good, too. But I didn't really like it. I felt a little slimy. I mean, they call you an ambulance chaser and they're kind of right. Wasn't for me. I like the sea, and I always loved boats and the few beach days we get. You know the old joke. Massachusetts—come for summer. July 15."

"Beach days are rare here, I'll grant you that," Rocky said.

Vince turned suddenly serious and shook his

head. "Rocky, we're not here to shoot the breeze, are we? What's up?"

Rocky met his eyes and spoke honestly. "You're looking suspicious as hell. You know this hotel—and the security system was knocked out here the same night someone set a fire on Devin's lawn and she ended up spending the night here. You were at the bar the night Brent Corbin was there and the dead woman's cell phone wound up in his pocket—something you somehow neglected to mention."

"Ah," Vince said.

"Got an explanation?" Rocky asked him.

"Yes, I was there. I had a date that night. I didn't mention this before because it has nothing to do with it—I was at dinner with a woman. She's married. After she headed home, I went to the bar for a quick drink. I was only there about fifteen minutes. I didn't see the relevance, so I didn't mention it."

"Identical murders point to a single murderer," Rocky said.

"And we were all there—when Melissa was killed," Vince said. He leaned forward. "Rocky, I didn't do it. I didn't kill any of them, I swear it. I can prove it. Well, I can't prove everything— but I can prove where I was when the last woman was murdered."

"You can?"

"That's good, right?" Vince asked.

339

Rocky lifted his hands. "The more people I can clear, the better I can concentrate on who the real killer might be."

Vince pulled one of the cocktail napkins on the table closer to him, drew a pen from his jacket pocket and began to write. He pushed the paper to Rocky. "Ellen Cahill. Give her a call. She's with Douglas Marine. I represented the firm recently, and she and I became . . . friends. We had dinner, then she went home. I had a quick drink at the bar before joining her at her place—I wanted to arrive there a little later so that it would look as if we'd had a business dinner. She's married, as I said, but separated at the moment, figuring things out. I'd rather you not— Well, I hope you can keep it under wraps. Anyway, I even saw her newspaper deliveryman in the morning. If you don't believe her when she tells you I was with her all night, I'm sure you can find out his name and check with him."

Rocky accepted the napkin. "Thanks," he told Vince.

"Be discreet—if you don't mind."

"I will," Rocky said.

"Well, what would you like to eat?" Vince asked him.

Crow, Rocky thought.

But had he ever believed it was Vince?

They were desperate for clues—real clues, solid clues.

"You look depressed," Vince told him. "But I'm not sorry. I'm really not a killer. What have you found out? Wait, you can't answer that. I wish I could help. Have you learned anything you *can* share?"

Rocky shrugged and leaned back. "You're distantly related to Devin's friend Brent Corbin."

"Yeah?" Vince asked. "Your other suspect? The guy who had her phone?"

"Yes, although to be honest, I don't think he did it, either." Rocky shook his head. "You have a legal mind. You've dealt with the good, the bad and the ugly. Why do you think someone would kill, then stage the victim so ritualistically?"

"The crimes aren't sexual in any way?"

"None of the women have been molested, no."

"The key has to be the ritual. The murders mean something to the killer," Vince said.

"What, though?"

Vince drummed his fingers on the table. "I don't know," he admitted. "Damn, Rocky, don't you think that finding Melissa the way we did had an effect on all of us? I've never forgotten it. I can still see her lying there. It's crystal clear in my mind's eye. Hell, sometimes, I can't remember what I had for breakfast in the morning, but I remember that sight as if it were burned into my mind." He went silent for a minute. "The victims weren't all from here, right?"

"Barbara Benton was from Ohio, but she had

family here back when the witch trials were going on. And our Jane Doe . . . who knows? I'm guessing she wasn't from the area or someone would have stepped forward to identify her by now, but until we know who she is I can't be sure."

"And they were killed like Melissa was?"

Rocky arched a brow at him.

Vince shrugged. "The details aren't in the news, but you know how it goes. A cop says something even if he's not supposed to, and lawyers are good at picking up the gossip. What I'm curious about is why the killer stopped for all those years."

"You tell me—what's your take?"

"Maybe the right people weren't around to kill," Vince said. "Like you said, you still don't have an ID on the one woman, right?"

"Nope," Rocky agreed. "But Carly Henderson was around here all those years. And how the hell would he even know Barbara Benton existed?"

"Maybe . . . Oh, hell. I don't know. I'm an attorney. My job is to take the truth and put a spin on it that helps my client. You have to deal with the truth as it is—naked and ugly." Vince looked at his watch. "Got to get back to work. Check out every word I said, Rocky. You'll find the naked truth."

Once Vince was gone, Rocky paid the check and stood. He didn't call the number that Vince had given him. Instead, he pulled out his phone and found the company address. The offices were on the wharf, within easy walking distance of the hotel, and he headed straight over.

Old figureheads, ships' wheels and pirate flags decorated the reception area. A pretty blonde woman sat at the front desk.

Rocky didn't produce his credentials; he asked to speak with Ellen Cahill. The blonde arched her brows in surprise. "I'm Ellen Cahill."

She smiled and he wondered if she saw in his eyes that he was somewhat surprised that Vince could have tried to pull off his date as a business dinner if Ellen was a secretary.

"I'm a paralegal," she explained. "Subbing for the receptionist. I thought you might be by and figured that I'd rather meet you at this desk myself."

Rocky smiled and offered his hand. "I'm Craig Rockwell. You knew I was coming?"

She nodded and rose to take his hand. "Yes, I've heard all about you. It's a pleasure to meet you. And thank you for not making calls and just . . . Well. I don't know where my future is going. But I am separated now—just not advertising what I'm doing."

"I guess you know that I'm an agent—in town because of the murders?"

She nodded somberly. "Yes."

"There was a murder the other night—the woman had been at a bar where you and Vince were the same night."

343

Ellen Cahill shuddered. "I know! I heard. That's so horrible!"

"Well, I guess I came to stress just how careful you need to be."

Ellen nodded fervently. "I know! And Vince has been wonderful. Thankfully, we were together that night and he called me earlier today—I won't be going home alone again until this whole thing is over. Thankfully that night . . ." She paused and flushed and started over. "That night, I left alone. But then, we were together when it was all happening. When I was talking to Vince today, he said that he won't let me be alone again!"

"That's good," Rocky said. "That's very good."

"You have to catch this horrible person," Ellen said.

"We're trying," he assured her. "But you're right. Don't be alone. And, I swear, we're doing our best to get him as soon as possible."

"Of course, and my prayers are with you!" Ellen said. "Lovely to have met you."

Rocky said, "Thank you, and I'm delighted to meet you, as well. Um, best of luck with whatever your decision may be."

"Thank you."

He left the offices, certain that the woman had been telling him the truth.

Standing on the street, Rocky felt compelled to call Devin and make sure she was all right.

She was.

She was at the cottage with Jane and Angela, who were, she assured him quietly, the best watchdogs ever.

Then she asked, "Did you talk to Sam?"

"Sam?"

"Yes, he was trying to reach you. He matched one of the fingerprints they lifted off my back door."

"Oh?" he asked sharply. He quickly looked at his phone and saw that he had missed Sam's call.

"It was Beth's. I'm sure it doesn't mean anything. She's been over here dozens of times," Devin said.

"Wouldn't she use the front door?" Rocky asked sharply.

"We've been friends since we were kids. If I didn't answer, I'm sure she would have gone around back."

Devin sounded defensive, Rocky thought, but she might well be right. Still . . . "Sure," he said.

"I don't like that 'sure,' " she told him.

"We have to follow every lead, Devin."

"Beth . . . come on, you know her, too, now. It's just not possible. You should have seen her back in school, Rocky! She was so shy and sweet—I'm amazed she's even managed to open a shop. She's come so far."

"Anything is possible. I'm just going to stop in at the store and see how she's doing," he said.

"Rocky . . ."

"Yes?"

"Please don't accuse her outright. I'd like to have a few friends left in the area."

"I'll be the model of courtesy and discretion," he promised her.

She sniffed. She didn't seem to believe him. "What else is going on? What about Vince—anything?"

"A verified alibi," Rocky said. "See you soon."

He hung up, then headed for Essex Street and Beth's shop. Beth was showing a couple, the only customers, jewelry from the counter display case, but she looked up and saw him, and waved.

He didn't see Theo or Gayle and assumed they were in the back, giving readings.

He began to look through the books displayed at the end of the counter, waiting for Beth to be free.

The couple bought an amulet and left. She caught his eye and gave him a radiant smile.

"I was in the area, thought I'd stop by," he told her.

"That was nice of you," she said cheerfully. Then her expression turned anxious. "Are you getting anywhere? Anything new?"

"No, I'm afraid not. I'm a little worried about all of you, frankly."

"Us?" Beth asked.

"Yeah, pretty young women with family histories that stretch back to the witch trials."

Rocky smiled and watched her. "Rebecca Beckett Masters," he said, thinking back to what Devin had told him and hoping he had it right.

Beth looked at him in surprise. "Masters?" she asked.

"She was your bunch-of-greats-grandmother. Born a Beckett."

"I think I have a family tree somewhere. I wasn't related to anyone interesting, though. Wait, that sounds terrible. I'm sure they were interesting people. But I wasn't related to any of the convicted 'witches' or their accusers, or to any of the examiners or magistrates or anything." She smiled. "My ancestors were apparently fond of living, and that meant staying as far away from controversy as they could."

"Smart," Rocky said. "You and Devin have been friends for ages, right?"

"Oh, yeah. Best friends."

He grew serious, leaning on the counter. "Beth, were you over at Devin's recently?"

"I go by a lot— What do you mean by recently?" she asked. "I was there last night, with everyone else."

"Before last night."

Beth pondered the question. "I think I went by a few days ago—but Devin wasn't home. I checked all around the house. I can't remember exactly when . . . maybe Gayle can. Oh! Or Brent. He went with me. I remember now, because I went around to knock on the back door and he yelled at me—you know, because the woods are right there."

"You must be worried about Devin, huh?" he asked her.

"Because the woods are so close and someone was already killed there?" Beth asked. "I am. But," she said, and paused, grinning, "I guess she has you."

"She does have me," he said.

As he spoke, Gayle emerged from the curtained-off area at the back of the store, accompanied by a young man, presumably a client. She told him to have a good day, then joined Beth and Rocky at the counter.

"Hi," she said, smiling. "Anything new?" she asked him.

"I wish I could say we'd caught him, but no," he said. "Hey, any new necklaces yet?" he asked Beth.

"No, I'm afraid not. I promised to let you know when I had some, and I really will," Beth said.

"Thanks. I guess I was just hoping."

"Aren't they a little feminine for you?" Gayle said. "And if you're thinking of getting one for Devin, she bought one just the other day."

"My mom," Rocky said. "She's not living in the area anymore, and I'd love to send her one."

"What a sweet idea," Gayle said.

"Hey, Gayle, do you remember what day Brent and I went by Devin's after work?" Beth asked her.

Gayle shrugged and shook her head. "A couple or three days ago, I guess."

"Yeah, that's what I said, but I was trying to pin it down," Beth said. She looked at Rocky. "Does it matter?"

"Actually, yes, but I can check with Brent later," he said flatly, then decided to go for it. "I'm trying to find out if you tried to break into her house and then set fire to her lawn."

"What?" Beth gasped.

Gayle sighed. "Beth, we're all under suspicion."

"Look," Rocky said to Beth, "you two are friends. Naturally, your prints are all over. We're eliminating people who are close—it helps, believe me."

"You have my prints?" Beth asked, frowning.

"He's the government, Beth. He has everything," Gayle said.

Just then Theo emerged from the back with his customer. Seeing the group at the counter, he joined them as soon as he showed his customer out. "Hey," he said, looking at Rocky expectantly.

"Hey. Business as usual, I see," Rocky said, shaking Theo's hand.

"People like their cards read," Theo said.

"Do they come to you to speak with the dead?" Rocky asked.

"Sometimes," Theo said. "But I don't do anything like that. A good tarot reader understands how the cards can guide someone, though. We're listeners, really. And cheaper than a psychiatrist." He shook his head. "Love affairs are my biggest dilemma. Anyway, I'm sure you didn't stop by just to chat, so what's up?"

"He's here because we're all under suspicion," Gayle said.

"Oh!" Theo said, clearly surprised.

"Just following through," Rocky told him.

"Big Brother has my prints, and they're all over Devin's house," Beth explained.

"I'm also back to warn Beth and Gayle to be careful and remind them not to go anywhere alone," Rocky said. "We think the murderer is targeting women whose family trees go back to the time of the witchcraft trials." He turned to Gayle. "Did you know you and Beth are distantly related?" he asked her.

"Half of Salem is related," Gayle said with a shrug. "Of course, aren't we all related way back when somehow?"

"Neanderthals," Beth said.

"Well, the point is that women who can trace their family history back that far need to be especially careful," Rocky said.

"Don't worry, Beth and I are being *very* careful," Gayle promised.

"I convinced the two of them to actually stay

together instead of just talking about it," Theo said.

"Thanks, Theo," Rocky said. "By the way—you had ancestors here at the time, too."

"Me?" Theo sounded surprised.

But was his tone sincere—or feigned? Rocky had to wonder.

"Yes, we found out while researching our theories about victimology," Rocky said. "Our Jane Doe is still a mystery, of course, but the last victim—Barbara Benton—was in Salem specifically because she had family here at the time of the witchcraft trials and wanted to find out more about them. Same with Melissa Wilson years ago, and Carly Henderson."

Beth looked worriedly at Gayle, then back to Rocky. "You weren't kidding. We really do have to be careful."

"Don't go anywhere alone," Theo said sternly.

"Keep thinking for me, will you?" Rocky asked them. "If you can remember anything at all that happened at the bar the night Barbara Benton died, it could really help."

"We'll try, Rocky. Honestly. We'd do anything to help you," Theo said.

Waving goodbye, Rocky left the shop, calling out his thanks and one last warning to be careful.

He couldn't help himself. He stood in the middle of the pedestrian mall on Essex and watched people go by. Some were heading to the

Peabody/ Essex Museum, some to the smaller "witchcraft" museums and some just to shop or find a restau-rant.

He heard snatches of conversation. Many people were excited and unworried, talking about where they were going next. But some were talking about the murders.

Couples held hands tightly.

Mothers walked close to daughters.

Fathers had wary eyes.

Rocky pulled out his phone and called Devin again.

"Do I still have any friends?" she asked.

"I was the perfect picture of diplomacy," he said, though he knew he was stretching the definition a bit.

"And?"

"Beth says she went by your house with Brent a few days ago and tried the back door."

"I'm sure she did."

Ignoring that, preferring to wait for facts and not emotion, he asked, "What are you up to?"

"We're at the cottage, creating cross-referenced family trees to show the connections between the murdered women, the people you and I know and Margaret Nottingham. Oh, and Sam and Jenna are here, too. They're still sorting through missing-persons reports from around the country."

"Jane Doe," he murmured.

"Are you coming over?" she asked him.

"Soon."

"Good. We'll pull something together for dinner," she said.

"Sounds good."

Rocky hung up and realized he was near Brent's Which Witch Is Which, and decided he needed to drop in.

Brent was there—glum and alone.

He looked at Rocky with weary eyes. "No tour tonight—I guess news of my visit to the police station got out."

"I'm sorry," Rocky told him. "You did have the cell phone."

"I was set up."

"By who?"

"I wish to hell I knew," Brent said.

"We'll catch him and this will end," Rocky said. "And then, who knows, your adventure might become a selling point."

"This from the man who ruined my life."

"Your life isn't ruined—the dead women are the ones whose lives have been ruined."

Brent swallowed and glanced at Rocky with a guilty expression. "Yeah, sorry, you're right."

"Did you go by Devin's with Beth a few nights ago?"

Brent frowned. "Yeah, but she wasn't there."

"Thanks," Rocky told him.

"Why are you asking?"

"Brent, I know you think I tried to ruin your life,

but there was nothing personal about it. It's just that the more we know, the easier it is to zero in on what we don't know and narrow down the clues to the ones that might actually lead us somewhere."

"So what do I have to do to get off your suspect list?" Brent asked. "You want me to wear an anklet that tells you where I am all the time?"

"Not a bad idea," Rocky said. "But not really legal, either."

"Hey, I'll report in any time you want. I'm not going through that again."

"Yeah, I understand."

"No, no, you don't," Brent said. "But I believe you're trying," he added grudgingly.

Rocky's phone rang, and he excused himself to answer.

It was Sam Hall. "Get over here now. We have an ID on our Jane Doe."

17

"Hermione?" Rocky said. He knew he sounded bewildered, but really? Hermione?

"Hermione Robicheaux," Devin said. "Her family moved south in the 1800s. But once Jenna found the missing-persons report with her picture, it was easy to trace her family history and end up right here in Salem."

"We contacted the Nashville police. They sent her dental records to the morgue in Boston, and the M.E. confirmed it. She's our Jane Doe," Angela told him.

"Hermione?" Rocky said again.

"Her parents apparently liked the name, even before *Harry Potter*," Sam said. "She was thirty—one of our older victims. And the reason we couldn't ID her sooner is she had vacation time coming and planned her trip here on her own to look into her family history. When she didn't show up at work a few days ago, her boss thought she had just up and quit—apparently they didn't get along too well—but her coworkers got worried. Her parents died when she was young, and she grew up in foster homes. But they contacted the distant cousin she'd listed as next of kin, and that's who filed the report."

"Makes her death even sadder," Devin said. "She was just looking for family—for people to love."

"Maybe she's finally found family," Auntie Mina said.

Devin looked over at her and smiled, then turned back to Rocky. "No one here reported her missing?"

"She might not have had time to check into a hotel. Besides, the people who work around here can see hundreds of people in a day. It's not surprising no one recognized her picture."

"So the victims weren't random," Sam said. "Whoever the killer is, he has a way to find victims who fit his profile."

"And he knew how to hack the surveillance system at the hotel," Jane pointed out.

"I'm impressed," Rocky said, looking around Devin's dining room table at the group that had gathered: Sam, Jenna, Jane, Angela, Devin—and Auntie Mina. "I'm impressed you were able to trace all those people that far back. Do me a favor and run through it again. Maybe something will jump out at me."

"Okay, this is what we know," Jane explained. "Devin is a descendant of Margaret Myles Nottingham. Brent Corbin and your friend Vince Steward can trace their lineage back to Elizabeth Blackmire—the first person to accuse Margaret Nottingham of witchcraft. Beth Fullway and Gayle Alden can both trace their lineage back to the same family. Gayle's ancestor was Mary Beckett—born Mary Nottingham. Beth's ancestor, Rebecca Masters, was born a Beckett. The two women were sisters-in-law."

Rocky sighed in frustration. "If we follow one train of thought, the murderer would be Brent or Vince, because they're carrying on a tradition of hatred or some kind of rite. But Vince has an alibi—a good one. And we pretty much ripped Brent's life apart and didn't find a thing to suggest he had anything to do with any of the murders."

"We have to figure out why Margaret Nottingham was murdered and who did it," Devin said. "I really think that will help us figure out the motive, and once we have the motive we can find the killer."

"True, but there could still be other motives," Rocky said. "Contemporary motives."

Angela shook her head. "Everything we've learned points to the past. The victims all had some association with Salem. They had family members here at the time of the trials. We haven't seen any other commonality between them, and the choice of victims isn't random, not given the witchcraft angle in the way he leaves the bodies."

"What about Beth's fingerprints being on Devin's back door?" Sam asked.

Devin couldn't help but tense. "She's my friend. Of course her prints are at my house. Besides, she had just turned fourteen when Melissa Wilson was murdered."

"It is incredibly unlikely," Sam said, "that a fourteen-year-old girl committed a murder that left no clues and was so cleanly executed. Even ignoring the fact that she probably wasn't tall enough, children do murder, but rarely in such a calculated manner, and rarely without leaving any evidence behind."

"I don't think Beth was even allowed out past nine o'clock at night back then. Her parents were pretty strict," Devin said.

"Puritanical?" Jenna asked with a smile.

"Just the parents of a teenage girl," Devin said.

"I agree. Nothing is impossible, but it's definitely unlikely. And given her friendship with Devin, I don't think we can read anything into her prints being at the house." Rocky paused thoughtfully. "Jack's people have pursued leads on some other names that have popped up in various places. So far, everyone has alibis that pan out and are clear. Of course, we're focusing on alibis for the one murder, now, really, and may have to expand, but I just can't believe my gut is wrong on this."

"So now we're looking at Theo, aren't we?" Jane asked. "He says that he's not from here, but his family was—and at one time so was he."

"We don't know how old he was when he went to the Midwest—we may be able to check tax records and establish that—but we know he came back here as an adult," Devin said.

Rocky nodded. "And the fact that he was gone for years actually addresses one of our biggest questions—why the killer stopped for so many years between Melissa and Carly. We definitely need to learn more about him. I'm certain we're on the right track. The personal connection helps explain burning a pentagram into Devin's lawn."

"A warning?" Sam wondered.

"Or maybe—as Margaret's descendant—I'm

supposed to be the grand finale," Devin asked.

"I don't think the killer wants you dead. I believe the fire was meant to scare you off," Jane said quickly.

"Maybe, maybe not," Rocky said. He looked at Jane and wondered if she had spoken just to allay Devin's fears. "We can't let down our guard, though."

"So," Devin said matter-of-factly, "you said you're going to concentrate on Theo, but what about Jack?"

"No one has worked harder on this case," Rocky said.

"She has a point," Sam said. "When you're working the case, you know everything that goes on with it, all the little details that are kept from the press."

"We all work on the premise that the more people we eliminate, the closer we get to the truth," Jane said. "And we really haven't looked at Jack."

"You're right," Rocky said. "It's just . . ."

"None of us want to think our friends could be involved in something like this," Jenna said.

"Right. None of us," Devin said.

"Okay, so we'll look into Jack. And now that we have a name, we show Hermione Robicheaux's picture all over town and try to find out where she was and what she was doing on the day she was killed."

"Her picture has already been out there, and no one has come forward," Jane said.

"But *we* haven't been out there with it, forcing people to take a close look," Rocky said. "We'll try to follow her footsteps. And we'll go back and retrace Carly Henderson's last day. We'll pound the pavement until we find something. Or . . ."

"Or?" Devin asked.

No one said anything at first.

Then Angela let out a soft sigh. "Or we wait until the killer strikes again—and we move as quickly as possible. He'll make a mistake."

"How do you know that?" Devin asked.

"All killers do—eventually," Sam said.

Auntie Mina suddenly spoke up. "You will find out what's going on," she snapped firmly, "and no one else will die."

With those ferocious words, she was gone.

Angela finally spoke. "Dinner. We have to eat, whether anyone feels like it or not. Everyone needs to keep their strength up right now."

"I'll set the table," Sam said.

"Sorry, guys, but it's just chicken," Devin said. "It's a good recipe, though—chicken and dumplings."

Jane laughed. "Why are you apologizing?"

Devin shrugged. "I guess because chicken's always boring banquet food."

Rocky smiled at her. "Chicken and dumplings sounds great."

● ● ●

They ate, cleaned up, gave Poe some attention and headed back to the hotel. Rocky was quiet, on edge. And yet, when they reached the room he turned immediately to Devin and drew her into his arms.

Neither one of them spoke. They simply held each other, made love, drifted into a doze wrapped up together, then woke and made love again, and finally lay silently in the darkness of their room.

She knew, though, that when he touched her, he was fully with her. That he felt the same arousal she did when their naked flesh touched, felt her lips, moved with her as if they were one.

But she knew, too, as they lay there together listening to the hum of the air conditioner and the slowing thunder of their hearts, that he was brooding on the case. She didn't speak, only lay with him and let him think. She thought he probably felt the same kind of numbness she did. It was impossible to believe that a friend could have committed murder.

They slept curled together. When they woke in the morning, she was spooned against him, comfortable in the feel of his arms around her.

"We're moving back to the house," he said, smiling as she turned to look at him in surprise.

"Um, okay," she said.

"Margaret Nottingham came to see you there," he said.

"And led me to a dead woman in the woods. I'm really praying she doesn't do anything like that again."

"I just think we need to be there," Rocky said. "Margaret's ghost may come or . . . I don't know. Just call it a hunch and leave it at that."

"Is everyone coming?" Devin asked. "It would be fine, of course. We'll fit them in somehow."

"Just the two of us," he said.

She grew momentarily serious at the thought, then reminded him, "It won't really be just the two of us, though."

He smiled. "Mina? Well, I suppose I can control my libido in the effort to save lives and provide us with a future."

Devin looked away quickly.

A future. It was a nice concept. But he was an FBI agent whose job took him all over the country. She wrote children's books and lived here in Salem.

"I'll be good, I promise," he said.

She looked up and smiled at him. "Oh, I'm not worried about you. It's my own desires I'm worried about. Never mind. The thought of Auntie Mina appearing is something I usually love—but not in my bedroom." She gave an exaggerated shudder.

"We'll both behave," he said.

"Are we bait?" she asked.

"I would never let you be bait," he said. "You'll never be there alone."

She rose up on an elbow and smiled at him. "I'm not afraid. Well, I *am* afraid, but not of going back to my house. Whoever this is, he's not relying on strength. He gets people out to the woods and then slips up behind them. He takes them by surprise. I don't think there's any way we can be taken by surprise."

"Not by surprise, no, but I've seen desperate killers do things no one would ever expect. But you'll never be alone," he swore.

He started to get out of bed, then looked down at her and rejoined her.

He touched her face gently, smiled slowly. Then he bent and kissed her, and when she rose to meet him she felt the hardness of his arousal.

"I guess you're happy," she murmured.

"Waking up with you makes me happy," he said.

She smiled. "I like that."

"I'm glad."

They made love again. Devin wondered what it would be like to have a day—just one day—to rise when they chose, make love, wander the streets, listen to music. . . .

Not today, though.

He rose regretfully at last and headed for the shower. She made a point of not following him. When he was done, she showered and dressed, then joined him at the table, where he was drinking coffee and speaking on the phone.

"I'm heading to the station," he said when he finished his call. "I'm going to do whatever I can to clear Jack, but I promise you, I won't let myself think that it's impossible for him to be involved, even if he is a dedicated police officer. Sad to say, he wouldn't be the first. Sam and Jenna are heading to Danvers—old Salem Village—to show Hermione's picture around."

He got up, stood behind Devin and put his hands on her shoulders. "What we need now is more knowledge about your ancestor—Margaret Nottingham. Why does she come to see you? To warn you? To help you? Because she's worried about you? Is she connected to the murders themselves in some way, or only to you?"

A knock at the door stopped him from theorizing any further. He looked through the peephole before opening it to the rest of his teammates, who were standing in the hallway.

"Ready to roll, if Devin is set," Angela said.

"Jenna and I are taking the team rental to the lab to find out if anything pertinent was discovered about the pentagram," Sam said.

"Angela, Jane, and Devin are going to do more research and get Hermione's picture out on the street, ask people if they saw her," Rocky told him. "I'm going to meet up with Jack at the station."

"And we'll all spread the word around town that

364

you and Devin are going to stay at the cottage tonight," Angela assured him.

"Good plan. Everyone keep in touch," Rocky said.

"We will," Angela promised.

Rocky met Jack at the station, and they started going through case files again, hoping something would miraculously jump out at them, something they'd somehow managed to overlook a dozen times before.

Jack leaned back in his chair. "Okay, we know that Vince has an alibi. We couldn't find a thing on Brent Corbin. We believe the killer was tall, which means we're not looking at Renee—though I suppose she could have been an accomplice, which . . . I'm not seeing it." He paused, staring at Rocky. "You would make a good suspect—except you were in California when Carly Henderson was murdered. So let's be up front here. It has to have occurred to you that it might have been me."

Rocky looked at him with a steady gaze. "Yes."

"I've got an alibi," Jack said. "Though I admit that Haley and I are collectors, and we own several athames we've picked up over the years. I've never owned a pentagram necklace, but I'll bet Haley has at some time."

"Just to cover all bases, let's trace your movements," Rocky said.

"I'm either on the job or I'm at home, with Haley." Jack laughed without any real humor. "Next thing I know, you'll tell me she's a suspect, too. She's tall enough. Hell, maybe she and I are in it together. Or maybe all of us take turns."

"When we were kids, any one of us could have lured Melissa into the woods. Haley was in great shape, tall and athletic. We were all big kids— you, me and Vince. The three of us didn't get together until she'd already been dead for several hours."

"And *you* found her," Jack reminded him.

Rocky nodded. "Don't worry. I'd suspect me, too."

Jack thought for a moment, then said, "It's possible the current killer's a copycat—someone who saw Melissa's body. But that brings us back to you, me and Vince. And none of us fit. I mean, the cops, the M.E., they saw her, too, but . . ."

"You're forgetting someone," Rocky said. "The murderer."

"Or murderers," Jack said. "Except," he added with a note of disgust in his voice, "it's hard enough for one person not to leave a scrap of trace evidence. Two?"

Rocky was thoughtful. "Maybe one person gets the victim out there and the other one does the killing."

Rocky pushed a folder forward. "Theo Hastings," he said.

"He wasn't here when Melissa was murdered," Jack said.

"We don't know that," Rocky said. "My team discovered that he's really from here, he just moved to the Midwest for a while."

"Let's bring him in, see what he has to say," Jack said.

They started with the shops and restaurants on Derby and Essex streets, splitting up, with Jane taking one side of the road and Angela and Devin taking the other. For the most part, people were eager to help, but despite that, no one recognized Hermione Robicheaux.

Eventually, though, Devin and Angela found a busy waitress who started when she saw the picture, then put down her tray to take it from them. "Yeah, I saw her—she was in here a couple weeks ago. She sat at the table by the window there. She was telling me that it was her first trip here, and she was really excited. She said that she could trace her roots back before the witch-craft trials." The woman paused. "Me, I can't trace my family back past my mom and dad. Well, I think my grandparents on my dad's came from Cleveland, but that's about it. Cool to know where you came from the way she did, huh?"

"Not always," Devin murmured.

"She didn't happen to mention any of her plans, did she?" Angela asked.

"Oh, she had lots of them," the waitress told them. "She was heading out to Danvers to visit the Nurse homestead, and she was going to do all the museums and take a ghost tour. She said she might take a couple, even if they all told the same stories."

Devin and Angela glanced at each other, thanked the waitress and left the coffee shop. Outside, they saw that Jane had just left a shop across the street and waved her over.

"Ghost tour," Angela said.

Devin looked at her watch. "I'm sure that Brent's opened the store by now. Let's go ask him if he saw her. Of course, he might lie."

"But he might not be a very good liar," Jane said. "Let's go."

They were standing on a playground in the midst of two dozen two-, three- and four-year-olds at the Salem Prep Preschool when Rocky's phone rang. Sam.

He excused himself, certain that Jack had indeed proved his point. They'd gone to the principal's office and confirmed that on the night Carly Henderson had been killed, Jack had been running the school carnival. He could account for his every movement from 5:00 p.m. until 2:00 a.m. Going by the M.E.'s time line, that meant that Jack Grail couldn't possibly have killed Carly.

Rocky was relieved—and vindicated. Even

though he knew he'd had to consider the possibility, it had still been all but impossible to believe that Jack could be their killer.

Sam was at the lab. "We have a report on the necklace found with the bones of the woman we presume to be Margaret Nottingham. It's as much as eight hundred years old, and the experts found some crisscrossing marks on the underside that might be a signature of sorts. One of the lab techs is into all kinds of pagan stuff, and he says a medallion like this one wouldn't have been considered evil by the maker. The pentagram goes back thousands of years, and it's only relatively recently that it's taken on its demonic reputation. Anyway, according to him, it was probably some kind of family heirloom that made its way to the New World when the colony was settled. It wouldn't have been a common piece of jewelry, and no one during the time of the witch trials would have worn one. The association between paganism and Satan was strong among the Puritans, as you know, and the pentagram was considered a mark of the devil by then. Who knows? Maybe her killer held to the old beliefs and thought it was a way of protecting her in death, or perhaps he thought it was a way to show she was marked for the devil."

"Eight hundred years old, huh?" Rocky said.

"Uh-huh. The composition of the silver matches that used by certain silversmiths in the

Mediterranean during the sixteenth and seventeenth centuries. The medallion might have been acquired by a knight or one of his retinue during the last Crusade and brought back to England, then given to someone as a trinket—way before the whole witchcraft craze swept Europe. I suspect it would have been a family talisman of some kind."

"Thanks, Sam."

"My pleasure," Sam told him. "Hey, what's going on there? Sounds like Custer's Last Stand."

Rocky laughed. "Nope, just a preschool. I'll explain later. Thank the lab guys for me."

"Will do," Sam said.

"Everything good?" Jack asked him when Rocky rejoined him.

"Fine," Rocky said. "Ready to go?"

"I just said goodbye to Jackie, so let's hit the road. Where are we heading?"

"Essex Street. We're going to do a little silver shopping," Rocky said.

Devin was surprised that Beth wasn't behind the counter when they entered the shop. It had been strange enough to get to Brent's store and find it closed and him not even answering his cell, but she'd figured he was just upset about being questioned and was hiding out to lick his metaphorical wounds. Beth's shop had been a logical next stop, since she might have seen him or at least have an idea where he might be. So where was she?

Beth didn't do readings herself. She'd told Devin once that understanding the tarot was hard work, and she preferred buying and selling, plus she had Gayle and Theo, who not only read the tarot but palms, as well, and could even interpret tea leaves.

Today Gayle was behind the counter, talking on the phone. She looked distressed, and lifted a finger to ask them to wait. A few moments later she hung up without having said a word and turned to them.

"Sorry, but I'm a little bit worried. Beth hasn't come in. I can't get hold of her, and it isn't like her not to show up."

Devin instantly felt a cold rivulet of fear snake up her spine. "I thought she was staying with you?"

"Yes, but she left ahead of me this morning," Gayle said. "She said she was going to stop and grab coffee and a breakfast sandwich, and drop a few things off at the cleaners, but . . . she should have been here by now."

"Was she walking?" Angela asked.

"Yes—I'm less than a mile away," Gayle said.

"Can you show me the route?" Angela asked.

"Well, actually, there are a few."

"Any with woods?" Devin asked.

Gayle went white. "Um, yes, just a block behind

Darby, toward the old jail. Not real woods, but a patch of trees."

Theo came out of the back room just then, saying goodbye to a client—an older woman who still had curlers hidden beneath a scarf.

"Not yet?" he asked Gayle anxiously.

Gayle shook her head.

Devin fumbled for her phone, about to call Rocky, but Angela was already calling. But just as she started to speak, Rocky and Jack entered the shop.

"Beth is missing!" Devin said frantically.

Rocky hurried forward and calmly told them not to panic. After Gayle filled him in, he pointed out that Beth's errands might simply have taken longer than she'd expected, and she could have accidentally left her phone somewhere. But, he said, they weren't going to take any chances, so they were going to go out looking for her.

He directed Jane to take one route, Jack and Angela another, and told Devin to come with him and they would check out the route past the cemetery and the trees. He took her hand, telling Gayle to call him the second she heard from Beth and promised that he would call her, too, if they found her.

Devin was truly frightened. *Her best friend was missing.*

"You think something's wrong, don't you?" she asked Rocky.

372

"I think something's off, yes," he said. "But this doesn't fit our killer's MO. He seems to like dusk and dark, times when his victims aren't expected anywhere and it will take longer for them to be found."

He was walking fast, though, and she was nearly running to keep up with him. That seemed pretty worried to her.

They neared the Howard Street Cemetery, and he slowed, looking down an alley. There were houses on both sides—and a tiny stand of brush and trees that lined the alleyway by one old house.

He headed down the alley and pushed into the trees, then stopped so short that Devin nearly collided with him.

She moved up next to him and followed his gaze. A woman was sprawled facedown on the ground near the bushes.

They'd found Beth.

18

Rocky was certain Beth was dead.

Dammit! Why had he brought Devin with him?

Before he could stop her, she was down on her knees beside the body, and in seconds he joined her.

He started to warn Devin not to disturb the body,

and then Beth let out a moan. Relief filled him.

She was alive.

"Beth!" Devin gasped.

Rocky had his cell out, calling for an ambulance, as Devin set a hand gently on Beth's shoulder and helped ease her onto her back.

Beth blinked and coughed and looked up at them with dazed eyes. She was clearly disoriented, with no idea where she was.

"Beth, it's okay, you're going to be all right," Devin assured her, then looked at Rocky, the anguish in her eyes asking for assurance from him.

"Ambulance is on the way," he said. "Devin, watch what you touch. Beth . . . can you talk? Can you tell us what happened?"

"What happened?" Beth repeated.

"Yes, what happened?"

Beth almost smiled. "No . . . I was asking you . . . what happened?"

"You didn't show up for work. Gayle was worried," Devin said.

"Work, right," Beth said, frowning. She tried to sit up, then went, "Whoa . . ." and lay down again.

"Do you remember anything?" Rocky asked.

"Um, yes . . . walking. And then . . . now I'm here."

He could hear the sound of an ambulance, and he felt frustrated. He needed more information, and that meant he needed more time. But her health came first; she needed to get to the hospital.

When the ambulance arrived, the EMTs set to work immediately, and Rocky and Devin were pushed back. He quickly called Jane, Jack and then Beth's shop, telling Gayle that Beth was going to be fine but she'd had an accident and was on her way to the hospital.

"What part of don't go anywhere alone did those two miss?" he muttered after he hung up.

"Rocky, it's hard to think that in broad daylight—with tourists everywhere—you're going to get attacked on your way to work."

"Stay together, I told people to stay together," he said, aggravated.

She didn't reply, because Beth was calling to her and Gayle was running down the alley toward them. Rocky went to intercept her just as Jack and the rest of the Krewe members arrived.

"I've got patrol coming to cordon off the area," Jack said.

"Agent Rockwell, we're going to take Miss Fullway now," one of the EMTs called to him. "Is anyone riding with her?"

"Please, someone, come with me," Beth said pathetically.

"I'll go," Gayle said.

"Devin?" Beth asked.

"Only one in the back," the EMT told Rocky.

"Beth, Devin and I will be right behind you," Rocky said. He looked at Jack.

"I'll handle the scene. We might get lucky and find something."

Rocky nodded and turned to Devin. "Let's go get the car," he said, and took her hand. She clutched his tightly, and they hurried toward the garage where he'd left his car.

Beth was going to be all right; the doctors gave her the thumbs-up after a thorough examination. Nothing was broken, though she'd sustained some bruising. They were keeping her overnight, though, just in case of concussion.

By late that afternoon Devin knew it was fine for her to leave. Gayle was sitting by Beth's side, holding her hand. Theo was there, too, after making an executive decision to close the store for the day. Beth was in good hands and didn't need her there, too.

She'd been gone a long time, she thought. Theo and Gayle were closer to Beth now than she was.

She also wanted to rejoin Rocky, who she knew was feeling both puzzled and frustrated.

Beth hadn't been robbed, and the only injury her attacker had inflicted was the blow to the head that had knocked her out and sent her into the foliage. She'd been unable to tell Rocky anything except that the attack had happened around 9:30 a.m. as she'd been on her way to get the store ready for her usual 10:00 a.m. opening.

That was it. She'd been walking along and

hadn't noticed anyone behind her. She hadn't even heard her attacker come up from behind.

That was all she could remember.

He'd pressed hard, until she'd started to look upset. Devin had stopped him then, and suggested quietly that maybe he could try again later, and he'd left the room to pace restlessly in the hall until Devin was ready to go.

When she joined him, he stuck his head into the room and told them to keep in contact, then started walking quickly toward the hospital garage.

Devin followed and kept silent. Clearly his mind was elsewhere.

"I don't understand it," he finally said when they were in the car. "She fits the profile of our killer's victims, but nothing about the attack fits, other than the nearby trees."

"Rocky, there *is* a possibility she was just attacked by a random mugger," Devin said.

"Except her purse was there, her cell phone . . . Not a lot of cash, but it didn't look as if the attacker even dug through her bag. He just knocked her out."

"Maybe he was trying to close down her shop for the day," Devin suggested.

"Because . . . ?"

"I don't know. I still don't understand any of this."

"I wish your ancestor would talk to us," he said. "Your aunt Mina is full of talk, but Margaret

Nottingham—who might actually know something useful—doesn't have a thing to say."

"Maybe she'll come to the house," Devin said hopefully. She hesitated, then said, "I don't know if anyone had a chance to tell you in all the excitement, but before we went to Beth's store we tried to talk to Brent, but his store was closed and he wasn't answering his cell." She took a deep breath. "We found a waitress who recognized Hermione Robicheaux and had even talked to her about her plans. Hermione was all excited. She said she was going to do everything—go to Danvers, go to the museums and take every ghost tour out there."

"I need to talk to Brent," Rocky said. "We'll start with the store. Maybe he just opened late."

Rocky found street parking on Derby Street and they walked up Essex to Which Witch Is Which.

It was open and full of customers, so they waited until Brent was done helping people.

Devin thought he was going to assume that they'd come to see him because of the attack on Beth, which he'd undoubtedly heard about by now. And that meant he was bound to be angry.

But he wasn't. When he finished his sale and turned to them, he was smiling and self-righteous. "I'm in the clear on this, and I can prove it. I was at Red's from 8:30 a.m. until after noon, doing paperwork for the store, and at least twenty people saw me. My waitress was named Gilda, and both she and the hostess can swear I never left my booth that whole time. Gilda and I started talking, and I may even have made a date."

"We tried to call you and it went straight to voice mail," Devin said, carefully steering clear of telling him *why* they'd called.

"Sorry, dead battery," he said, pointing to his phone charging beside the register.

"No worries, Brent. We didn't come to accuse you of anything," Rocky said.

"No?" Brent said, surprised.

"We need help. I think that phone really was slipped into your pocket, probably by someone who knows you usually go for a drink when your tour is over. Meanwhile, we have an ID on our Jane Doe."

"Ah yes, Hermione Robicheaux." At the startled look on Rocky's face he said, "Your friends were in here already. Don't you guys communicate?"

"We've been at the hospital with Beth," Devin said.

Brent nodded, then looked at Rocky. "I told them I *think* I remembered her. I guess the thought must have been rolling around in my subconscious since the cops first released her picture. I have a full tour almost every night, so I see a lot of people and forget most of them. I went through my credit card receipts and couldn't find her name, but a lot of people just pay me cash."

"Do you think she might have gone to the bar after the tour?" Rocky asked him.

Brent was thoughtful for a long moment, then let out a breath. "Honestly? I don't know for sure. But I do suggest that place to people. It's right there on the corner, so it's convenient, it's good, the prices are reasonable, so yeah, I generally tell people to stop in if they're thirsty. I do it so often I get my drinks free sometimes."

"Thanks," Rocky told him.

Brent stared at Rocky. "You're really not taking me back in or anything?"

"No," Rocky said.

"You haven't even checked my alibi— Oh. I told the other agents the same thing, so one of them probably did that already."

"Probably," Rocky said with a smile.

Brent grinned. "I should really hate your guts. I don't know why I like you."

"You're okay, too," Rocky said. "Well, I guess we'll get out of here, let you get ready for your tour tonight."

Brent nodded and looked at Devin. "Beth really is okay, right?"

"She really is," Devin said.

"Well, I'm here if you need me," Brent told Rocky. "And I'd like to stay here, if it's all the same to you, but I'm happy to answer any other questions you come up with."

"Thanks, Brent," Rocky said. "Oh, can you hold me four places on tonight's tour?"

"You're coming back?" Brent asked. He didn't sound particularly pleased.

"No, but Angela and Jane don't really know the area, and Sam and Jenna could use a break. I think they'll all really enjoy it."

"Oh. Okay," Brent said.

"We think you're being set up, Brent. We're just going to keep an eye on things," Rocky said.

"You planning on sending someone every night?" Brent asked, blinking.

"No, just for a few nights," Rocky said.

"And then . . . ?" Brent asked.

"By then I hope we'll have caught a killer."

Brent nodded. "See you later, then."

Devin gave him a kiss on the cheek, and then she and Rocky left the shop.

"The cottage?" she asked.

"For now."

"And then?"

"I think we should drop in on our friendly local bar."

Auntie Mina was delighted to hear that she was going to have company again. She did, however, smile and giggle and then try to look entirely somber when she asked Devin about their sleeping arrangements.

"The whole Krewe isn't sleeping here—not

tonight, anyway," Rocky said. "I want anyone who's interested to think we're still using the hotel as our base."

"Oh," she said, sounding both puzzled and just a touch worried.

"I'll be using your room, Mina, if that's all right," he said.

"Of course," Aunt Mina told him. "I mean, if that's what you really want."

Rocky and Devin managed to keep straight faces. "We'll be most comfortable that way, Auntie Mina," Devin said.

"Of course, dear, of course." Auntie Mina seemed disappointed.

"Excuse me, I have to make some phone calls," Rocky said. He pulled out his cell and wandered toward the front, trying for a decent signal.

"You should hang on to that one," Auntie Mina told Devin, nodding gravely.

"Auntie Mina, he has his job, and it's an important one that takes him all around the country."

"Things work out, child. Things work out. Remember, home isn't where you are, it's who you're with."

"It's who you're with . . ." Devin repeated. "Auntie Mina . . . where are our family records? Shouldn't we have an old Bible?" She walked over to the bookshelves, filled mainly with history books and a few old novels, along with an old journal her mother had kept, but as far as she knew, they didn't have anything that dated back to the late 1600s.

"If there ever was a family Bible, it was gone long before I was born," Aunt Mina told her. "The closest thing would be . . . let me see . . ."

Aunt Mina's spirit swept across the room and joined Devin in front of the shelves. "Ah, there," she said, pointing.

"*The Chronicles of Narnia?*" Devin asked, looking at her curiously.

"Don't be silly—the next book."

"*Meet Me by the Hanging Tree?*"

"Yes, that one."

Devin pulled it out. As she held the book, she remembered leafing through it when she'd been younger. She looked at Auntie Mina, frowning.

"It was written by someone in the 1800s. An ancestor of ours, right? Percy Ainsworth—one of dad's great-greats?"

"Yes. There were probably about a hundred copies of it at one time. I don't think Percy was ready to hit the world of publishing, but he did have a lot of opinions on what happened here in Salem. There's some family history in it."

Devin took the book to the sofa and started reading through it. At first there was a lot of disorganized rambling. Percy had been convinced that Puritanism still ruled in Salem but that religious diversity was—and should be—on the way. But as she read further, she decided she would have liked old Percy. He was a forward thinker for his day.

She read aloud to Aunt Mina. " 'One of the things that must be remembered is that the people of Salem lived in a dark atmosphere of fear. While greed and hatred and the power that came with land ownership might well have influenced who was and who wasn't accused, it was a time when society at large believed with full sincerity in the devil and the evil that the devil could do. Anything that hinted of a link to Satan was illegal to own. To curse a neighbor was an act of witchcraft, and by the laws governing the colonies, the practice of witchcraft was punishable with death. The people saw witchcraft in the same way that we see a disease that we know transfers from one man to another. In their minds, a person tainted as a witch might well convince another to sign the devil's book. A mole or a freckle might be the devil's work, as could any talisman. Handmade dolls could signify to the examiners that a person meant to prick or torment the dolls as the symbol of a real person, causing that person great harm or even death. Possession of medallions, toys and other objects from the West Indies, where voodoo was practiced, could mean arrest for a man or woman.' "

Devin looked up and saw that Auntie Mina was gone but Rocky, sitting across from her, was listening intently. "Sam found out something interesting earlier. That medallion you found buried with Margaret? It's as much as eight hundred years old. It had probably been in her family—or someone's, anyway—for generations."

"So you think Margaret owned the pentagram herself?" she asked. "And someone—Elizabeth Blackmire—saw it and accused her of witchcraft. And if she was going to be arrested—"

"Someone might have been afraid of what she would say when she was examined. Who she would accuse," Rocky said.

"But whether that's the reason or someone just wanted to spare her a hideous death, how is her death connected to the current murders?" Devin asked.

"Theory," Rocky said. "Maybe one of her descendants is carrying out some kind of twisted revenge, trying to pin the murders on Wiccans because he blames the witchcraft hysteria for Margaret's death. Maybe he even believes the accused really *were* witches, so he thinks blaming Wiccans for the murders will end up wiping them all out, much more efficient than going after them one by one himself."

"All right," Devin said, smiling, "here's another theory. Maybe Margaret knew a dark secret about someone important, something that could have gotten them killed—maybe even that someone no one suspected really was practicing witchcraft—

and she was killed to keep her from talking. And now she sees someone else killing to keep people quiet and feels compelled to step in."

"But how does either of those theories relate to all the victims having ancestors here back at the time of the witch trials?" Rocky wondered. "Okay, let's say Margaret's killer really was practicing black magic. Maybe the answer to the current murders is the obvious one. Blood ritual."

"So these women are being sacrificed?" Devin asked.

"Possibly," Rocky said. "In Margaret's case, the killer might have accomplished two things. He kept her from talking, *and* he carried out a blood sacrifice." He shook his head and took a deep breath. "Now we just have to figure out how either a sacrifice or a mercy killing from the late 1600s connects to the present."

Just then his phone rang. He answered, listened, said, "Gotcha," and hung up, then met Devin's eyes. "That was Sam. They showed Hermione's picture around the bar, and Judah and one of the waitresses remember seeing her there. They're meeting up with Brent soon, so we're going to grab some dinner, then meet them all there after the tour." He gave her a wry smile. "So much for a quiet night at home."

19

Angela, Jane, Jenna and Sam went on Brent Corbin's tour that night. Rocky and Devin went to the bar early, before it filled up, and so they had time to eat dinner and be waiting when the tour was scheduled to end.

Rocky was starting to feel like a regular, he knew the staff so well.

Apparently they felt the same, because they were ready to help him. Although, he supposed, maybe that had more to do with him being part of the FBI. Judah Baker walked out from behind the bar to greet them. He called Brenda over, and set them up at a long table in the back, where they could observe both the bar and the floor. There was plenty of room for Brent and the Krewe to join them when they came in after the tour.

Before Brenda left, Rocky asked her, "If you see anyone you know was in here the night Barbara Benton disappeared, can you let me know, please? Same thing for the night Hermione Robicheaux was in."

"Absolutely," she promised.

"We're on this," Judah said. "I'm escorting half the staff home after work these days. Husbands and boyfriends can't always make it. I can't wait for you to get this guy."

When Brenda came back with their drinks she asked Devin about signed books for her children. Devin promised to bring them by, then smiled at Rocky after Brenda left and said, "I feel like a real local tonight."

"A local celebrity," he said, smiling back. "Meanwhile, let's order—I'm starving."

They ate and talked about anything but the case. Soon after they finished, Brent and the Krewe joined them.

They talked about the tour and the history of Salem, but mostly they kept their eyes on the patrons. Finally it was almost closing and the crowd began to thin out.

Judah came over to the table and asked Rocky, "Anything else here? Last call coming."

"We're good. And I take it you haven't seen anyone or anything noteworthy?"

Judah shook his head. "No, it's been a nonlocal night. You guys are the only people who came in here I know—or have even seen before."

Rocky thanked him and looked around the table. "Well, I guess that's it," he said. "Whenever you all are ready . . ."

He paid the check, and then they hung around on the sidewalk until the last customers had left. Brent thanked him for the drink and headed off down Essex.

"Disappointed?" Devin asked Rocky softly.

He shook his head and smiled at her. "Some-imes, nothing is something," he told her.

"Oh?"

"Yeah," he said, grinning.

"What something would tonight's nothing be?"

"I'm not sure yet." He raised his voice and said, "Okay, guys, we'll convene at the cottage in the morning. Everyone keep your—"

"Cell phones close by," the others said in unison.

Rocky flushed slightly. "Sorry."

They all said their good-nights. The Krewe members set off walking. Rocky and Devin headed for the garage and his car. He took her hand, and then, in the midst of the pedestrian mall with its lights casting an eerie glow over them, he hesitated.

"What is it?" she asked.

"Nothing."

"A nothing that might mean something?"

"Uh-huh."

Hand in hand, they walked to the car. At the house, Mina was waiting for them. "Anything new?" she asked anxiously.

"Not tonight, Auntie Mina," Devin said. She went into the kitchen and came out with treats for Poe. "You're a good old bird," she said.

"A dear bird, and I'm so pleased you're caring for him so well," Auntie Mina said. "Oh, dear. Here it comes. I feel myself fading."

Devin laughed. "Oh, Auntie Mina! Now I'm picturing the witch from *The Wizard of Oz* saying. 'I'm mellllllting.' "

"No one likes a smart-aleck, missy," Auntie Mina said. "And I *am* fading!"

With that, she disappeared.

Rocky laughed. "I do believe that Mina is doing her best to throw you into my arms."

"Possibly," Devin said, heading quickly to her room. "But I don't trust her. See you in the morning."

Rocky grinned. "Okay. See you then."

"First one up brews the coffee," she told him, then entered her room and closed the door.

He smiled. He was really going to miss her tonight.

But he was glad just to be near her.

He didn't go to bed right away. He sat in the living room.

Listening.

Waiting.

Hours went by and nothing happened.

He picked up the book that Devin had been reading earlier, *Meet Me by the Hanging Tree.*

Percy Ainsworth had been one heck of a scholar, he thought as he read. The old guy made frequent references—complete with footnotes— to medieval devil worship.

Not paganism or anything that resembled modern Wicca.

Devil worship.

There had been cults at work in Eastern and Western Europe, arising almost simultaneously with Christianity itself. Of course, primitive peoples around the world had practiced blood sacrifice. Percy Ainsworth had found that in the 1500s—even as the so-called "burning times" were taking hold—a secret group called the Strega of Satan had been recruiting followers worldwide. According to Ainsworth, they might have come together in self-defense, on the theory that if a man was going to be accused of witchcraft, he might as well be a witch, practice some black magic and see what it got him.

Rumor had it that in the early 1500s the first European Inquisitors had come out of Spain and Italy—six exceptionally vicious men who had been known to rip people to shreds on the rack, pierce them, skin them and leave them hanging from the gibbets to be eaten by crows. After that, the number six had become the acceptable sacrifice to Satan to win his protection. Six was also the basis of the devil's sign: 666.

Fragments from journals kept by those who were members of the Strega of Satan confirmed that the followers who delivered up unto their master the blood of six innocents would find what they sought: lives free from fear, filled with riches and a place in the house of Satan when they died, where wine, women and all earthly pleasures would be theirs for eternity.

After a while the words on the page began to blur. He yawned, stood and stretched, then walked over to check on Poe. The bird appeared to be peacefully sleeping.

He walked around the house, checking all the locks again. When he returned to the parlor he saw Mina standing there, smiling beatifically.

"I'm here, so go to sleep," she told him.

"Thank you," he said.

Mina wagged a finger at him. "And don't let anything happen to her."

"I won't. I swear," he said.

"Get on then, go to bed."

Who was he to argue with a ghost?

Maybe it was because Auntie Mina had made her think about *The Wizard of Oz.* Whatever, Devin's mind had gone into theater mode.

She slept easily—not as easily as when she was curled up against Rocky, but easily enough, knowing he was near. And in her dreams, she was at the theater.

Perhaps the first play should have been *The Scarlet Letter* or *The Crucible.* But she had gone into the Shakespearean realm instead.

Macbeth.

Three witches stood over a cauldron, stirring away. "Double, double toil and trouble."

Then the Shakespearean part was over as the

witches turned to look at something glowing red in the background. They bowed and scraped, and the steam issuing from their great cauldron took on a misty red hue . . . a crimson glow, as if blood had painted the very air. Then the red mist began to fade, and Devin saw what the witches had been staring at. A giant, horned goat-god, crimson and terrifying, perched upon a throne with a staff in his hand.

Satan, as the Puritans had envisioned him.

The crones continued to bow and scrap before the devil. Then they offered up chalices filled with the molten red liquid from their cauldron.

Fire burn, and cauldron bubble. . . .

The words resonated in Devin's ears.

And then, one by one, the witches spoke.

"For life eternal."

"Riches eternal."

"Luck and love eternal."

The giant red goat-god stood and took the offerings. He began to move, and Devin saw herself as if from above, sitting in the audience, watching, and yet, as she watched . . .

The goat-god turned to her.

And smiled.

She woke with a start, gasping for air.

She was in her own room, of course, and she realized she hadn't screamed or Rocky would have been there already, no doubt with his gun drawn. A glow through the curtains told her that the sun was rising.

She stood up, walked to the windows and opened the drapes. She could see the garden, wilted from the summer heat, the little stone path that led to the road . . .

And the forest off to the left.

Someone, she thought with complete certainty —and not the innocents who had died—*had* been practicing black magic in Salem.

And they had gotten away with murder.

The rest of the Krewe arrived just as Devin and Rocky began making breakfast.

She had told him about her dream, and Auntie Mina had materialized to listen in, then told her to study her dreams, because dreams were often a result of the subconscious mind trying to put together what the conscious mind was also attempting to puzzle out. And then Devin's stomach had growled. Embarrassed, she said it was clearly time for breakfast.

Luckily she had shopped recently. When she'd told him she was going to make omelets—her forte—and he'd told her the Krewe was coming early and they should go somewhere, she'd been able to smile and tell him they had plenty of food. He put on coffee, worked the toaster and dealt with the bacon, while she whipped up fluffy omelets filled with cheese, veggies and bacon to order.

As they ate, everyone reported that the night had been quiet.

"Have you spoken to Jack? Were they able to find out anything about the attack on Beth Fullway?" Sam asked.

"I'll call him after breakfast, but I'm pretty sure they've come up empty," Rocky said. "If they had anything, Jack would have called me."

"What's on the agenda for today?" Angela asked him.

"I'm going to pair you and Jane up to reinterview Carly Henderson's family and see if we can trace her movements. It made sense that Barbara Benton and Hermione Robicheaux were anxious to take a tour. They had roots here but didn't really know the area," Rocky said. "But Carly lived here, so I can't see her paying to walk around town with a bunch of tourists and listen to a lecture on history. We need to find out where she was before she was killed, and so far no one has come up with anything. I'm not saying the police didn't try and try hard, but I'm hoping you guys can come up with a new angle. Her family and friends were used to her going to work and coming home, or maybe going out with friends first, but something different happened that night, and I'm counting on the two of you to figure it out.

"Sam, you and Jenna need to hit the local streets again—you may have better luck than the police finding out what happened to Beth yesterday."

"Gotcha," Sam said.

Once their assignments were settled, Rocky told them about the book he had been reading.

"Would someone *really* have dared to practice black magic here in the middle of the witch trials?" Jane wondered.

"I'm pretty sure someone did," Devin said. "I'm not a hundred percent sure how I know that, I just know I do. And if there *was* a member of the Strega of Satan here at the time and they needed their six victims . . ." She looked around the table, then started counting. "One—Margaret Nottingham. Two—Melissa Wilson. Three—Carly Henderson. Four—Barbara Benton. And five—Hermione Robicheaux."

"So . . . one more to go," Rocky said. "We have to find out what's going on before there's a sixth victim. I started thinking last night that our killer began with Margaret Nottingham but didn't get any further. Maybe he was arrested, maybe he fled to avoid arrest. Maybe he just chickened out when he discovered killing someone wasn't as easy as he thought. Then, years later, someone decided the world wasn't going well for them—someone seriously warped, obviously—decided that he could have power and riches in hell if he finished the sacrificial cycle."

"So he killed Melissa," Devin said. "But that was thirteen years ago. And then he stopped. Why?"

"Maybe he was afraid of being caught. Or things

changed. He got sick or something. And then recently everything fell back into place," Rocky said. "Or maybe we're looking at Theo. I'm going to ask Jack for more help on that angle."

"We do know our killer knows his history," Jane said.

"So where do we find you?" Sam asked Rocky.

"I'd like to stop by the hospital," Devin told Rocky. "See if Beth needs a ride home or anything."

"Of course." He turned to Sam. "After that, we'll be hanging around Essex Street, just watching and listening. Let's pray that one of us finds something tangible today."

They never made it to the hospital. Rocky was driving and Devin was next to him when her phone rang. It was Beth sounding cheerful and completely recovered.

"I'm out! They let me go first thing this morning."

"That's great, Beth," Devin said, looking at Rocky and waving a hand in the air to signify that they were no longer going to the hospital. "But you were hit pretty hard. You have to take care of yourself."

"I'm fine."

"And don't be alone!"

"I'm not alone. I'm with Gayle and Theo at the store."

"I'm not so sure you should be at work so soon," Devin said.

"You want me to be alone at home? Gayle has to be here. I don't want to go broke on top of this—I have to keep the store open. So just come by and see me, why don't you?"

Rocky must have heard Beth speaking, because he smiled at her and nodded.

"We'll be there soon," Devin told her.

A few minutes later they reached the parking garage, and as they got out of the car, Devin asked, "Explain to me exactly what we're doing today?"

"Just keeping our eyes and ears open, stopping in to see people just to read how they're doing. And if you don't mind, at some point I want to visit a cemetery," he said. "I'd like to bring flowers to Melissa."

"Of course."

They walked along the street—busy by day—glancing into the shop and museum windows. When he laughed at the cheesiness of some of the gorier museums, she pointed out that they did a booming business with teenagers. And while some of the others might not have a lot of money behind them, they still did a great job at accurately presenting the area's history.

When they walked into Beth's shop, she was sitting in a chair behind the counter. Theo was nearby arranging dried herbs in a display case.

Devin tried not to stare at him suspiciously—or to shout, "Dammit! Are you the killer?"

She managed to call a quick hello to Theo, then hurried over to give Beth a hug.

"Look at me," Beth said. "I look good, right?"

"Fantastic," Devin assured her.

"You'd never know a thing happened to her," Theo said, coming over.

Beth smiled at Rocky. "You know, I never thanked you two. I could have lain there forever!"

"Actually, you would have come to eventually—though with a hell of a headache," Rocky said. "Just don't overdo it today, okay?"

Gayle emerged from the back, smiling. "She's amazing, our Beth. A real trouper."

"Since you're here . . ." Rocky said, smiling as he leaned on the counter and looked over at Gayle. "When am I getting my pentagram necklace?"

"Rocky! You sound like a broken record," Beth said. "I told you. As soon as—"

"I wasn't asking you, Beth. I'm sorry—I was asking Gayle," he said.

"What?" Gayle said.

"You *are* the artist, right?"

"No, no, I—" She broke off and stared at Rocky. "Okay, I'm the artist. How did you know?"

"The way you looked at Beth that day when I asked," Rocky said pleasantly. "And you do know a lot about them. Make one for me, will you—please?"

Gayle flushed. "Yes, yes, of course. You know you can buy them all over Salem."

"Not like yours."

Rocky really was very good, Devin thought. If she hadn't already known he was playing Gayle, she never would have noticed.

"That's very sweet of you," she said.

"Nope—just true," he said. "You're a terrific artist. You should stop hiding your identity. Let people know who you are. That would mean—"

"That I'd be swamped," Gayle told him. "Please, keep it a secret."

"All right, I promise," Rocky said solemnly. He chatted with her for a few more minutes and then said, "Well, we're off. We're visiting a cemetery."

"Historic?" Gayle asked.

"Anything from the past is historic, isn't it?" Rocky asked lightly. "Melissa Wilson was a friend of mine. She was the first victim of the killer. We're going to visit her."

"I remember," Beth said. "I was only thirteen or fourteen, but I remember."

"I'm really sorry you lost a friend," Theo said to Rocky.

"She was a good kid," Rocky said. "But enough about sad things. What are you all up to now that Beth's been sprung?"

"Hoping for a busy day here at the store, and tonight, after we close, some cleaning," Beth said.

"I promise I'm going to sit in my chair and supervise."

"Cleaning? Really? That's the best you can come up with for your first night out of the hospital?" Rocky asked.

"Why? Do you have something more exciting to offer for the evening?" Theo asked.

"No, not really. I think Devin wants to do some housecleaning, too."

"What about your fellow agents?" Beth teased. "Don't they want to party?"

"They're pretty exhausted, to tell you the truth. Working this case has been stressful. I expect they'll be heading back to the hotel to get some sleep," Rocky said.

"I talked to your friend this morning—Jack Grail," Beth said. "They still don't have anything on what happened to me. I know the attack on me might not be related to the murders, but if it is . . ." She trailed off and shivered. "I was very lucky."

"You definitely were," Rocky agreed. "But now we really have to go. We'll see you soon."

Devin and Beth hugged goodbye, and then he put his hand on Devin's shoulder and guided her out of the store.

"Cemetery?" she asked.

"In a little while," he told her. "I just want to check in on one more person."

"So we're saying hi to Brent again?"

"Yep."

Brent smiled when they walked in and chatted comfortably. He definitely didn't seem to be expecting to be invited down to the station again.

They didn't stay long, and their next stop was the florist a few doors down, where Rocky bought flowers.

They had lunch at a place just off the pedestrian mall, and then drove out to the cemetery. Melissa Wilson had been buried in Peabody, alongside various members of her family.

There were already flowers in a metal vase by Melissa's headstone, though they were beginning to wilt. Rocky knelt down and replaced them with the fresh ones, then remained down on one knee for a minute.

When he stood, he looked at Devin. She realized he was waiting.

"Anything?" he asked her.

She shook her head and looked around the old cemetery. A huge oak dipped long branches toward the ground. The scene was both beautiful and forlorn. She knew he was hoping she could see Melissa—that perhaps, though he obviously couldn't, she could somehow communicate with his long-gone friend.

But the cemetery was empty.

"I think you should be glad," Devin said softly. "She's gone on. Wherever she is, she's at peace. Maybe she's even praying for us here."